Beginnings

An Erica Murray Mystery

J E Nice

First published in Great Britain in 2018 by
Write Into The Woods Publishing.

ISBN 978-1-912903-00-9

Cover design by Jenny Lewis,
Write into the Woods.

www.jenice.co.uk
www.writeintothewoods.com

For me mam, Vivien Erica,
and my grandmother,
Minnie Murray.

Other Books By J E Nice

Matter of Time
Despite Our Enemies
In My Bones

Steve

The house was too quiet. The baby was asleep after a night full of screaming and tears. Steve sat at the kitchen table, baby monitor next to his hands, resting on the table top. He listened to his son's breathing, feeling his own body relax and his eyes close. Everything ached. He'd never been much for crying. It just wasn't done in his family. He had shed multiple tears as the midwife had handed a newborn Joe for him to clumsily hold for the first time. He seemed to remember getting a little watery-eyed when Rachel had agreed to marry him. The only other time he could remember crying was when he was small and had fallen off his bike. His dad had picked him up, roughly brushed him down and plonked him back on the saddle. Steve wondered briefly what he would do when Joe fell off his bike.

The emptiness of the house brought him back. The silence itself was a sound, reverberating off the walls. Joe could certainly hear it. He had been such a quiet baby when they'd brought him home. He cried when he was hungry, or needed changing, but otherwise seemed an unnaturally happy, gurgling baby. He hadn't even woken when Steve's mates had come round to watch the World Cup, cheering, supping at their beers.

Now Joe cried and cried. He screamed, he sobbed, he hiccupped until he passed into a fretful sleep. Steve knew he should sleep when Joe slept, but he couldn't.

The amount of tears he had cried these past few months had more than made up for a lifetime of not crying. It wasn't over yet.

At first, Steve couldn't sleep because when he closed his eyes, he saw her face. Now he couldn't sleep because of what might wake him.

Still, his mind grew fuzzy, his heavy, exhausted eyes closing properly, his brain shutting down to sleep.

The baby monitor crackled.

Steve's eyes opened, staring forward, past the baby monitor on the table and into the hallway. It was real. He hadn't dreamt it, he hadn't imagined it. He wasn't having delusions. He knew in his gut that this was real, this was happening.

Holding his breath, he looked at the monitor and watched the light flicker as the noise grew. It sounded like white noise, the crackling of empty space when an old analogue television couldn't be tuned in.

A flash of light caught the corner of his eye and Steve looked back up to the hallway. There was only darkness.

Then Joe's crying broke through and Steve was on his feet, knocking the table, causing the monitor to fall over as he ran up the stairs. The crackling on the monitor quietened until the only sounds in the empty kitchen were the muffled whispers of Steve calming his son.

1

Erica couldn't see clearly as she ran down the stairs, nearly falling at the last step and knocking into a suited man and his cup of coffee. Breathing an apology, she pushed through the doorway and slammed into a door. Fumbling for her security pass, she opened it and went through, into the fresh air of the world.

The office windows looked out over her so Erica didn't feel she could just put her hands on her knees and breathe without someone asking questions.

Oh, to hell with it.

She put her hands on her knees and took a couple of deep breaths. Let them ask questions. It would be wonderful for someone to ask her what's wrong. What's wrong? she would say. What's wrong? She would tell them what was wrong. A rejection email, that's what was wrong. From her own manager, telling her she wouldn't be getting that promotion. Four years of hard work, four years of overtime, working during the weekends, of fighting to be heard and straining to come up with good ideas which were then ignored. Four years of her life that she'd put into this job and all Erica could see when she read the email was that it was four years wasted.

Tears pricked at her eyes. She blinked them

back, stood straight and sucked in more air. It wasn't fresh. It was fresher than the air in the office which was continually turned around by the air conditioning unit, but the air outside was filled with the stench of exhaust fumes from the adjacent busy road. The same road that meant that there was no peace to be found here either.

Erica took out her phone and reread the email.

Dear Miss Murray

Thank you for attending an interview for the position of Senior Account Manager at Goldbrick Communications.
Unfortunately, you were unsuccessful at this time.

We hope you will apply again in the future and good luck.

Yours Sincerely
Carl Bower
Director of Marketing

Unfortunately, she had been unsuccessful at this time.

Unfortunately.

Erica read that sentence over and over.

The email was so short, so impersonal.

'Four years,' Erica murmured. The shock was turning over and pitching into anger. She wiped under her eyes with the tip of her finger, slid her phone back into her pocket and made her way back into the office.

She silently walked up the stairs. In the depths of the ladies toilets on the second floor, Erica wiped her tears and blew her nose. As she washed her hands, she stared into her own eyes in the mirror. Four years. How long would she have to wait? Another four years? That would be four years with someone else as her supervisor, someone else doing the job she had worked so hard for. Had they hired internally? Would she be working for someone she knew? Or would they be new? Erica's mouth twisted. She knew what that would mean. If they were new, they wouldn't understand the role. No one new to an organisation knew the ins and outs immediately. Erica would end up doing some of the work, work that she wouldn't be getting paid for, for the job that should have been hers in the first place.

Now the anger began to burn in her belly and she snarled at her reflection.

She wouldn't do it. She wouldn't sit at that desk for another four years, working hard only to be rejected again.

Erica left the toilets and made her way back to her desk. Keeping her head down, avoiding eye contact with anyone who passed. She didn't want to talk. The soft rock music that pumped through the Goldbrick Communications office seeped into her ears and her right eye gave a subtle twitch in response. The office itself was littered with brightly coloured chairs and large desks. Big leafy plants were stationed at either end of every desk, towering over the Macs with their shiny screens. The carpet was coloured too, a bright blue that the CEO spent good money on keeping clean every month. His semi-private office, made pointless by the large glass wall separating him from his employees, was empty. He was in Italy, skiing.

Thankfully, Erica's team was currently re-presented by a load of empty desks. Her manager was in a meeting. A few were on holiday, one was on maternity leave, others were in meetings and one was off sick with depression. Erica considered that. Would the doctor sign her off sick? She sighed. No. That wasn't who she was, it wasn't what she wanted.

She fell into her chair and stared blankly at her computer screen. After a quick glance around, Erica loaded up the screen, typed in her password and opened the search engine. She paused and looked over at the empty desk next to her. Pouting, she pulled out her phone again and sent a quick message.

I didn't get the job.

Placing the phone carefully on the desk where she could see it, Erica began a job search. The rock music grated at her. The office had seemed wonderful four years ago when she'd first stepped foot inside as a marketing assistant. She'd had a plan. She would work hard, have wonderful, original ideas and be promoted within her first year. Within five years, she'd be creative director, in charge of all the marketing accounts within the agency.

Of course, maybe she wouldn't stay at this particular agency, but her progression would be so swift she wouldn't have time to move to another employer.

Her phone buzzed against the wood.

What?! That's insane. Do you know who got it? Do you want to have drinks tonight?

Erica grinned. Thank the powers for Jess. She looked back at her friend's empty desk. Maybe she should go part-time too. The week would certainly be more bearable without a promotion if she was only in the office at the same time as Jess.

It had taken two years to get the promotion to account manager. That was fine. A vacancy simply hadn't come up and Erica was learning so much. She enjoyed the work and they'd put her through college for her qualifications, paying for all of it. She owed them. So she hadn't even entertained the idea of leaving. It would be fine, she'd thought. In two years, she'd be a senior account manager and then the marketing manager. So it would take her eight years instead of five to become creative director. She could handle that. Except that it would take longer now, wouldn't it. This was the second time she'd applied for the senior role. The second time she'd been interviewed by her own manager. The second time she'd been rejected. Yet, when she asked him about it he could only tell her what wonderful work she was doing.

She bashed out a reply.

No idea. And yes yes yes please. I'll come to you.

Going back to her job search, Erica saved the links for two managerial jobs. The pay wasn't enough. Was it her or were salaries decreasing? They wanted previous managerial experience as well. How was she supposed to get that when the people who knew her and what she was capable of wouldn't give her a chance?

Her phone buzzed.

Great. I'll get the alcohol. Come for dinner. 6pm.

Erica gave her phone a smile and went to reply when it jumped and buzzed in her hand. Erica managed to not give a surprised squeal as "Mum" flashed up on the screen. All thoughts of the rejection, anger and alcohol were replaced with a splash of fear. Sliding the green button, she held the phone to her ear, moving her chair to turn her back on the office.

'Hello. Everything okay?' she asked.

'We're all fine,' said her mum. 'Your grand-mother's gone missing again.'

Erica exhaled slowly.

'Have you checked the cemetery?'

'Of course. First place we looked. She's not there. Has she said anything to you recently?'

Erica looked over her computer screen as her manager came back to his desk, smiling, deliberately avoiding eye contact.

'Oh no! That's awful!' Erica exclaimed. Her manager peeked over at her. 'I don't know. I'll see what I can do. I'll be there as fast as I can.'

'What? You don't need to come, Ric. I was just wondering if she'd—'

'Yep, as fast as I can. I'm on my way.'

'You didn't get the job did you?' A lump rose in Erica's throat. 'Oh, sweetie. I'm sorry. Screw them. Come home and we'll sort out a little search party.'

Erica nodded and then realised her mother couldn't see that.

'Okay. Love you.' She hung up and began to

tidy her desk away. 'Mark?' Her manager turned to her in his swivel chair. 'I don't know if you heard any of that.'

'Family emergency?' he asked, biting into an apple.

'My grandmother's gone missing from her nursing home.'

'Didn't she do that last month?'

And last week, thought Erica.

'Yes. She does it a lot. She's what's known as a flight risk. Apparently. My work is all up to date.' It always was. 'I don't have any meetings. But I'll keep my phone on.' Erica wondered why she said that. Why did she always have to make herself available to these people?

'Please make sure you do. I hope you find her. Maybe you could work from home if you find her quickly?' Mark raised his eyebrow expectantly.

Something inside Erica screamed but instead of letting it out, she held up her laptop case.

'Packed up and ready to go. See you tomorrow,' she added quickly. Mark nodded as she turned and walked as fast as she could out of the office and towards her car.

Once in her sky-blue Mini Cooper, Erica relaxed back into the seat and pulled out her phone.

Gran's gone missing again and isn't at the cemetery. I might be late. Will let you know.

She turned on the engine and music blared into the car. Pushing away thoughts of the rejection email, Erica replayed her last conversation with her grandmother as she drove out of the car park and towards home.

Her phone buzzed as she drove. That would be Jess replying, she thought, so she ignored it for now.

2

Her phone tucked away in her pocket, Jess held five shopping bags in her arms, slammed the car door shut with her hip and somehow managed to find the lock button on her car key. The car blipped and seemingly went to sleep. Jess took a deep breath. The bags were getting heavier. That would be the potatoes. And that bottle of wine.

Still, she thought, I'm on my own driveway leading up to my own front door with my own shopping. It made her smile and the bags seemed a little lighter. But only a little.

She staggered sideways, turning to face said front door when a slam made her look up.

On next door's driveway a large man was doing the same as her, his arms comfortably full of shopping bags. Jess didn't bother to count whether he was carrying more than her. It was hard enough wrenching her gaze from his face.

He caught her eye and for a moment they stared at one another.

'Hi.' He nodded at her.

Jess managed a smile, feeling the bag with the potatoes slipping from her grip. The big man with short dark hair shaven close to his scalp, biceps bulging under the weight of shopping, turned and walked into her neighbour's house.

Jess struggled down her own driveway and stared at her front door.

Her neighbour was an elderly man who had glared at them from the window on the day they'd moved in. When she'd gone round to introduce herself, he'd snidely remarked that he hoped her child would be quiet and that she wouldn't be bringing strange men into the neighbourhood at all hours. Jess had avoided him after that, giving herself a mental note to interrogate the neighbours next time she was buying a house.

Was this the neighbour's son? Who else could he be? And how was she going to open the front door?

With an exasperated sigh, Jess put down all five bags and unlocked the door, pushing it open to reveal the stark white walls of her new home. With a grin, big handsome man not forgotten but pushed to the back of her mind, Jess took her shopping in and unpacked.

Flicking the kettle on, Jess sat at her kitchen table. A row of cabinets and the oven in front of her, large fridge to her left and a wall of glass looking out onto the garden behind her, Jess checked her phone. Erica hadn't replied. She considered calling her. No. She would be driving, or busy. She'd give it another hour. Except that in an hour she'd have an unruly four-year-old at home. Jess checked her phone again. It was nearly time to pick Ruby up.

৪০০৪

'But then Miss Crabby said I did it when I didn't. She made me sit away from everyone, which wasn't nice of her. Can I watch TV?'

Jess blinked. Her daughter had been a fountain of words since Jess had met her at the school gates. She had so much to say since she started school.

'Hang on,' Jess told her, taking off Ruby's coat and hanging it up. 'So many things are wrong with what you just said. Firstly, it's Miss Gabby, not Miss Crabby. Never call her Miss Crabby because one day you'll accidentally say it to her face. Secondly, did you do it?'

Ruby stared up defiantly at her mother.

'Of course not. Can I go watch TV?'

'Of course not. We're not done yet. Do you know who did do it?'

Ruby shrugged.

'Charlie did it.'

She was lying, Jess knew, but she didn't want to say that outright because parenting books and advice columns sometimes said that was a bad thing to do. Jess frowned as her daughter looked up at her.

'Sometimes we get punished for things we didn't do,' Jess murmured, her mind springing to her own job.

'That's not fair.'

Jess cocked her head at her daughter.

'Did you do it?'

Ruby threw up her arms dramatically.

'Maybe!'

Jess smiled. There it was.

'Well then. Don't put paint on the walls and then blame someone else. Be glad all Miss Gabby did was separate you.' Jess hesitated. 'What was the point of separating you?'

'Charlie dared me to do it. Can I go watch TV

now?'

Jess had to stop herself from laughing.

'Nope. Look, Ruby, we've got this lovely house now with a lovely garden. You can watch TV later but for now go and change out of your uniform and then why don't you go play in the garden?'

'I can watch TV later?'

'Yes.'

Ruby looked sceptical.

'Can I stay up late?'

'No.'

'Can I have ice cream?'

'Possibly.'

Ruby considered this.

'Okay.' She jumped over her bag on the floor and ran up the staircase, her footsteps echoing around the hallway. Jess picked up the bag and took it into the kitchen to dissect its innards.

She was just peeling a flyer for a school fair and a permission slip for a visit to a farm from one another when Ruby flew past her, through the open patio doors and into the garden.

'Careful!' Jess shouted after her, sniffing at the sticky substance on her fingers.

സൗൽ

Her mum was always telling her to be careful. Ruby sometimes listened. When she was climbing a tree or there were strange people around. But this was her garden. She didn't need to be careful. She had big plans to bend this patch of green lawn and empty flowerbeds to her will. Her mum said she could have a swing and that they'd start a vegetable patch. Ruby's plans involved slugs and snails more than anything else.

Without thinking, she headed straight to the broken fence panel at the back right of the garden. Next door lived a horrible old man and the urge to peer into his garden and at his creepy windows was often too much to bear.

Ruby stopped so suddenly that she nearly toppled forward from the leftover momentum. Through the broken fence panel was a large man with a shovel. Ruby eyed him and then glanced up towards the neighbour's house.

'Hello,' she said. The man jumped and turned to look at her, bending a little to see her through the fence.

'Uh. Hello.'

His voice was deep. Deeper than her dad's. She liked it. It had a strange but soothing quality to it. Unfortunately, his height and size weren't quite as soothing.

'What are you doing?'

The big man looked down at his shovel. There was mud all around him where the neighbour's nice lawn had been dug up.

'I'm taking up the lawn.'

'Why?'

'Because Mr Horton wants me to put gravel down instead.'

Ruby looked up at the man with large eyes.

'But why?'

The man shrugged his broad shoulders.

'Some people think gravel is easier to maintain than a lawn.'

Ruby did an exaggerated eye roll. The man chuckled. 'What was that?'

'That's what Mummy will do when she finds

out.' Ruby tutted and rolled her eyes again. The man grinned at her. Ruby looked down at the mud on the man's shovel.

'If you put gravel down instead of grass, where will the worms go?'

The man followed her gaze.

'They live in the dirt underneath the gravel.'

'They'll still be able to come up and breathe?'

The man shifted his weight thoughtfully.

'Well, I need to put a layer down between the dirt and the gravel, to stop the weeds coming up and the grass growing back.'

'So the worms won't be able to get out? They'll be trapped?' This was awful news. Ruby had to do something. Throwing handfuls of mud at Mr Horton's window was the first thing that came to mind.

The man looked at her kindly, but not with the annoying patronising expression that most adults gave her.

'They'll find their way out,' he told her. 'They'll dig under the fence to your garden, if they know what's good for them.'

Ruby shook her head.

'Worms usually don't know what's good for them.'

The man tilted his head at her.

'I tell you what, kid. You go get me a bucket or something, something your mum won't mind getting dirty, and any worms I find, I'll put in the bucket. Then when I'm done, I'll slide it back onto your side of the fence and the worms can live happily in your garden. What do you think?'

Ruby pursed her lips.

Jess stretched her arms above her head, turning to look out of the window and check on Ruby. She lowered her arms. What was that girl doing? She was talking to their horrible neighbour through the fence. Well, whatever Mr Horton was saying to her little Ruby, Jess wouldn't be having it. She stormed out through the patio door.

'Ruby!' she boomed in her best motherly authoritative voice. Ruby snapped round to face her. Taking long strides, Jess reached her daughter's side and towered protectively over her child. She faltered when she saw it was the big man from earlier and not Mr Horton on the other side of the fence.

He gave her a small smile.

'Hello.'

'Err, hello,' said Jess. She looked down at Ruby. 'What's going on?'

'He's taking up the grass, Mummy. Mr Horrible told him to take up the lawn.'

'Stop making up names for people,' Jess muttered, peering through the broken fence slats to the garden beyond.

'He's replacing the lawn with gravel,' the man confirmed.

Jess tutted and rolled her eyes without thinking. The man and Ruby exchanged a grin. She would have to question Ruby on that later.

'I'm concerned about the worms,' Ruby declared. Jess couldn't help but smile.

'Of course you are. How will they breathe under all those stones?'

'Exactly.' Ruby beamed up at her mother. The

man on the other side of the fence watched with a bemused glint in his eye.

'If she has a bucket, I've offered to save any worms I find. I'll push the bucket through the fence when I'm done for the day and she can give them a new home.'

Jess stared at the man a little too long.

'What a wonderful idea,' she breathed. 'Go get that disgusting – I mean – lovely pink bucket your dad bought for you last year. The one you've never used. Quickly.' Jess gave Ruby a little pat on the back and the girl sprinted into the house. Jess glanced back to the man. 'Thank you. For indulging her.'

The man's broad shoulders heaved in a shrug.

'It's sweet.' He looked over the broken fence. 'I can get this fixed for you, if you like.'

'Is that not part of the lawn arrangement?' Jess frowned. 'I offered to pay to get it fixed but Mr Horton said he'd do it.'

'He hasn't mentioned it to me. I'm Mr Horton's handyman. Marshall.'

Jess's lips twitched and she gave a small smile.

'Jess.' She straightened her thoughts. 'A handyman. So you were doing his shopping earlier?'

'And now I'm sorting out his garden.' Marshall nodded. 'I'll ask him about the fence.'

'Oh, thanks. Only, I don't want to be a bother. I mean, I've found that he can be quite... ' Jess's voice faded as she struggled to find a polite word.

'Difficult?'

'Yes! Difficult. At times.'

Marshall gave her a lopsided smile and Jess bit her lip.

18

'I'll be diplomatic, don't you worry.'

There was a pause between them. A heavy silence that dragged at Jess. Just as she opened her mouth to say things she really shouldn't, Ruby came running back into the garden shouting that she'd found her pink bucket.

She passed the bucket through the fence slats to Marshall, who took it with that lopsided smile on his face.

'Thanks, kid. I'll collect all the worms and if you check out here later, say, maybe, at six? There'll be a bucket of worms on your side of the fence. Okay?'

Ruby nodded. Marshall looked back up to Jess and she had to quickly tear her eyes up to meet his gaze. 'And I'll let you know about the fence.'

'Great. Thank you. So much.' Jess gave him a smile, her hands on Ruby's shoulders. She opened her mouth to say more, anything to keep the conversation going, when a cheerful tune began playing in her pocket. 'Oh. That's me. Sorry.' Jess pulled out the phone, expecting to see Erica's name. She frowned. It wasn't Erica. 'Excuse me. I think I need to take this.' Giving Marshall one last glance, she herded Ruby back to the house and answered the phone.

'Hello?'

'Jess? It's Steve.'

'Hi.' Jess had a moment of panic. 'How are you doing?'

'Not great.'

'No.' Jess closed her eyes. Of course he wasn't. 'Is there anything I can do?'

'Actually, I think I'm going insane. I don't suppose I could borrow you?'

'Of course. Coffee? I can do tomorrow morning.'

'No. Now. Is that okay?'

Jess looked over at Ruby, standing in their kitchen, watching her expectantly. She put her hand over the phone's mouthpiece.

'Okay. Go watch TV.'

Ruby ran off into the house. Jess settled back at the kitchen table, facing into the garden this time, eyes fixed on that broken fence panel. 'I can't, Steve. There's no one to watch Ruby.'

'Bring her.'

'Steve, I can't—'

'Please, Jess. Bring whoever you like or need to. I need to talk to someone about this.'

Jess sighed. Wasn't there some sort of charity, who didn't have four-year-olds to look after, who dealt with situations like this?

'Look, Steve, I understand you need someone to talk to. Of course you do, but I can't bring Ruby into that situation. She's too…bouncy. Not to mention prying. It's not fair on you or her, and I don't have anyone to look after her right now.'

'I think my house is haunted,' Steve blurted. That stopped Jess. She held her breath for a moment.

'What?'

'I said it. There it is. And I need someone to tell me I'm not going mad.'

'But…what? Why do you think the house is haunted?'

'Please, Jess. Tonight. Come tonight if that's better. That's when it mostly happens anyway.'

Jess rubbed the space between her eyes.

'Okay. I'll see what I can do. I'll let you know.'

'Please, Jess.'

'Yes. I'll come, but I need to find a sitter for Ruby. I'll let you know.'

There was a pause.

'Thank you,' said Steve. 'See you later?'

'See you later. Bye.'

Jess hung up and heaved a sigh, wondering if Erica had found her grandmother yet.

Steve

Steve hung up the phone and stared at it. The silence in the house was heavy, weighing on him, pushing him down to the floor. He wanted to take a deep breath but didn't feel able to open his lungs.

He shook his head.

He was being ridiculous.

From the baby carrier on the chair next to him, Joe began to grumble. Steve glanced at him, his heart sinking as the baby began to cry.

He felt it too. Steve knew he did.

In one swift motion, Steve stood and picked up the baby carrier, striding towards the front door. Placing the baby down carefully, he grabbed his coat, keys and the bag his wife had so lovingly picked out to celebrate being six months pregnant. She'd been so proud of it, showing it off when he'd come home from work that night.

'Look, Steve! It's perfect.'

'For what?' Steve had grinned. He remembered it well, although he wondered at times if he'd changed his memory since his wife's death. In reality, his grin hadn't been that big. He'd had a bad day at work and had wanted to be alone when his wife had shoved the bag in front of him, nattering on about her day. Work had been hard then, and the idea of her spending yet more money hadn't helped his mood. But those parts of the memory had faded weeks after her death, to be replaced with a big grin and how he should have reacted on that evening.

'It's for nappies and wipes and the bottle and everything else we'll need when we go out with the baby. Trust me. You'll thank me. When you want to go out, you'll be able to just pick up this bag and the baby and out we'll go.'

She'd been so happy, and she was right, the bag was useful. It had been worth every penny, and the memory of himself scoffing at her, struggling to pay her attention, made him so guilty he wanted to vomit.

Laden with everything he needed, Steve picked up the baby carrier and headed out of the door.

The hall lights flashed on and off.

Steve stopped and hung his head. His instincts screamed at him to run, as fast as he could. Instead, he stood his ground. Heart pounding, cold sweat prickling at his hot forehead as his stomach twisted and bowels loosened, Steve turned around.

There was nothing there.

He wasn't sure what he'd been expecting. Maybe to see her standing there, her arms crossed against her chest, an eyebrow raised as if to say, 'See, I told you we'd use that bag.'

She wasn't there.

He wasn't sure if he was relieved or not.

His head snapped up as the lights flickered on and off again. Maybe it was just the electrics. He should really call the developer, get it all checked out. There would be a logical and reasonable explanation.

Again, the lights flickered.

'Stop it!' Steve shouted without thinking. He span round, his grip on Joe's carrier tightening until his whitened knuckles ached, and ran out of the house, pulling the door shut behind him with a slam.

3

Erica went to the cemetery first. Her mother said she'd already looked there but there were places she didn't know about. Places Erica's grandmother had shown her. She parked her car in what constituted a car park but was actually just a large area of gravel. There were a couple of other cars, most likely belonging to the volunteers who couldn't walk there, and one truck with a back full of lopped branches.

Erica stood by her Mini Cooper and took a deep breath. Despite the nearby main road, the cemetery was quiet except for bird song, and the air smelt fresh. There was something about this cemetery. Erica had always felt it as a child when her mother and grandmother had brought her here to visit her grandfather's grave. Erica gave a small smile and began a slow walk down a path off to the left. The cemetery was old and had at one point been left to ruin, so instead of gravestones in smart rows, huge trees filled the site with shrubbery growing between tombstones placed there centuries ago. Magpies cackled overhead as Erica moved into what had become a small woodland, the floor littered with old grave markers. There was an area cleared for the recent graves, those who had ancestors already buried in the cemetery, or who had strong local connections and had donated funding to the volunteers who worked to keep the site preserved. Erica trailed her fingers through the leaves of a bush as she passed. Her grandfather had tended the woodland. He had been part of the conversation about whether the trees would be felled and the area cleared to its former glory. He had argued against it, preferring to allow nature to keep its hold.

'After all,' he had told Erica. 'We all go back to nature in the end.' That was her strongest memory of the man. That, and the smell. Earth and dog and cigar smoke. That was her grandfather.

Standing in front of his grave, Erica wondered whether her mother had stood in the same spot earlier that day during her search.

'Is she there, Granddad?' Erica asked, a smile playing on her face. 'Who is she talking to?'

No one answered. No one ever did.

Erica moved past the grave, kissing her fingers and pressing them against her grandfather's gravestone as she passed it.

Towards the back of the cleared area, where the majority of the new graves were, was a brick wall covered in ivy. Erica walked along it until she reached a wooden gate. Most people assumed it was locked or out of bounds so the volunteers called what was behind the gate the Secret Garden. Not that imaginative but it was a perfect description. Erica opened the creaking latch and eased her way through, closing the gate behind her.

The cemetery was quiet but the Secret Garden was silent. The birds still sang but their song was softer. The chatter of the magpies was in the distance and the road noise was just a memory. The cemetery was in the middle of the city, but Erica could easily have been stood in the countryside. Lost, forgotten among the trees, shrubs and long grass. The volunteers had lovingly turned the space into a garden. The grass was kept long, for the wildlife, but a path had been mown through it. Erica walked through, searching the darkness between the close tree trunks for movement.

Trees lined the edge of the long grass and beyond them was another wall and a gate leading onto a small Victorian chapel. Erica followed the winding mown path round to the left as it diverted, one way leading further into the garden, the other towards the chapel. Erica stayed in the garden, around the trunk of a large yew tree and there, against the far brick wall, sat on a bench, was her grandmother.

Minerva Warner was eighty-nine but didn't look a day over sixty. She didn't act a day over twenty. Her long skirt brushed against the short grass upon which the bench sat. Her fingers tapped against the arm of the bench, her face held up, eyes closed, a smile on her lips.

'Hi, Gran.' Erica stood in front of her grandmother and waited. Minerva opened her watery blue eyes and gazed up at her granddaughter.

'Erica. You found me.'

'It was easy, really.' Erica sat next to Minerva as her grandmother patted the bench beside her. 'Have you been speaking to Granddad?'

Minerva gave a single nod.

'He asked after you.'

'What did you tell him?'

Her grandmother turned and looked her in the eye. Erica never had been able to withstand that for long.

'You didn't get the job.'

'How did you…?' Erica shook her head. Her grandmother always knew these things, Erica didn't know why she even questioned it anymore.

'He told me. He told me to be kind to you, because the bastards had screwed you over. Again.'

Erica laughed.

'Yeah. Pretty much.' She looked up into the garden, through the long grass to the yew tree. 'Why did you leave the home, Gran?'

Minerva waved away the question.

'Why do I do anything? Because I wanted to. What do you want to do?'

Erica's gaze fell to her feet.

'I don't know. Hey!' She looked back up to her grandmother who was gazing at her with a sparkle in her eye. 'Don't change the subject. What are you doing here?'

'I needed to talk to them.'

'Them?' Erica knew who she was talking about. She held the sigh in.

'You're in need of guidance.'

'You didn't know that when you left the home.'

'No. I was in need of guidance then.'

Erica shifted so she faced her grandmother.

'Why did you need guidance?'

Minerva didn't respond. She looked up at the yew tree.

'They told me that you shouldn't worry about your job. Because something big is coming. Something good.' She held up a finger. 'But big. It'll be scary, but you're more than strong enough.' She faced her granddaughter and smiled. 'Your life is about to change, Erica.'

Erica didn't return the smile. Instead, she frowned as a heavy weight dropped into her stomach.

'A new job would do,' she managed to say. 'Is this bigger than a new job?'

'By the sounds of it. Have you quit yet?'

'What? No! I haven't got another job to replace it yet. I can't leave.'

Minerva rolled her eyes.

'I have money. You can have it to live off until this big thing happens.'

'I'm not taking your money, Gran.'

'You will when I'm dead. Why not now?'

'Gran! Don't talk like that. Oh.' Erica took out her phone and quickly called her mother. 'Hi mum. I've found her, safe and sound. I'll make sure she gets back to the home. Hmm? She was at the cemetery, you must have just missed her.' Minerva shot Erica a warning look. 'Oh. Okay. Sure. I'll bring her home then. I'll text when we're on our way. Love you. Bye.'

Erica hung up and stayed staring at the time on her phone as the light dimmed, feeling her grandmother watching. It was too late to do any work now, and the longer she stayed here the later it would be. 'Mum wants me to take you home instead. She's making a big dinner.'

Minerva nodded.

'That'll be lovely.'

'I probably can't stay. I'm meeting Jess tonight.'

'Jess can come too. Your mum won't mind. Jess and her little 'un. They mentioned her too, you know.'

'They mentioned Ruby?'

'No. Jess. They mentioned Jess. This big change

that's coming? It involves her.'

Erica sat back.

'Maybe we're both going to be made redundant.'

'Would you like that?'

'It would be nice to be paid to leave.' Erica shrugged. 'Jess has wanted to leave for ages.'

'I didn't realise she was stuck looking for something new too.'

'Not stuck. She doesn't want another job, she wants to start her own business but couldn't do it properly until her mortgage was through. Her new house is nice, you'll have to come see it sometime.'

Minerva grinned.

'That would be lovely. I can anoint it. Make sure it stays a safe, happy place for them. Jess could do with some happiness.' She glanced at Erica out of the corner of her eye. 'As could you.'

'Couldn't we all?' Erica asked.

'You know, they once asked me to go with them.'

'You've told me.'

'Yes, but it's a good story, don't you think? Romantic. Being asked to leave this world and travel to theirs. One of them wanted to marry me. He was kind and sweet. I nearly said yes.'

A warmth travelled through Erica at the thought of it, but also from the comfort of hearing this story yet again.

'Why didn't you?'

'I would have had to become one of them. I would have been stuck in their world. Can you imagine? Life as a fae. Immortality, constantly living with the seasons, having sex all the time.'

'Gran,' Erica said without much conviction. Minerva beamed.

'It would have been amazing. But if I'd done that, I wouldn't have had your mother, or your uncles. I wouldn't have had you.' Minerva planted a kiss on Erica's head. Erica leaned into her.

'No. You would have had other children. Other grandchildren.'

'It would have been awful,' Minerva agreed. Erica took her hand and squeezed.

'No regrets?' she asked.

'No regrets.' Minerva squeezed back. 'Plus, it turns out you don't have to be a fae to have sex with them,' she whispered.

Erica froze and then carefully disentangled her hand from her grandmother's.

'That's why you came here? To have sex? If I'd arrived a bit earlier, would I have interrupted?' Erica's voice was becoming shrill. She coughed to bring it down. Minerva was practically cackling.

'It's not why I came here. This time.' Minerva gave Erica a sideways glance. 'They're quite handsome, the fae men, if you're in need of—'

'No.' Erica interrupted. 'I am not in need of. I'm definitely not in need of.' She bit her lip. That was a lie. She was completely in need of, but the idea of even meeting her grandmother's fae friends sent nervous shivers through her. For now, she could still tell herself that it was all in her grandmother's head. But if she met them? What would she have to think then?

'You will meet them one day,' said Minerva, as if reading her mind. She stood with a creak and a groan. 'Come on, then. Let's get home.' She began walking down the mown path, back towards the gate and her late husband's grave.

Erica watched her for a moment. A breeze swam

through the garden, shaking the blades of grass and lifting the leaves. Erica held her breath and cocked her head. Was it her imagination or could she hear someone laughing? She looked around. Visitors, perhaps on the other side of the wall. Except the laughter was soft and came from all around, finishing in the trees to the side. A ray of sunshine fought its way through the clouds and landed on the yew tree. Erica watched, dazzled.

'Are you coming?' Minerva's voice broke through the reverie.

'Yes.' Erica stood up. 'Here I come.' She took a couple of shaky steps when something made her stop. Every part of her body wanted to turn around, to face the trees. Someone's watching you, her mind told her. Somebody's there. Turn around.

No, thought Erica. No, no, no.

She jogged to catch up with her grandmother. Minerva's gaze went past Erica to the line of trees. She gave a subtle nod and then put her arm around her granddaughter, leading her away.

As Minerva eased into Erica's car, Erica couldn't help but look around again at the cemetery. The awkward feeling was gone, no one was watching them now. The steady roar of the main road was back. The wind must have changed direction. Off to one side, the magpies argued in the tree tops. Erica climbed into the driving seat. Her phone rang, making Minerva jump and swear.

'Sorry,' Erica mumbled, pulling her phone out. She answered. 'Hey, Jess. You okay?'

'Hey,' said Jess. 'I'm great. Except I think I might be in a porn film.'

Erica blinked.

'Excuse me? What...? Is this about work?'

'What? No. Of course not. I'll explain later. I just had a call from Steve. Do you remember Steve?'

'Steve. The guy you used to work with, with the new baby who…oh.'

'Yeah. That Steve. He just called me and he wants me to pop round tonight.'

'How come?'

'Well, he's worried he's, erm, going insane.'

'That'll be the grief.'

'Yes. That's what I thought, so he just needs some reassurance.'

'Okay. Do you want me to come with you? I'm sure my mum will watch Ruby if you like? Then you can come back to ours for dinner. I'm just taking my grandmother home now.'

'You, Erica Murray, are magical.'

Erica laughed.

'Well, there's no way I'm letting to you go alone to the house of a man who's worried he's going insane.'

'There is that. But there's also…'

'Yeah?'

'You're not going to like this, but it's the other reason I'd quite like your company.'

'Go on.'

'He thinks his house is haunted.'

There was a long pause while Erica took a deep breath.

'I'm going to join you because I love you and I want to make sure you're safe,' Erica told Jess carefully. 'And that's it.'

4

'Ruby! We're going to be late.'

'The worms, Mummy,' came Ruby's voice from the kitchen. Jess, waiting by the front door, stopped and blinked.

'You what?'

'He left the worms. I can see the bucket.'

'Oh. Oh, well. Good. They'll be okay until later, we'll deal with them then.'

'But won't the birds eat them?' Ruby appeared at her mother's side. Jess looked down at her.

'Fine!' Jess cried, throwing her arms up in exasperation but grinning all the while. Ruby jumped up and down, and followed her mother to the patio doors and out into the garden.

There was the pink bucket, pushed through the broken fence panel and into their garden. Jess suppressed a smile. 'Go on then. Go get the bucket. Let's see what we've got.'

The bucket, which Ruby held up proudly for her mother to inspect, had a large pile of writhing worms at the bottom. Jess was impressed. The worms ranged from pink to brown and varied in thickness and length. Clods of dirt stuck to some, hiding their true size. 'In the corner.' Jess pointed. 'On the empty flower bed, there.'

Ruby pulled a face.

'I can't just dump them. The birds will eat them.'

Jess sighed.

'They bury into the earth, sweetie. That's what worms do. It'll be fine. Empty out the bucket and we'll get going.'

Ruby stuck out her bottom lip in defiance. 'Don't make me tell you again, Rubes,' Jess said in her firm mother voice. 'Even if birds do get some, that's what life is. Imagine if birds didn't get any. The birds would starve.'

Ruby's eyes widened a little.

'I don't want them to starve.'

'No. So let the worms go free, let them bury themselves and live, and if a bird chooses one, then that means a bird gets to live.'

Ruby nodded gravely and Jess watched as she emptied the pink bucket of worms onto the flower bed. She put the empty but dirty bucket back by the fence panel. 'You're putting it back?' Jess asked.

'Yes. So Marshall can put tomorrow's worms in there. He isn't finished,' Ruby told her, peering through the fence panel.

'Fair enough.' Jess reached out to her daughter. 'Come on then.' She led the way back into the kitchen, pausing to lock the patio doors, and then through the house.

There was a knock on the front door just as Jess and Ruby reached it.

'Oh, for the love of—' Jess was beginning to wonder if they would ever leave. She peeked through the peephole and took a sharp breath. It was Marshall.

She rocked back on her heels.

'Mummy? Are you going to open it or are we not

home?' asked Ruby.

Jess exhaled slowly and opened the door. Marshall smiled at her, the smile falling as he looked from Jess to Ruby.

'Are you on your way out?'

Jess blinked and glanced down at little Ruby beside her with her yellow backpack.

'Yes. Yes, we're just leaving.'

Marshall gave a nod.

'I'll be quick then. Mr Horton says he won't be paying to fix the fence.' Marshall screwed his face up as if in pain. 'Sorry.'

Jess laughed and then stopped, wondering what Marshall must think of her.

'Oh, don't be. I never expected him to pay for it. What's annoying is that I've offered to get it fixed, pay for it and everything, about three times since I moved in and we only moved in a week ago.'

That smile was back on Marshall's face. Jess had a tough time not staring.

'I can fix it for you.'

'That would be fantastic,' Jess gushed. 'How much, do you think?'

Marshall hesitated.

'Forty quid?'

Jess paused.

'Really?' She narrowed her eyes. 'Are you sure?'

'Yeah.' Marshall flashed his teeth in a grin. 'Did you find the worms I left you?' he asked Ruby before Jess could respond.

Ruby nodded emphatically.

'We put them somewhere safe. On a worm flowerbed,' she told the big man.

'A worm flowerbed. Sounds like a worm

paradise,' Marshall told her. Ruby nodded and then looked up at Jess.

'Can I do that, Mummy? Make it into a worm paradise?'

'Of course.'

'With flowers and a swimming pool.'

Jess narrowed her eyes.

'I think worms just like mud. Maybe we'll look up more about worms and see what they like to eat.'

Ruby nodded.

'You have to have snacks while you're by the pool.'

Jess and Marshall stared at Ruby for a moment. That's her father, Jess thought. That's what he does when he takes her away on holiday. She resisted rolling her eyes and instead looked back up at Marshall. At his tanned skin and short dark hair. Those dark eyes caught hers and his lips twitched.

'So, when would be a good time to come fix that fence?'

'When you've gotten all the worms,' said Ruby before Jess could answer. Jess put her hand affectionately on Ruby's head.

'Anytime. I'm around most of tomorrow.'

'Great. I'll get the panel in the morning and let you know when I have a moment spare.' Marshall smiled at them and gave Ruby a nod. 'See you tomorrow, then.' He turned and walked away down the driveway towards a white van parked outside the neighbour's house.

'Yup,' murmured Jess, watching him closely.

'Mummy? Mummy? Are we going or not?'

'Shit. Yes. We're going to be late. Quick, quick! Get in the car.' Jess pressed her car key and the car bleeped as it unlocked. She stepped out and turned to lock the front door to find Ruby staring up at her, still in the house. 'What? Come on!'

'You swore, Mummy.'

Jess bit her tongue to stop her swearing again.

'I did, didn't I. I'm very sorry, Ruby. That was very naughty of me.'

'Yup.' Ruby walked out of the house and straight to the car. Jess locked the front door and heaved a large sigh.

ಬಂಡ

'So, when Steve says he think he's going insane, he means…?' Erica drifted off, checking her wing mirror before moving into the outer lane.

'I don't know. He just said he thinks the house is haunted,' said Jess.

They were in Erica's Mini, driving down the dual carriageway that led to the new housing estate where Steve and his wife, Rachel, had bought their first family home.

'He thinks his wife is haunting him?'

Jess shrugged.

'It makes sense, don't you think? If I died, I'd sure as hell come back and haunt Ruby's dad.'

'It's a bit different. From what you've said, Steve's wife actually liked him.'

'I meant so I could see Ruby,' Jess said. 'She left behind her newborn baby. If that's not unfinished business, I don't know what is.'

'I guess,' murmured Erica. Jess looked at her. Erica glanced sideways but otherwise didn't take her eyes from the road.

'I never understand your scepticism,' Jess said.

'Really? You really can't understand it?'

'No. If I'd grown up with your mum and grandmother, I'd believe it all the way.'

'And do you?' Erica asked. 'Do you believe in ghosts?'

Jess shuffled in her seat. To be honest, she wasn't sure.

'Maybe. We'll see what Steve says.' She wondered what she was hoping for. The idea of a real haunting fascinated her, but the idea of the woman coming back to haunt her husband and watch over her baby was a little too much to bear. Jess suddenly had the strong urge to turn around, grab Ruby and go home. Home to her broken fence panel and a bucket waiting for more worms. 'Anyway, I think I might be in a porn film.'

'Oh yeah!' Erica grinned. 'What's that about then?'

'I came home today to find this man helping out Mr Horrible Next Door.'

'That grumpy old man?'

'Yeah. Anyway, turns out this guy is his handyman.'

'So?'

'So, you should see him, Ric. He's gorgeous. He's big and tall and his arms... And he's a handyman.'

'I don't get it.'

'Oh, come on. He's coming round tomorrow to fix our broken fence panel. You still don't get it? The sexy handyman coming round to fix the horny single mother's fence panel?'

Erica's cheeks flushed a little and she shook her head.

'Okay. I get it.' Her grin fell. 'That's not what he's actually doing, though. Is it?'

'He's literally fixing the fence panel. There'll be no sex on the dining table.'

'That was a tad specific.'

'Was it? Well, I certainly haven't given it any thought whatsoever.' Jess cleared her throat. 'It's just off here. Over there.' She pointed.

Erica chuckled, turning the Mini around a roundabout and into the new estate.

The houses, painted in soft pastel pinks, blues and yellows, were narrow and tall, each with three levels and terraced. The front doors were white and clean. The windows on the top level were floor to ceiling and some were lavishly decorated with long curtains and tall lamps. Jess could almost be envious, if it wasn't for the fact that those beautiful windows looked out onto the dual carriageway and a building site. No, her little detached house with normal windows and long driveway was so much better. She wondered how big the gardens were behind these houses.

Jess glanced down at the address on her phone screen and directed Erica to park outside one particular house. It was painted a pastel blue. All of the windows were dark except for one on the ground floor, and through the net curtains Jess could see kitchen units and a dining table. There was movement and a suggestion of a man walking through.

Jess climbed out of the car and made her way to the front door while Erica got out more slowly, studying the house.

Jess knocked softly on the door, mindful of the baby behind it. A silence followed.

'Why do they have to put new houses so close to each other?' murmured Erica in her ear. Jess shrugged.

'Makes them more money, I guess.'

Erica shook her head, looking down the street.

'You'd think the logic would be that people would spend more for more space, rather than everyone living on top of one another.'

Jess opened her mouth to reply when the door opened.

The hallway was brightly lit, so the man standing at the door became silhouetted. Still, as Jess blinked up at him, her eyes grew accustomed and she could make out some features. His hair had grown shaggy, although not yet long, and he had a beard where he hadn't before. His hair was chestnut, but grey was peeking through at the sides. His green eyes were rimmed red and looked exhausted. In fact, everything about him screamed exhaustion. His skin was pale and dehydrated. Jess frowned.

'Hi, Steve.'

'Jess, thank you so much for coming. Come in, come in.' Steve stepped aside to make way.

'Thanks. This is Erica. She's a friend of mine. She has some, err, experience…so I thought she could help.'

Steve nodded sagely as the women entered the house. 'Where's the baby?' Jess asked. Steve closed the front door.

'Asleep, upstairs.' He nodded to the staircase.

Jess gave an awkward nod and waited, unsure of what to say. Thankfully, Steve had enough wits about him to lead them into the kitchen where he offered them seats at the table. They sat and Jess accepted an offer of tea, although Erica declined. The women glanced at one another as Steve turned away to make the drinks.

A baby monitor sat in the centre of the table but no noise came from it. Jess searched for the little light that said it was on.

'Is this working, Steve?' she asked without thinking. He looked over his shoulder to her, glanced at the baby monitor and went back to making the tea without reacting. Jess caught Erica's eye. 'I can go check on him, if you like. Give you a little break?'

'No. He's okay. I checked on him before you knocked. He's fine.' Steve placed the tea cups on the table and sat, looking down. He took a deep breath, reached forward and turned the baby monitor on.

Jess sat back.

'I'm always here, Steve,' she murmured. 'If you need help or just a break. You just have to call me.'

Steve gave a small smile.

'Thank you,' he whispered. 'How's work?' He looked up, his voice back to normal, looking from Jess to Erica.

'It's fine,' said Jess, noncommittally.

'You hate it, don't you?' Steve gave a small laugh which Jess echoed.

'Yeah. I do. But I've just bought my own house, so it has some benefits.'

'You work together?' Steve asked, glancing at Erica.

'Yup. Partners in crime.' Jess smiled at Erica affectionately and Erica attempted a warm smile back. Yup, thought Jess, this is still too awkward. 'What's going on then, Steve?'

Steve's gaze flickered to the baby monitor. Jess and Erica followed suit. Jess tapped her finger against her cup. 'What's going on?' she whispered.

Silence filled the room. Jess sighed. 'Seriously, Steve.'

Steve blinked.

'Maybe it's because you're here,' he said. 'Maybe that's why it's not happening.'

'Why what's not happening?' asked Jess.

The baby gurgled through the monitor and then began to cry. With a heaving sigh, Steve scraped his chair back. 'I'll go if you want,' Jess offered gently.

'No. No, it's okay. I'll go. I'll be right back.' Steve left the room, leaving Jess and Erica staring at the baby monitor.

'Maybe I shouldn't have come,' murmured Erica. 'Maybe it's because I'm here, he's not opening up. I can wait outside?'

Jess opened her mouth to speak when there was a sharp crack. They both snapped to look at the baby monitor. The crying had quietened and had been replaced with roaring white noise.

'Err, does that happen with baby monitors?' Erica asked, leaning back.

Jess cocked her head at the device.

'Sometimes wavelengths get crossed over. You pick up other people's monitors. It's terrifying. It sounds like someone's in your baby's room comforting them. It only happened the once. I chucked the monitor and bought a different brand. Didn't have a problem after that.' Jess gave a nervous laugh. 'It's the ones with screens that I don't get. Stupid idea. I've seen too many horror movies to put up with that.'

Erica did an attempt at a laugh but the white noise became louder and drowned her out. Just as quickly as it had started, the noise stopped and silence filled the room. The sound of the baby crying filtered down the stairs.

'Ah,' said Jess. 'It's broken. That's all. That must have been its last legs.' She leaned forward to pick up the monitor. As her fingers brushed against it, it sparked back to life with a bang sending Jess jumping backwards. Erica leapt to her feet, her chair falling over.

'Are you okay?' She jumped over the chair to Jess's side, her hand on her friend's shoulder.

'What the fuck was that?' Jess growled, standing straight and checking her hands. 'Did it just blow up?'

'Are you okay?' Steve trotted down the stairs, hanging onto the banister to peer into the kitchen. 'I heard a bang?'

'Your baby monitor exploded,' Erica told him. That brought Steve into the kitchen.

'It what?'

'It made a crackling noise and then exploded.'

Steve looked to Jess who nodded.

'Was it new? You should take it back and get a refund. That's disgusting! Is the monitor upstairs okay? Steve? Are you okay? You don't look okay.'

Steve had paled further as Jess talked. Silently, he ran back up the stairs and returned with the other baby monitor in one hand and a basket holding his son in the other. He placed them both on the table.

Jess had never been one for babies. Ruby had been something of an accident. Jess had struggled through baby-parent classes and meet-ups when she'd first become a mother, before admitting that the only baby she liked was her own and that she generally preferred the company of other grown-ups. Still, she worked hard on her relationships with other parents. Ruby had friends, after all, and you never knew when you'd need to call in a favour for a babysitter. It meant that Jess glanced over at Steve's baby boy, but she didn't feel the need to coo over him. He was tiny, wrinkled and soft looking. Far too fragile, she thought, remembering Ruby at that age. She'd been terrified to hold her for fear of breaking her.

'It's working fine,' said Steve, gesturing to the second baby monitor. His voice repeated through the monitor and for a moment it felt like Jess's heart had stopped.

'How is it doing that?' she asked.

Erica took the monitor from Steve and spoke gently into it.

'Hello?'

The word echoed around the room as it sounded through the blown monitor. There was a pause. Even the baby was silent.

'But. But it blew up?' Jess murmured.

'Do you mind if I take a look?' Erica asked. Steve shook his head.

'Be my guest. It's been acting strange ever since…' Steve looked down at his son as Erica got to work taking the back off the blown monitor. 'It worked fine when we bought it. It started making strange noises the first night after she…passed away. At first I thought it was what you'd told me, Jess. Crossed radio signals and all that. But it happens every night. Every. Single. Night. And sometimes during the day. That, and the lights.'

'What about the lights?' Jess asked.

'They flicker. I've had an electrician out to look at them. He says there's nothing wrong, that it must be a power surge. But you don't get that many power surges, do you? And not every night. I can't

48

sleep. I forget to eat.'

'I don't think you'd be doing those things anyway,' Jess murmured without thinking, watching Erica and the baby monitor closely.

'Well, yeah. I thought it was the grief at first. It does funny things to your head, doesn't it? But this isn't the grief, Jess. You're not grieving her but you heard it. Erica didn't even know her but she heard it too. It's not just me. I'm not going crazy.'

Jess looked up at Steve and sagged. The poor man. They hadn't been overly close at Jess's last agency where they'd met and worked together. They'd sat next to each other and made jokes, shared problem clients and helped each other out. Jess had listened to the wedding plans and then the pregnancy updates until the day she left. Then they'd only shared customary likes and comments online until Steve's wife had been hit by a car. Even then, they'd only messaged each other, except for one meeting over coffee the day after the funeral. Steve had needed the company and the baby needed the fresh air.

'You're not going crazy,' she murmured to him, gingerly placing a hand on his arm and squeezing. He looked down at his baby boy and blinked a few times, evidently holding back the tears.

'No. Definitely not,' muttered Erica. She looked up and caught Jess's eye. Jess edged closer as Erica shielded what she had found from Steve. She had removed the back from the monitor to reveal the batteries. Or, at least, where the batteries should have been. Instead there were two pillars of silver dust.

'What in the hell?' whispered Jess.

'But it's still working,' Erica whispered back.

The two women looked at one another.

'What do you think?' Jess asked her. Erica shrugged.

'What is it?' came Steve's voice over their shoulders, making Jess jump.

'The batteries are gone,' Erica told him, carefully showing him the insides of the monitor. Steve leaned over to look.

'But it's working still?'

'Yes.'

Steve turned to Jess with wild panic in his eyes.

'It's not me?'

Jess shook her head, resisting the urge to hug the man.

'It's not you. This isn't you. Look, why don't we take the monitor and look into this further. I'll let you know how we get on and I can come round tomorrow morning, if you like? Give you a hand with anything.' She wanted to offer to take the baby, to give him a break, but she had her own child to get back to.

Steve only nodded.

'Thank you. We're okay. I just wish this would…stop.'

'I know,' Jess said gently. 'We'll do everything we can. I promise.'

Steve flashed her a sad but thankful smile.

'Why do you want the monitor?' Erica asked Jess as they left the house.

Jess turned back to Erica.

'Any chance your grandmother will know anything about this?'

Steve

Steve climbed the stairs and paused to listen in at the nursery. Satisfied that Joe was asleep and breathing, he turned to go into the bathroom.

He stopped, his breath rushing out at once.

Had he imagined that noise?

He turned to face the landing and listened.

There.

He took an involuntary step backwards, into the bathroom.

A voice, high-pitched and soothing.

'Hello?' he called quietly. Without thinking, he strode into his son's nursery, pushing the door open so hard it crashed into the wall with a bang.

There was no one there other than the baby who began to cry. Steve picked him up, murmuring to him as he studied the room. There was nothing out of place. The window was still closed and locked. Holding his baby close, Steve breathed a sigh of relief.

It was all in his head. Maybe he was going mad. He kissed his son's head. No, not mad. It was the grief. Just the grief. This would pass. It had to.

Steve placed a now quiet Joe back into his cot. His bladder, now certain that the danger had passed, was cramping urgently. He promised Joe he'd be back soon and almost ran across the landing to the bathroom.

As he flushed the toilet, the noise sounded again, louder this time, from the other side of the bathroom door. A woman's voice, talking to someone in a calm tone. It ended just as Steve registered it, so he stopped, holding his breath, urging for the toilet to be silent.

The voice was quiet, until Steve turned to leave.

Was that? Steve shook his head but every part of his body knew it was true. It was her voice. He'd know it anywhere, despite it being muffled by the door. Despite her talking so low. Steve made his way carefully onto the landing.

The voice, his wife's voice, was singing now. A gentle lullaby coming from the nursery. Steve could see the cot and his son, but he couldn't see if there was anyone else there. He tried to make out the words of the song, but the voice was too low. A whispered hush. But he knew the tune. It was the tune his wife had hummed to her swollen, pregnant belly as she'd gone about her day. The same tune she'd sing to lull Joe to sleep when he was days old.

A lump rose in Steve's throat, tears blurring his vision.

His chest tightened as a shadow fell across the nursery floor and then disappeared.

'Rachel?' Steve called, his voice cracking. The light above his head flickered. He walked into the nursery but there was no one there. Just Joe, sleeping in his cot. Steve brushed the tears from his face with his sleeve and took a long sniff.

When would this grief fade?

He looked down at his baby boy, letting a hand hang into the cot. His fingers nudged something hard. Frowning, Steve carefully pulled the blanket away and lifted the culprit up.

A bracelet. A thin silver band.

Steve's hand flew over his mouth and he fell to his knees, the tears coming freely, his body wracked by huge sobs. It was no use swallowing them down, no use attempting to hold them back. He cried, loud and horribly, waking up the baby whose cries and yells joined with his own. In his hand, clutched against his aching stomach, he gripped his wife's bracelet.

5

Erica drove home slowly. Jess sat in the passenger seat in silence. Both were lost in their own thoughts. Erica imagined her thoughts would be slightly more awkward than Jess's. Was she a sceptic? She'd never thought of herself like that. Jess was right, how could she be a sceptic? No, sceptic wasn't the right word. So, why didn't she believe in this ghost? Even when she'd looked into that baby monitor and had seen the batteries turned to dust, she'd not been scared. She'd just known. That was it. The supernatural was a truth and this wasn't the truth Jess wanted it to be. Erica frowned.

'Let me show the batteries to my gran,' she told Jess. Jess seemed to startle out of her thoughts.

'Okay.' She paused. 'What do you think it is?'

'Honestly? It's not what you'd classify as normal,' Erica said, pulling up at red traffic lights. She sat back in her seat.

'It's something paranormal?'

'If by that you mean not normal, then yes. It's not necessarily a ghost though.'

'Oh? Why not?'

Erica looked at Jess.

'I can't say.'

Jess narrowed her eyes.

'Well, now you realise you have to tell me.'

Erica looked away. It had been a long time since she'd admitted these feelings to herself, never mind to someone else. But if she was going to say it out loud, it might as well be to Jess. It should be to a believer.

'Okay. Here goes.' Erica took a deep breath, staring out of the window, avoiding Jess's gaze. 'I didn't feel anything.' She snapped her mouth shut.

The air between them became heavy but Erica daren't look at her friend.

'What do you mean, feel anything? You couldn't feel a ghost?' Jess shifted her weight to lean closer to Erica. 'You can feel ghosts?'

Erica pulled a face.

'Sometimes.'

'Like, you can see dead people?'

This made Erica face Jess.

'Of course not. Can you imagine?'

'Absolutely terrifying.' Jess agreed with a nod.

'I can't really explain it. Gran can do it, Mum can do it, I can do it. I think a lot of people can. Maybe you can too.'

'But I didn't grow up in a house full of ghosts.'

Erica gave a small smile.

'It was Gran's house that was full of ghosts, not mine.'

'But still.'

Erica sighed, looking out the driver's window into the evening and rush hour traffic. Were these lights stuck on red?

Movement caught her eye and she watched as a man in a long, dark brown trench coat walked past the queues of vehicles, hunched over, hands deep in his pockets. It wasn't raining, it wasn't even that cold. Was he hiding from something? She noted the police station behind him. Had he just left there? He looked up for a moment, checking the lights, and she caught sight of his eyes. He didn't see her, didn't even glance at the car, but still something in Erica's stomach twisted.

'Ric. Lights.'

Erica looked up at the green light with a snap, quickly putting the car into gear and moving away. 'You okay?' Jess asked.

'Hmm? Oh, yeah. Just…lost in my thoughts.'

'Yeah. I'm sorry I dragged you into this.'

'What? No. Don't be. I'm glad I came. It was all a bit freaky. I wouldn't want you doing something like that on your own. Hopefully Gran can shed some light on the situation.'

ಸಾಡಿ

Erica's family home was a bustle of activity when they arrived. It usually was. Erica often expressed dismay at still living with her parents despite being in her thirties, but in truth she wasn't sure she'd cope on her own. It'd be far too quiet.

As they walked through the door, the two Labradors came running at them. The gangly black puppy leaped up at Erica while the older golden dog trotted over, wagging her tail. Erica greeted both of them with cuddles, pushing the puppy down.

'Ric? That you?' came her mother's voice.

'Yes!' she called back.

The smell of cooked chicken filled the house and they followed it into the kitchen, shadowed by the dogs.

Ruby sat drawing at the large oak table that dominated the small dining room, just off the kitchen. Beside her was Erica's grandmother, furiously colouring at a piece of paper with a crayon, the tip of her tongue poking from the corner of her mouth. Erica's mother, Esther Murray, stood at the oven, checking on the steaming vegetables. The back door opened and closed bringing a rush of cool air and Erica's father.

'Evening, girls.' He nodded to Jess and gave Erica a hug. 'How did it go?'

Erica and Jess exchanged a look.

'It went okay,' said Erica.

'Okay? It was downright weird.' Jess had moved into the dining room and planted a kiss on Ruby's head. The little girl didn't even glance at her, instead scribbling with her crayons.

'Weird?' Esther turned to look at them, her gaze lingering on her daughter. 'So the poor man is being haunted?'

Erica chewed on her bottom lip and sighed.

'Oh dear.' Her mother and grandmother glanced at one another. 'Do we need to discuss it?' her mother asked.

'Please,' said Jess.

'Maybe. Maybe we just got swept up in the whole thing. He was pretty distraught. Those strong emotions could have had an effect on us.'

'Grief is a powerful one.' Minerva nodded knowingly.

'A powerful what?' Ruby asked.

'Emotion.'

'Can emotions be powerful?'

'My dear one, emotions can be so powerful that they can change the course of history.' Minerva glanced at Erica.

Ruby looked up at her mother.

'It's true,' Jess told her. 'My love for you changed my life.'

That made everyone smile, although Ruby pulled a sick face.

'Tea's ready,' said Esther as she poured the vegetables into a dish. 'Clear the table, please.'

Erica moved to help set the table as Ruby and Jess tidied up.

'So, what was weird?' Erica's father asked as he and her mother laid the food on the table. They all took their seats.

'It was the baby monitor,' Erica told them. She quietened as she looked at Jess. Her friend had a sparkle in her eye. She wanted to tell this story and she'd do so with more passion than Erica, so Erica let her. Jess started right at the beginning, from when Steve had contacted her saying he thought he was going insane, and ended it with them leaving his house.

They were half way through their meals by the time she'd finished.

'What awful grief is the man suffering?' Minerva asked.

'His wife was killed,' Jess told her. 'A few months ago. A car crash.'

'And they have a baby.'

Jess nodded.

'It's awful. Steve was so excited when he met her, never mind when they got engaged and married. I still remember the day he told me she was pregnant. She was only seven weeks gone but he couldn't contain himself.' Jess glanced sideways at Ruby. 'It's one thing deciding to be a single parent, totally another thing to have it foisted on you,' she added quietly.

'Such a tragedy,' Minerva agreed. 'I should like to take a look at this baby monitor.'

'Mum, you're not a detective. You barely know how to work the remote control. What makes you think you'd understand the baby monitor?' Erica's mother said, filling her fork with chicken and potato.

Minerva rolled her eyes.

'Sweetheart, it's not the technology I want to look at. It's the dust. And I would think I know more about strange dust in technology than techno-men know about it.'

Erica smiled to herself.

'I'll show you when we're done,' she assured her.

Minerva narrowed her eyes at her granddaughter and leaned forward.

'What did you feel, Ric?'

Erica blinked.

'Nothing.'

'Erica?' came Minerva's warning voice.

'Honestly. There was nothing.'

A pause stretched out across the table.

'What does that mean?' Jess asked, chewing slowly. Beside her, Ruby shovelled the last forkful of food into her mouth.

'Highly unlikely to be a ghost.' Minerva sat back and sniffed. 'Not if Ric felt nothing. She always was good at sensing the supernatural.'

Erica frowned.

'Then how do you explain the dust?' Jess asked.

Minerva waggled a finger at her.

'Ah, well. We'll find out after pudding. And if we can't figure it out, I know some people we can ask.'

Erica's stomach twisted and she snapped a look at her mother.

'No,' said Esther.

'What?' Minerva furrowed her brow, as if having trouble hearing.

'You're not asking the damn fairies.'

'Manners, Esther,' Minerva snapped. 'And they're fae, not fairies. Have you forgotten what I taught you?'

'Oh, I remember. I remember all too well. And I remember telling you I don't want Erica involved with them. And you certainly shouldn't be talking about it when there are young people in the room.' Esther gestured subtly at Ruby. Ruby didn't seem to notice.

'Jess has a new fancy man,' Erica blurted out. She immediately regretted it. Jess widened her eyes, as if caught in headlights, as everyone turned to look at her. Erica flashed her an apologetic smile.

'Oh? Who is he?' asked Minerva.

'What's a fancy man?' Ruby asked.

Jess glowered at Erica, who sank low into her seat.

'It's nothing,' Jess told Ruby. 'And he's no-body,' she said to the room. There was an awkward pause as everyone looked down at their plates. Jess sighed and shrugged. 'But, in news entirely unrelated.' Jess nodded subtly in Ruby's direction without her daughter noticing. 'Next door has hired a handyman.'

'Oh.' Minerva and Esther exchanged a smirk.

'Is that the worm man?' Ruby asked.

'Should we ask?' said Erica's father, pulling a face at Ruby who stuck her tongue out at him.

'He's pulling up next door's lawn and Ruby was

worried about the worms. So any he finds, he's putting into a bucket for her, through our broken fence.'

'That's still broken? I can still come fix it for you,' Erica's father offered.

'No, thanks. Marshall's going to do it.'

'Oh. Marshall, is it?' said Minerva, the smirk still twitching at the corners of her mouth.

'Don't go paying a man. I'll do it for free,' said Erica's father. His wife elbowed him gently.

'That's not the point,' she murmured to him.

'By the sounds of it, he's giving me a heavy discount, so it's no problem,' Jess told him.

'I bet he is,' said Minerva. They all looked at her until she cackled and shovelled another forkful of food into her mouth.

After pudding, Ruby was convinced into helping Erica's father wash up, leaving the women to gather in the living room. Erica carefully showed them the dust filled compartment of Steve's baby monitor.

Esther sighed.

Minerva whistled through her dentures.

'It could well be a spirit,' she said, taking the monitor from Erica. Erica collapsed back into her seat, glad to no longer be touching the thing. Jess leaned forward, eager, eyes wide.

'You really think it could be a ghost?'

'It might not be a spirit,' Esther told them. 'Grief could have done this. Not a spirit.'

Minerva twisted her lips.

'True. True. But look. The insides are completely frazzled. Nothing but dust left. I've never known grief to do that. Grief can move objects, it can kill batteries, but I've never known it to rot them away to dust. And it must have been quick. A short, sharp burst.' She held the monitor to her nose and gave it a quick sniff.

'Does it smell of sulphur?' Jess asked.

'No.'

Erica gave Jess a look. Jess had no idea what she was talking about, but she was saying all the right things. The very idea made Erica's stomach clench.

'Maybe we shouldn't be getting involved,' she murmured.

'What? You saw poor Steve. There's a baby in that house. We have to help them,' Jess said. 'If not us, then who?'

Erica shrugged and looked to her grandmother for help but Minerva ignored her.

'You should help the poor soul,' she murmured. 'I can't feel much coming off this.' She looked up at Erica. 'You said you felt nothing?' Erica nodded. 'Interesting.'

'So, how does it work?' Jess asked. 'How would a ghost turn batteries to dust?'

'Oh, it's simple. A ghost isn't a person. It's the remnants of them. And what are all living beings made up of? Energy! A spirit is basically a big ball of energy and depending on the strength of that energy, they can do different things, like move objects, control technology or talk to us.'

'But if they're not a person, how can they talk to us?'

'They were a person once. The energy, if strong enough, will have their memories.'

'But not their consciousness?' Jess asked. Erica could have sworn she sounded disappointed.

Minerva looked up at the ceiling.

'It's a tricky one. Everything I've been taught

says no, and yet sometimes you have these experiences…' she trailed off, turning her attention back to the baby monitor.

'So, what do we do to get this over with as quickly as possible?' Erica asked. Out of the corner of her eye she saw Jess shooting her a look.

Minerva blew out her cheeks, which wasn't a good sign.

'You need more information, Ric. I'd say a full investigation of the house, research the history and an interview with the victim. At the very least.'

Erica groaned but Jess sat bolt upright.

'Yes! We can do that. Can't we?' She turned to Erica.

'Why are you so excited about this? What about your new house and your handyman and Ruby and work? Aren't we busy enough?'

Erica sagged under the withering looks being shot at her.

'C'mon, Ric. You need a distraction. It'll be fun.'

Erica raised a finger at Jess.

'No. It will not be fun. Fun is not what these things are. Maybe if—' Erica stopped herself and sat back. The three women watched her, waiting.

'Maybe if…?' Jess encouraged.

'I don't mind helping,' Minerva offered.

'No.' Erica waved her away. 'No. It's fine. We'll do it.'

Jess bounced in her seat.

'What do we do if it is a ghost?' she asked Minerva, eyes shining.

'That depends. Sometimes just a little chat makes a world of difference. Other times, a full exorcism is needed.'

Jess clapped her hands and turned to Erica.

'I'll let Steve know. When should we go round?'

Erica took a deep breath.

'Whenever. Whenever you like.'

6

Jess sat down at her dining table and took a deep breath. The scent of coffee filled her nostrils and the morning light was warm against her face as it filtered through the window. She smiled. This should be my life, she thought. Every day. Work from home while Ruby was at school and then spend the rest of the day with her daughter. Her smile faded as she opened her emails and the reality of agency life came back to her. She gave the emails a cursory glance, checked there was nothing urgent and then opened a new window and searched "baby monitor haunting".

Her stomach twisted as videos popped up.

"Baby Ghost Climbs Into Son's Cot"

"Spook Caught On Couple's Baby Monitor"

"Eerie Sounds Come From Baby's Monitor"

Jess clicked on that last one and sipped at her coffee as the video loaded. She turned up the volume on her laptop. The video started and then so did the sound. A soft whistling, barely audible, followed by a loud happy gurgle of a baby. Jess's heart pounded as both sounds were cut off and replaced by a white noise. The same white noise they'd heard at Steve's house.

Jess jumped as there was a knock at the door. Hand smashing down onto the laptop, she paused the video.

Glancing out of the window, she couldn't see a delivery van. Jess opened the door with a frown and froze at the sight of Marshall with a fence panel.

'Good morning. Oh, did I come at a bad time?'

'What? Oh, no. No.' Jess shook her head and smiled. 'Morning. Sorry, I was just lost in, err, work.'

Marshall gestured at the fence panel.

'So, now is a good time?'

Jess nodded.

'Yes. Please. I'll go open the back gate for you.'

Marshall flashed her a toothy grin and turned away to rest the fence panel by the gate. Jess closed the door and breathed for a moment.

Marshall wasn't there when she opened the back gate. She peered out and spotted him emerging from his van with a tool box. Jess fought back a smile.

This is ridiculous, she told herself. Fancying a handyman. Whatever next? And what did she think would happen? She wondered what she'd like to happen. Really. Marshall was a big man, intimidating in many ways, and she knew nothing about him. Except that he seemed good with Ruby.

'And those arms,' Jess murmured to herself.

'Hmm?' Marshall appeared in the garden carrying the fence panel.

'Nothing,' said Jess quickly. 'Can I do anything?'

'No. You're okay. I'll get this sorted and let you know when I'm done. Don't want to interrupt your work.'

Jess searched Marshall's face for any sign of sarcasm or mockery but he appeared genuine.

'All right. Thanks. I'm just in there.' She

gestured to the dining table beyond the windows. Marshall nodded and moved past her to get on with the job.

Jess stepped through the sliding doors and sat back at her laptop. She closed the browser, hiding the videos of hauntings, and stared at her emails. With a sigh, she glanced to her right and watched Marshall dismantling the old fence panel.

She turned away sharply as he straightened and looked directly at her.

'Emails,' she muttered. 'Work. Clients. Come on, Jess.' She cleared her throat, sipped at her cooling coffee and opened the oldest, unread email. Her eyes scanned the words but her brain didn't make sense of them. She read it again. A client wasn't happy with the proofs they'd been sent by the agency's designer. Jess rolled her eyes. This client was never happy. She forwarded the email, typed in the designer's name, edited the email to show just the client's requests and typed out a message. She hit send and opened up the next email.

Again, her eyes scanned it but her brain didn't make sense of it. Instead, she found her head turning back into the garden and to Marshall, who was preparing to fit the new fence panel.

'Oh, this is ridiculous.' Jess pulled a face at her lukewarm coffee and scraped back her chair. She poured the coffee down the sink and climbed the stairs to the bathroom. Hefting down the washing basket, she plonked it in front of the washing machine back in the kitchen and began piling clothes inside. She measured out the washing liquid, shoved it on the top of the clothes and slammed the door shut. Looking back up into the garden, she watched Marshall sliding the new fence panel into place as she switched on the washing machine.

It didn't beep.

She looked down at it. No lights came on. She pressed the On button again. Nothing happened.

She could have screamed. She could have kicked the damn machine, punched the wall and yelled at the top of her voice. Jess wanted to do all those things, but she didn't. She stared at that On button and pressed it hard, growling as her finger ground into it, and she let rip a series of curse words precisely summing up how the washing machine could burn in hell.

Then she turned around and put the kettle on. Her hands leaning on the counter, Jess wondered when she'd have the chance to go look for a new washing machine. Ruby was with her father at the weekend. She'd have to go then. Did Ruby have enough clean clothes to last her until Tuesday?

A tap on the window behind her made Jess turn with a small squeal. Marshall waved apologetically at her.

Jess slid the door open.

'Sorry. I didn't mean to scare you.'

'Oh, it's okay. Lost in my own world. My washing machine's broken. It's been playing up for a while and I guess it's just given up. I'll have to go find a new one at the weekend. Forty quid, right? Hang on, I'll go get it.'

Marshall was studying the washing machine.

'Hmm? Oh, don't worry about it.'

'What? The fence looks good as new. Well, I mean, that part is new. I'll go get the money.' Jess smiled at Marshall and felt herself doing the flirty smile she'd practised so hard during her twenties.

And we all know where that landed me, she thought.

'Do you want me to take a look at the machine?' Marshall offered. 'I might be able to fix it.'

'Seriously?' Jess grinned. 'You lay lawns, do the shopping, fix fences and now you can fix machines? Wow. What can't you do?'

Marshall's eyes softened and they stared at one another. Jess's mouth opened, her breath coming hard, as she silently panicked, wondering if she should be doing something, wondering if he would do something.

Marshall was the one who broke the tension. He gave a short laugh and looked away, back to the machine.

'I might not be able to fix it. Sometimes you're better off just replacing the whole thing. Especially the newer models. But I'll take a quick look.' He bent down before Jess could argue. She fetched her purse and the two twenty pound notes.

'Here. For the fence.' Briefly, she considered giving him more.

'Thanks. I can fix your machine.' Marshall stood and gently took the money. 'It just needs a new button, that's all. Easy. I can get a new button this afternoon and get it fixed for you by tonight.'

'Really? You're not busy?'

'Just laying Mr Horton's gravel. That's all. Right next door. It's not a problem.'

Somehow Jess hadn't noticed before just how big Marshall's brown eyes seemed.

'That would be wonderful,' she said, stopping before she embarrassed herself.

Marshall folded up the twenties and shoved them in his pocket.

'I'll try and get back to you about – what would be a good time?'

Jess shrugged.

'I'm picking Ruby up from school at half three.'

'So, four?'

'Great. That would be great.'

Again, they stared into each other's eyes and the silence stretched. This time Jess broke it. She coughed, wrenching her gaze from his. Marshall turned away, back to the garden, his tools and the old fence panel.

'I'll just clear up and be out of your way.' He glanced at the laptop on the table. 'What do you do?'

'I'm an account manager at a marketing agency.'

'Oh.' Marshall raised his eyebrows.

'It's not as fancy as it sounds. Actually, it's awful. I keep meaning to quit but, you know, new mortgage to pay, child to keep supplied with crayons and food. It's a tricky one.'

'So, you're job hunting?'

'Sometimes. When I can. I like the idea of being self-employed.'

Marshall nodded.

'It's great. I earn more being self-employed, but I guess that depends on what you do.'

'What did you do before you became a handyman?'

'Security. I worked in a warehouse for a while. Any boring minimum wage job you can think of, I did it. Then I trained as an engineer.'

Jess's eyes widened.

'You didn't like being an engineer?'

Marshall smiled.

'I did, for a while. I got made redundant and

found it hard to find work after that.'

Jess nodded, knowingly.

'I think a lot of people have had that problem recently. The last agency I worked for went under. We all lost our jobs with no notice.'

'But you managed to find another agency.'

'And yet I get the feeling that you're happier than me. So what does that tell you.'

Marshall laughed.

'I don't know. You got a nice house out of it.'

'Yeah.' Jess looked around her kitchen. 'It's a lovely house. And now it has a proper, fully fixed fence. Thank you so much for that. Although Ruby might get annoyed that you can't pass her any more worms.'

Marshall gave that serious consideration.

'I can leave the bucket by your back gate, if she wants? And you don't mind?'

Jess resisted an overwhelming urge to throw herself into the man's arms.

'She'd love you for that,' Jess told him. Marshall grinned.

'I'll be back later, then. To fix the machine.'

'Wonderful. Thank you.'

Jess watched Marshall leave before collapsing back into her chair. Her laptop broke her reverie with the bing-bong of a new email. The designer wasn't happy. Jess gave a groan and placed her forehead on the table

෨ඥ

Ruby sat at the dining table eating a banana sandwich and giving the fixed fence panel a dirty look.

'What about my worms?' she asked her mother.

'Don't talk with your mouth full. And Marshall said he'd put your bucket by the back gate instead. Okay? You can ask him about it later, if you don't annoy him.'

Ruby gave her mother a shocked look.

'Do I annoy him?' She put her sandwich down.

'Oh, baby. Of course not.' Jess gathered her daughter up and squeezed her, before stealing the leftover crust from Ruby's sandwich and shoving it into her mouth.

'Oi!'

'Snooze, you lose.' Jess blew her daughter a kiss and moved towards the front door as there came a knock.

Marshall gave her a lopsided smile as she opened the door and Jess tried to subtly wipe the crumbs from the corners of her mouth.

'Is it a good time?' Marshall asked.

'Of course. Please.' Jess stood aside, allowing him in. She closed the door behind him and led him into the kitchen.

'Hello, Ruby,' he said.

'Hello, Marshall. Mummy says you're still going to collect worms for me.'

Jess turned the kettle on.

'Ruby. Leave the poor man alone.'

Marshall laughed.

'No. It's okay. Of course, I'll collect as many worms as I can until the job's done. Probably another day. I'll leave the bucket by the back gate. Is that okay?'

Ruby nodded

'Yes.' She glanced at her mother. 'Thank you.'

Jess winked at her. Good girl.

Marshall placed his toolbox by the washing machine.

'Would you like a drink?' Jess offered.

'A coffee would be lovely,' Marshall told her. 'It's been a long day.'

'Oh, I hope you haven't gone to much trouble with this.'

'No, no.' Marshall waved away her protests. 'I like being helpful.' He began taking the front of the washing machine off. 'Did work go well?' he asked. Jess hesitated and glanced over her shoulder to him.

'It went okay, thanks. How was your day?' Her chest fluttered as she looked from Marshall to Ruby.

'It's been a good day.' Marshall glanced up at her and gave that lopsided smile again.

'I've had a good day at school,' Ruby announced.

Jess and Marshall chuckled and Jess had to turn away to hide the grin on her face. She made the coffee and passed Marshall his cup.

'I really do appreciate the help. How long have you been working for Mr Horton?'

'Oh, not long. He hired me a couple of weeks ago to trim back the shrubs in his front garden. I noticed he had some trouble walking so offered to do his shopping.'

'You like helping people,' said Ruby with a nod.

'Yeah. It helps that he pays me too.' Marshall rubbed at the back of his neck, glancing at Jess.

'How nice to get paid for doing what you enjoy,' Jess murmured wistfully. She snapped out of it. 'Although I'm sure doing a food shop isn't a passion of yours.'

'No. But machines are.' Marshall bent down to

return to work on the washing machine. 'I like using my hands.'

There was a pause as Jess pondered that, again working at keeping the smile from her lips.

'Don't you love what you do?' Marshall asked over his shoulder.

'School's okay. Drawing is better,' said Ruby. Jess looked fondly at her daughter.

'And you?' Marshall asked her with a grin.

'I used to.' Jess shrugged. 'My friend, who I work with, she's all about the work. Very career driven. I used to be like that. I wanted to run my own agency at one point.'

'You don't anymore?'

Jess shook her head.

'I see what it does to people. How it takes over your life.' She looked over at Ruby. 'I have more important things in my life now. And the clients are just... It would be nice to be able to pick and choose my clients.'

'Yeah, that is a bonus.'

Was it her imagination or did Marshall just look Jess up and down? She shifted her position, stroking the warm ceramic of her coffee cup with a finger. As the pause lengthened, her mind wandered back to Steve.

'I would like to do something different.'

'Like what?'

'I don't know.' Jess frowned. 'I haven't figured that one out yet.'

There was a knock at the door and Ruby jumped to her feet. 'You go get it, love. That'll be your dad.'

Ruby ran out of the kitchen and Jess moved to tidy her things from the table. 'He's having her this weekend. He usually takes her on a Friday but he's got tomorrow off so said he'd take her tonight. Which is nice.' Jess stopped talking. She didn't know where she was going with this.

'Sounds like a good arrangement,' said Marshall. Jess looked over at him, wondering how much to say.

'Mummy! Mummy look!' Ruby's shrill voice ran through the house. Instinctively, Jess leapt forward. Marshall jumped up and looked ready to join her but seemed to stop himself, staying back in the kitchen while she ran to the front door.

'What? What is—'

Paul stood outside on the door step. The expression on his face said it all. He knew she would be angry. Ruby was bouncing around the hallway, pointing down at the large, fluffy black, brown and white puppy at Paul's feet.

'It's a puppy!' Ruby screeched. The puppy reversed, ears back.

Jess grabbed hold of Ruby and kept her still.

'Yes, so shush. Be quiet. You're scaring the poor thing. Go get your bags, now.' Jess gently pushed her daughter towards the stairs. Ruby went reluctantly, glancing back at the puppy every couple of steps.

Jess waited until she was out of earshot.

'You got a puppy?' she asked Paul, crossing her arms. Boy, that puppy was cute. She liked to think she was crossing her arms to be firm against Paul but really it was to stop herself from reaching down to sink her hands into that adorable puppy fur.

'Sort of,' said Paul. 'I got her for Ruby.'

All thoughts of puppy cuddles fled from Jess's mind. She stared at Paul wide-eyed.

'You fucking what?'

Paul flinched.

'I bought Ruby a puppy.'

'Without talking to me first?'

'You bought a house without talking to me.'

Jess opened her mouth but no words came out. Finally, she threw her arms up in the air.

'Oh, I am sorry for putting a permanent roof over your daughter's head. What a terrible mother I am!'

'And I'm a terrible father for buying my daughter a puppy?'

Jess took a deep breath, trying to calm the panic in her mind.

'So, the puppy is staying at yours?'

'Well,' Paul started with a sheepish look.

Jess rolled her eyes. She knew it.

'I knew it,' she muttered. 'You want the puppy to live here?'

'You're home more often. I figured that would be the kindest thing to do.'

'And you didn't think it would be kind to talk to me about this beforehand?' Jess hissed. 'And what breed is it?' It's a Bernese Mountain Dog, she thought.

'Bernese Mountain Dog. Pedigree. Purebred,' said Paul proudly.

Jess clenched her eyes shut.

'You realise how big they get, don't you?'

'A nice big, cuddly playmate for Ruby.'

'I – what? It's not a teddy bear, Paul! Dogs are a big responsibility.'

'You always wanted a dog.'

Jess resisted the urge to punch the man.

'What's really going on here, Paul? You didn't just go out and buy a really expensive puppy on a whim.'

Paul looked down.

'Katy wanted it. But when we got it home, it peed in her shoes and now she doesn't want it.'

Jess ground her teeth.

'Your girlfriend is a horrible human being, do you know that?'

Paul held out the lead to Jess. 'No.' Jess crossed her arms again. 'You can return it to the breeder.'

Paul didn't say anything. He didn't have to. The puppy at his feet whined and looked up at Jess. It was all Jess could do to not think of the poor creature in Paul's house, his young girlfriend screaming at the baby for doing only what came naturally. Paul was right, she had always wanted a dog.

The animal looked so frightened. Weren't puppies supposed to want to meet new people? It seemed transfixed by Paul's side, looking between them with big, sad eyes.

'How old is…is it a boy or a girl?' Jess asked softly as Ruby ran down the stairs with her bag.

'A girl. Just gone twelve weeks old.' Paul held out the lead again. 'Fully vaccinated. I'll go get the paperwork from the car.'

'Are we keeping her, Mummy?' asked Ruby, visibly stopping herself from dancing.

Jess stared at the lead in Paul's outstretched hand. With trembling fingers, she reached forward and took the lead, and the puppy. Ruby punched the air.

The puppy didn't move.

Jess crouched down low, facing the dog.

'Go with your dad then, Rubes. Have a lovely time.' Jess outstretched her arms. 'Come on, puppy.

It's okay.'

The puppy trotted forward and into Jess's waiting arms. She stayed there, crouched, stroking the soft, sweet smelling fur.

'Actually, about that. It turns out this weekend's no good, kiddo,' said Paul.

Jess looked up at him, holding her breath. No. No, not again. Paul looked down at her. 'Sorry. Something came up, last minute. It's work. Next weekend, though?'

'But this is your weekend with your daughter,' said Jess, trying hard not to sound angry. She glanced at Ruby who had sagged, dropping her bag to the floor.

'But you don't want to come with me this weekend when you've got a new puppy to play with,' said her father. Ruby looked at the puppy.

'I guess,' she murmured. Her little voice broke Jess's heart.

'Go back in the kitchen. See if Marshall needs help,' she told her daughter.

'Marshall?' Paul's eyes snapped back to her. Jess took a small amount of pleasure from the tone of his voice.

'Come on, Ruby. I could use an assistant,' came Marshall's voice from behind them. How long had he been standing there, Jess wondered. How much had he seen or heard? The big man was looking right at Paul and seemed to stand at his full height. He reached out, almost protectively, to Ruby and guided her back to the kitchen.

Jess watched them go, her chest fluttering.

'Who the hell's that?'

'What business is it of yours?' Jess asked Paul, standing straight and taking a bit of pride when the puppy moved to stand behind her.

'You didn't have a boyfriend last week. You've already introduced him to Ruby?'

Jess nearly laughed.

'He's the handyman, Paul, not my boyfriend. And in fact, Ruby introduced me to him. He's fixing our washing machine. I know you might not understand that concept, of being helpful around the house. Now, don't you have work to do? Isn't that why you can't spend time with our daughter? I think you should go. I'll call you tonight to arrange next weekend.' Jess stepped forward and took hold of the open door.

Paul looked from the kitchen, where Marshall and Ruby had disappeared, back to Jess.

'I'll go get the dog's things.'

'You do that,' said Jess, amazed at how strong she sounded.

Jess walked into the kitchen, leading the puppy. Ruby sat at the dining table, despondent. Marshall stood with his back leaning against the washing machine, his big arms crossed.

'What shall we name the puppy, Rubes?' asked Jess. Ruby didn't say anything.

Jess handed the puppy's lead to Marshall and moved to sit next to her daughter, wrapping her arms around her. 'It's okay, baby. We'll have so much fun this weekend. What would you like to do? Your choice. Whatever you want.'

Ruby shrugged.

'Do you want to go watch cartoons? And then later tonight, we'll have your favourite dinner and make cakes. Chocolate ones. How about that?'

Ruby brightened, sitting up and nodding. Her

eyes were watery but she hadn't shed any tears. Jess gave her a big kiss on her cheek, gripping her tight, making Ruby grin. 'Go on then. Go watch cartoons in the living room.'

Ruby jumped up. She spent a minute stroking the puppy, the little animal snuffling and licking at her hands. Ruby, giggling, left the room leaving Marshall and Jess both staring at the puppy.

'Are you okay?' Marshall asked.

'I have no idea.' Jess's eyes began to burn and she hurriedly forced the tears away. Not now. Not in front of Marshall. She reached down for the puppy. 'I'll be okay. Not the first little bundle of joy that's come into my life as a surprise. I'll make it work. I always do.'

Marshall gave a nod.

'Well, the washing machine's all fixed. Let me know if you have any trouble with it. Here.' He handed her a card. 'My number. In case you need any other help. Although.' He rubbed his hand down his stubbly face. 'I'll be dropping off worms for Ruby. If that's still okay?'

'Of course! Please do. She's so happy about the worms.'

There was a pause.

'I know it's not my place to ask but…does he do that a lot?'

'Let her down? Well, no. Well, sort of. Let me down? Yes. Constantly. Just one of the very many reasons we're not together.'

Marshall gave another nod.

'Okay. Well. Let me know if you need any help. With anything.' He caught her eye and held it. There was such meaning behind that look that Jess had to catch her breath.

'Thank you,' she managed. 'Oh. How much for the washing machine?'

'Oh, don't worry about it.' Marshall waved her away.

'What? No, no. Please. How much?'

'It's on me.'

'But—' Marshall turned and looked at her. 'I don't want to owe you anything. And you've been so kind. Please.'

Marshall relented.

'A tenner. For the new button.'

'And your time?'

'Was mine to give,' said Marshall. The tears did well in Jess's eyes then. She blinked them back and nodded, not trusting herself to talk. Marshall frowned. 'Call me. Anytime.'

That was the moment the puppy gave a small cry, squatted and urinated over the kitchen floor.

Steve

Steve had an hour before Jess and her friend were due to arrive. He'd carefully placed Joe, asleep, in his cot and now kneeled on the landing, just outside the nursery. On the floor was Rachel's favourite novel, the silver bracelet and a lit candle. Steve wasn't sure what he should be using, or even if he should be doing this, but he felt like a book and a candle were necessary somehow. Even if it was a romance novel and a cinnamon scented candle leftover from Christmas.

He closed his eyes and inhaled slowly. The heavy smell of cinnamon filled his nose and he stifled a cough as it tickled the back of his throat.

'Rachel?' he said tentatively.

There was no response.

'If you're there, please answer. Give me a sign. Please.'

After a moment, Steve opened his eyes, fully expecting Rachel to be sitting on the floor opposite him.

There was no one there.

'Rachel?' he called again. 'If you're here, I need to know. I need to know that you're okay. Are you alive? Are you stuck here? Have you come back for Joe? Please, Rach. I'm scared.' Steve stopped, biting his lip, holding back a fresh wave of tears.

'You're scaring me,' he murmured.

There was a crash from the nursery. Steve jumped up, nearly knocking over the candle, and rushed into the room.

'Rachel?'

Again, there was no one there. Nothing was out of the ordinary, except for the lamp. The little bedside lamp, with its dark blue lampshade covered in green dinosaurs, was lying on the floor. Hesitantly, Steve picked it up and placed it back on the shelf where it belonged. His fingers trailed over the wood of the shelf, as if that would give up some sort of clue. As if he could somehow reach her through the wood.

Had the lamp toppled over? Someone must have knocked it, surely. Steve looked down at the floor, searching. Was that a footprint in the new, plush carpet? He carefully put his own foot against the fading mark and gave out a sob as the footprint came up smaller than his own. He looked around the room again.

'Rachel, if you're here, tell me. Clearly. Appear in front of me. Tell me it's you. Please. Please.'

He sat down in the rocking chair. The chair Rachel had chosen for nursing the baby in the middle of the night and during the afternoon, as shafts of light fell across the room. He had sat here staring at Joe on the day of her death. Unable to move, unable to breathe, unable to take his eyes from his son. The loneliness had swallowed him then. The idea of raising a newborn on his own while dealing with this grief had been over-whelming, despite the offers of support from family and friends.

Now, as he sat in the rocking chair, the loneliness was ebbing away. She was here, he was sure of that. Whether physically or in spirit form, his wife was somewhere in this house and he had to find her.

7

'Are you sure your mum's okay?' Jess murmured as Erica pulled the car up to Steve's house.

'Of course. She loves Ruby. My whole family loves her. You're practically my sister according to them. And you might not be getting that puppy back. But don't worry, if you do, she'll be another step closer to house trained. Mum has a knack with these things.' She flashed Jess a smile but Jess didn't return it.

'I don't want to take advantage.'

'Don't worry about it. We'll make it up to them when we report back.'

That made Jess look at Erica.

'So you believe there'll be something to report back on? You do believe?' she asked with a smile.

'I didn't say that.' Erica stopped the car and pulled up the handbreak. 'I said they believe.'

'But you think we'll experience something tonight.' Jess undid her seatbelt.

Erica didn't respond. She got out of the car and looked up at the townhouse. The sky was already dark, the stars beginning to appear through the wisps of cloud. A cold breeze moved over them, bringing up goose bumps on Erica's skin. A shiver running down her neck as she looked up at the dark top floor windows. She half expected to see a face looking back down at her but there was nothing.

A light flickered in the background and Erica jumped a little. It must have been the hallway light as the front door opened and Steve appeared. Jess was already at the door, ready to meet him.

'Hi. Everything all right?'

Steve looked between them and nodded, moving aside to let Jess in. Erica followed, flashing Steve a nervous smile.

'Thanks,' she murmured as she moved passed him. She stopped in the hall and held her breath, but there was nothing. Jess looked back at her questioningly. Erica shrugged.

'Has there been anything else strange happening since we last came?' asked Jess, moving into the kitchen.

'Every night,' said Steve.

'Where's the baby?' Jess surveyed the room. Erica watched with a raised eyebrow. She'd been watching too much TV. You didn't need to study a room to know if there was a spirit present. Erica shook her head to dislodge those thoughts. Jess gave her a curious look which Erica ignored.

'He's asleep upstairs. I'll take him with me when I go.'

'You're leaving?' Erica asked.

'Yes. Jess told me I should.' Steve looked between the women again. The whites of his eyes were red, the shadows on his face getting deeper.

'When did you last sleep, Steve?' Erica took a step forward. There was no baby monitor on the table, she noted.

Steve shrugged.

'I sleep here and there. You have to with a baby, right?' He looked at Jess who nodded. She opened her mouth but stopped herself, closing it again and turning away.

Especially as a single parent, Erica thought. That was what she was going to say. Of course Steve wasn't sleeping. He didn't need a ghost to keep him awake.

'But the strange things happen mostly at night?'

'Yes. Although they've begun happening during the day.' Steve glanced up from the floor and met Erica's eyes. 'What does that mean? It's getting worse. You're an expert in this, aren't you?'

Erica exchanged a glance with Jess who nodded and smiled encouragingly. Erica gave a sigh.

'It depends.'

There was a pause. They wanted more but Erica kept her mouth shut, instead looking out of the door and back into the hallway. Did that light just flicker?

'Depends on what?' Jess asked.

'What kind of spirit it is, if it is a spirit.'

'You think it could be in my head?' Steve asked. His large tired eyes seemed to burn into her and Erica waivered.

'There are some things in this world that do their best work in our heads,' she told him. Beyond, she spotted Jess taking another sheepish look around the kitchen, as if something could be lurking behind the toaster.

'What's been happening?' Erica asked before Steve could dwell on what she'd said.

'Erm.' Steve clenched his eyes shut. 'During the day? Things moving around. I left my keys on the table and when I came back, they were on the worktop.' He stared at the table a moment. 'And there's been a voice.'

Jess perked up at that.

'A voice? You heard it talking?'

Steve nodded.

'I couldn't make out the words, but it was a woman's voice.' He glanced up at Erica who stared him down.

'Steve. Was it your wife's voice?' Jess asked kindly. Steve looked away.

'I think so. I mean, it sounded like her.' He took a breath. 'I'll go get the baby. We'll leave you to it.'

'Wait.' Erica stopped him. 'Where did you hear the voice? Where were you?'

'On the landing,' Steve told her. 'Is that important?'

'Near the baby's room?'

'Yeah.'

Erica caught Jess's eye.

'And when we were here last there'd been strange noises on the baby monitor.'

'Before it blew the batteries to dust,' agreed Jess. 'You think it's connected to the baby?'

'It's her, isn't it?' Steve whispered.

'We can't say,' Erica told him. 'But I do wonder if tonight might be more productive if you and your son stay put.'

Steve and Jess stared at her.

'You want us to stay? While you hunt for ghosts?' Steve looked ready to argue his way out of the door.

'Whatever is doing this to you is connected to you, Mr Green' Erica told him. She didn't feel comfortable calling him Steve, not when she was inwardly questioning his own belief in what he was seeing. 'The happenings could stop when you leave. They could even follow you. Then tonight would be pointless, all it would prove would be that whatever's happening is connected directly to you. We'd have to come back and do it all again with you here. It'll be better if you could stay.'

Steve looked back to Jess who attempted a reassuring smile.

'Is it safe?' Steve asked.

Erica shuffled her feet.

'I don't see why not.'

'What if you make her angry?' Steve looked back to Jess again.

'We don't want to do that,' Jess told him, giving Erica a secret stricken look.

'If it's your wife, I doubt she would hurt you or your son. Does she have any reason to hurt either of you?' Erica suggested. Her patience was wearing thin.

Something caught her eye, making her look back into the hallway. She was sure the light flickered that time. Cocking her head, she moved forward to investigate. Steve and Jess fell quiet, watching her.

Erica leaned out of the kitchen doorway and glanced around, peering up the stairs.

'What is it? Is something there?' Jess hissed in her ear, making her flinch. 'Any balls of light? Strange shadows?'

Erica turned to look her friend in the eye.

'What have you been watching when Ruby goes to bed?' she murmured. Jess had the decency to look guilty. Erica turned back to the kitchen and Steve.

'Nothing there. Just my eyes playing tricks on me, and that's what we need to figure out. If your grief is playing tricks on you. And we need you and your grief here for that.'

'Except that we all heard the noises on that baby monitor, Ric,' Jess reminded her quietly. 'Even your grandmother saw the dust.'

Erica couldn't argue that. She moved her head in ascent but kept quiet.

'Okay. We'll stay.' Steve sighed, rubbing at his arms.

'Don't worry. We'll keep you safe,' Jess told him. 'Won't we, Ric?'

Erica nodded.

'Of course.'

'And you really know what you're doing?' Steve asked her. Erica twisted her lips but Jess replied before you could.

'Her grandmother's a witch, so's her mother. Ric grew up in a house full of spirits. Her grandmother says she has a gift. Right, Ric?'

'Can't deny any of that,' said Erica.

'There's something else,' said Steve. They watched him, waiting for him to continue as he pulled something out of his pocket. It was a silver band.

'This was Rachel's. I found it in Joe's cot, after…'

'After?' Erica urged.

'I heard her voice.'

Steve reluctantly passed the bracelet to Erica as she held out her hand. She studied it for a moment. There was no information she could get from it. She wondered if she should be feeling a rush of energy emanating from it. She gave it back.

'You heard the voice on the stairs? Then I suggest we start up there.' She turned, blowing out her cheeks as soon as her back was turned, and climbed the stairs. Behind her, Jess told Steve to put the kettle on and relax. They'd be back soon.

'You really don't believe? Still?' Jess hissed as she joined Erica on the landing. There was a soft scent of cinnamon which Erica found curious. She checked behind the closed doors, orientating herself.

'Have you ever met a ghost, Jess?' she asked, discovering the bathroom.

'Not that I know of.'

'Then you haven't.'

'And you know because you have met a ghost?'

Erica stared at the last closed door. That must be the baby's room.

'What you told Steve is exactly right,' she murmured. 'When I was little, Gran's house was full of spirits. So yes, I've met a number of ghosts. Not all ghosts are the same. Not all are equal. And not all are, strictly speaking, ghosts. I'm not saying I don't believe. Of course I do. How can I not? I'm just saying that there is so much more to this world than ghosts. And we don't know what this is. Emotion is such a powerful thing. It can move keys, it can pull pictures off the wall, it can create the illusion of voices and, yes, it can do strange things to electrical items.' Erica took a step towards the baby's door when the light above their head flickered. They both stared at it.

'You mean, like that?'

'Exactly like that. The lights downstairs were flickering too. I wonder if it's the whole house that's flickering. It can't just be power surges. Maybe there's an electrical fault with the hallway circuit.'

Jess raised an eyebrow.

'I didn't know you understood electrics.'

'First rule of ghost hunting.' Erica allowed herself a small, knowing smile. 'Always check out the most boring, obvious solution first. I know Steve's had an electrician round but maybe we need a second opinion.'

'You know, I know a handyman who could check that out.'

The women grinned at each other.

Erica turned the handle on the baby's room door and pushed it open. She stopped mid-step when she saw the silhouette by the cot. There was a flash of blinding light, forcing Erica to hold her arms up to her face and clench her eyes shut. When she opened them, colours danced in front of her. The room was dark although the coloured shapes seemed to throw shadows into the corners and across the carpet. The silhouette was gone.

'Did you—did you see…' Jess trailed off.

'What did you see?' Erica asked quietly. She found the light switch. Jess immediately pushed forward to the cot as the baby began to cry.

'Everything okay up there?' came Steve's voice from the bottom of the stairs.

Jess picked up the crying baby, whispering soothing words.

'You better come up,' Erica called back.

They left Steve in the nursery, rocking and soothing his baby boy back to sleep. But they didn't go far. Erica pulled Jess to the other side of the landing and whispered in harsh tones.

'What did you see?'

'You mean apart from a bright light? Which, let's face it, is terrifying in itself.' Jess took a deep breath.

'Did you see anything before the light?'

Jess studied her.

'I saw a person, Ric. By the cot.'

Erica nodded.

'Me too.'

'Shit.'

'Yeah. Shit.'

'Is that normal ghost behaviour?'

'Standing by the bed of a sleeping person? Definitely. It's an annoyingly common habit, as far as I'm aware. Disappearing in a flash of bright light? Nope. Never heard of that one.'

'But if ghosts are made up of energy, as your gran says, then surely they're capable of creating a bright light.'

'I guess. That makes sense. I've just never heard of it before. I've definitely never seen it.' Erica's brow creased in thought. What else could it be though?

'Did you see her?' Steve asked, his son awake but quiet in his arms.

Erica and Jess exchanged a look.

'We don't know,' Jess admitted.

Steve's eyes widened in alarm.

'She was here? This is real?'

'No. Wait.' Erica held up her hand but stopped herself from mentioning that the person might not have been his wife. 'Maybe we need to set up a camera. Try and catch it—her—on film.' Steve nodded. 'Then we can see if it really is her.'

'What about a séance?' he asked thoughtfully. 'So I can talk to her, maybe?'

'No.' Erica snapped. She softened as Steve looked at her. He looked ready to crumple on the floor. 'Not yet. We need more information before we try and make direct contact. But you can try talking to her just in the house. Here. Now. Have you tried that before?'

Steve nodded.

'A few times.'

'Did you hear anything back? Did you feel anything?'

Steve appeared uncomfortable.

'No.'

'No chills, no strange noises, even at the edge of your hearing?' Again, Erica was aware of Jess watching her from the corner of her eye.

Steve thought for a moment and then shook his head.

'No. There was nothing.'

Erica looked around the landing, her gaze landing on baby Joe.

'Do you ever encounter anything strange when you go out?'

'You mean, is she following me?'

Erica didn't respond, but waited. Steve looked down at his son in his arms. 'No. Not that I've noticed.' He met Erica's gaze. 'Is it her?'

Erica's shoulders sagged.

'Do you want it to be her?' she asked, slowly walking past Steve and into the nursery. She stood where she had seen the figure, searching the carpet by her feet and looking around the room. Steve remained quiet.

'You think there is a ghost, whether it's her or not?' Jess asked.

Erica glanced at her over her shoulder.

'We both saw something,' she said. 'You stand here when you come in the room?' she asked Steve, gesturing to her own position.

'What? Yeah, I guess.'

Erica brushed some hair from her face and rubbed at where it had tickled her cheek.

'Why?' asked Jess, moving forward into the room.

'There are indentations in the carpet.'

'So?'

'So, this is where the figure was standing. And ghosts don't generally weigh that much.'

'Ghosts can leave footprints,' Jess countered. 'I've seen it. I mean, I've heard of such cases.'

'Hmm. Sometimes. Depending on the spirit.'

Jess nodded, appearing to have won that argument. Erica turned to Steve.

'Why don't you take the baby downstairs, let us look around here for a moment.'

Steve took Joe into the kitchen without another word. Erica stared at Jess until her friend met her eyes.

'Do you want it to be his wife?' she asked.

'What? I don't know.'

'Why are we here, Jess? What's going on?'

'We're helping a friend. You know about this stuff.'

'No. It's more than that. You're just using that as an excuse.'

'Or a reason,' Jess said, cutting Erica off. 'And you know what? You're good at this, Ric. You're putting the same thought and consideration into this as you do any work with clients. You could be in your element.'

'But I'm not. You think I'm enjoying this?' Erica hissed. Jess gave a small smile and Erica felt a ball of anger growing deep down in her stomach.

'I think you are.'

'Well, I'm not. Haven't you ever considered that

maybe there's a reason I'm not like my mum? Or Gran? That maybe I made a conscious choice to not go down the same path as them?'

Jess's expression hardened.

'Do you want to help Steve or not?'

Erica could tell those weren't the first words Jess had thought of. She was glad she'd chosen them, though. The anger was still building. Erica clenched her fists at her sides.

'Not really.'

Now Jess was getting angry.

'Fine. If you're not going to be helpful, then we should just go. Maybe I'll ask your grandmother to help instead.'

'And why do you want to help so badly?' Erica asked, aware that she needed to keep her voice down.

'Because.'

'Because what?'

'Because the man has lost his wife, Ric. He's lost the mother of his child. He's been left all alone with a tiny baby. He's got all the new baby woes of constant feeding and no sleep, and he's doing it all alone. And on top of all of that, he's grieving the woman he loved. And that baby is grieving too. He's wondering where the woman he was attached to for nine months is. They're both struggling and I can't even begin to imagine what that feels like, but I do know something about it. And when Ruby was a baby, I was grateful of every ounce of help I could get. If I can help Steve, no matter how small or how strange, then I want to help. Because that's what decent human beings do. I think the question here is why won't you help? What's so bad about this that's holding you back?'

Erica rocked back on her heels. Her cheeks flushed, heart pounding, her fists remaining clenched.

'Fine,' she muttered. 'You're right.' She ignored the last question.

'Are you going to help or what?'

'I'll help. But you have to do what I say. And this isn't going to affect my job.' Jess opened her mouth, thought better of it and closed it again. 'What?'

'Nothing,' Jess said with a shrug.

'No, say it. What were you going to say?'

'Oh, come on. You don't want this to affect the stupid job where they won't even promote you despite all your hard work? Do you even know who got the job yet?'

'No. Do you?'

'Nope. But I bet we won't agree with the decision. I can't remember when we last agreed with a decision from management.'

'All right. Fine. Then I don't want this affecting my job hunting,' Erica muttered. Jess gave a self-satisfied smirk.

'Great. Deal. So, what now?' Jess glanced around the room and shivered. Erica narrowed her eyes. 'Did you feel that? There was a chill.' Jess asked, looking at her with wide, excited eyes.

Erica moved over to the window, fiddled with the latch and, with a bang, closed and locked it.

'Yup. It's a bit breezy out there.'

Jess deflated.

'It was open?'

'Not that you could immediately tell, but apparently, yes.' Erica looked out the window. 'Bit chilly to leave the baby's window open, isn't it?'

'It is,' Jess agreed, joining her to look out of the window. 'You don't think our ghost is a real person, do you? Climbing in through the window to stand over a baby's cot? Ric, that's more terrifying than the idea of a ghost.'

Erica agreed whole-heartedly.

'We'd need to tell the police, if that were the case.'

Jess glanced at her.

'Should we tell the police?'

'Do you think Steve is in any frame of mind to make those sorts of decisions? It being his house and family, and all.'

'No.'

'No. I didn't think so.' Erica rubbed at her forehead. 'If it was a real person, how did they create that light?'

'Really? That's your question? Ric, we're two floors up. How did they get out of the window, almost close it behind them and not kill themselves from the fall?'

They both looked out of the window again, peering down to the road and Erica's car below.

8

Jess didn't sleep well that night. After an hour of tossing and turning, seeing silhouettes standing over her bed every time she opened her eyes, she ended up on the landing, standing outside Ruby's door. She watched her daughter sleep for half an hour before attempting to go back to her own bed. That hadn't worked. She couldn't even close her eyes, but neither could she bring herself to wake her daughter. So she had opted for the only viable and good parenting option, which had been to stand guard over her daughter's bedroom door for most of the night, sleeping in fits only to be woken by flashes of light and her own thudding heartbeat.

So, it was understandable that the morning had been a long one. Jess could feel in her bones that it wasn't even ten o'clock yet, despite her stomach and mind suggesting that it must be lunchtime by now. She stumbled over a stick on the pavement and swore under her breath. Her arms ached, the bags of shopping she'd thought would be a good idea to pick up on the way home from dropping Ruby off at school seemed to be getting heavier. The tired puppy had been left sleeping at home, and Jess knew she should pick up the pace. If the puppy had woken up, who knew what she'd chewed through by now. What if Jess had missed a wire when she'd hastily puppy proofed the room? Her legs refused to move faster, instead she stumbled again, the bags growing heavier with each step. Then there was her laptop, sat on the dining table in the kitchen, filling with emails from clients and her manager, waiting, demanding, to be answered.

Jess stopped walking. After a moment, she placed the bags on the ground, keeping her eyes straight ahead and tried not to cry.

'Miss Tidswell? You okay?'

Normally, Jess would have jumped, but the exhaustion had numbed her. Instead, she calmly turned her head to the house she was standing outside of. In the driveway was a large white van, and next to the open door was Marshall.

Jess blinked. She looked down at her bags of shopping.

'Oh. Yes. Yes, I'm fine. And please, call me Jess. What are you doing here?'

Marshall approached, thumbing back towards the house.

'Doing a little maintenance job. I just finished up.' He looked down at her bags. 'Do you want a lift? I'm going back to finish Mr Horton's garden, so I'm headed your way.'

Jess could hardly say no. Not that she wanted to say no. She smiled up at Marshall.

'If you're sure, that would be fantastic. I've left the puppy alone and who knows what she's up to right now.'

Marshall laughed.

'She doesn't have a name yet?'

'No. Ruby's working on it, apparently.'

Marshall shook his head and easily picked up Jess's shopping. She tried to avoid staring at his arms but failed.

'That's a great kid you've got.'

'She's incredible. But I'm biased. I do sometimes wonder what goes on in her head.'

'A lot of thinking, by the sounds of it. She's smart. Like her mum.' Marshall glanced at Jess from the corner of his eye and flashed her a sweet smile. Jess's breath caught in her throat and she swallowed hard on the giggle that rose up.

Marshall carefully placed Jess's shopping in the back of his van. She sneaked a peek and saw her bags nestled between a tool box and a pile of gardening tools lying down, their wires carefully wrapped and stored.

'To be fair, I am forced to acknowledge that she has some of her dad in her. You know, because of science,' she said.

Marshall gestured to the open passenger door as he slammed the back doors and made his way to the driver's side. Jess considered the steps up to the passenger seat. She needed to take her time. The worse thing that could happen at this point would be to misjudge those steps, slip and fall down them. No, she had to do this with dignity. After a moment's pause, she heaved herself up and plonked into the seat. Marshall was already in the driver's seat, closing his door and switching on the ignition. Jess had to reach so far to slam her own door that she nearly fell out. Door closed, she leaned back and took a deep breath. She'd made it through without making a fool of herself. The heavy musky scent of man, testosterone, dirt and tools filled her senses.

'What happened between you two, if you don't mind me asking?' Marshall reversed out of the driveway.

'Hmm?' Jess was busy looking over the dashboard, covered in dust with a mud smear across the glove compartment. There was an old SatNav attached to the windscreen and an even older air freshener hanging from the rear view mirror. In the footwell by her feet were piles of paperwork.

'You and Ruby's dad. You don't have to say, I shouldn't have asked.'

Jess looked at the side of Marshall's face as he concentrated on the road. His eyes darted to her but quickly returned to face forward. His hair was so short it was almost stubble, and there was stubble on his chin. Dark with the odd glint of grey. The skin on his cheeks was weathered and looked warm to the touch. Jess averted her eyes.

'No. It's okay. It's never been a secret. I'm pretty sure even Ruby knows the kid-friendly version of it, although I don't know if she should. We met about six years ago. We worked together at this marketing agency. Horrible place. In hindsight, I think I covered how much I hated it there by putting all my attention onto him. He was nice and made me laugh, and then he asked me out. We were together for a couple of months when we had a big falling out. We got on but it didn't feel right. So we broke up. Then, of course, I found out I was pregnant. He wanted us to be a family. I think he got scared and I got hormonal, and, well, we ended up moving in together.' Jess shrugged. 'It was hell. We just weren't right for each other and I think there's a lot to be said for pregnant women being surrounded by people who actually love them.'

Marshall smiled.

'He wanted you to be a family but didn't love you?'

'He loves Ruby. He thought that would be enough for him. And maybe it was. But it wasn't for me.' Marshall nodded, not taking his eyes off the road. 'Anyway, about four months in I'd had enough. But we decided to stay living together because he wanted to be a part of the pregnancy, and he wanted to be there when Ruby was born. We moved apart when Ruby was about three months old. He wasn't exactly great with the newborn stuff.'

'That's good that he wants to be a part of her life.'

'Oh, yeah. Being a single dad doesn't go well with his lifestyle, though. It never has. He's a bit of an all or nothing man, so sometimes he lets Ruby down. Which is understandable, but sometimes I think he forgets the pain I want to inflict on anyone who hurts her.'

Marshall laughed.

'Duly noted.'

Jess smiled at him, her chest fluttering.

'Oh, you're the Bringer of Worms. Right now, I think you're good.'

Marshall flashed her a look and then turned back to the road, smiling to himself. The silence was palpable and Jess caught herself wondering if they could just pull over somewhere quiet. Just for five minutes. Five minutes of his lips on hers, of his hands touching her. She straightened in her seat and looked out of the window.

'So, now you work at a different agency?' he asked. Grateful, she looked back to him.

'Yeah. Another marketing agency. It's actually a nice place. Or it was. They just overlooked my friend for a promotion after she's spent the last three or so years working her socks off for them. There was a rumour last year that our CEO was having an affair with an intern. I think the whole place might be going down the drain, to be honest. We've had a few people leave.'

'Is that why you're not happy?'

'I thought so. But recently I've been wondering if it's actually just that I hate working in agencies now. Not just agencies. I'm tired of having to juggle Ruby around an office job. It's exhausting.'

'So what do you want to do?'

'I don't know.'

'Do you want to stay in the marketing world?'

'Not really. I quite like the idea of doing something completely different.'

Marshall smiled.

'I know the feeling. There's something to be said for trying new things.'

'Oh, yeah.' Jess shifted her position so she was turned towards him. 'What was your favourite of all your past jobs?'

Marshall took a deep breath, pulling up at traffic lights and tapping his finger against the steering wheel.

'I liked most of them, to be honest. Working security was fun to a point.'

'The authority that came with it?'

Marshall grinned.

'Yeah. That. Got a lot of attention from the women, too. I was young and better looking back then. But after a while I got tired of drunken men thinking they could take me on.'

Jess gazed over Marshall's bulk.

'You could always take them?'

Marshall shrugged.

'They were usually drunk off their tits. I was cold sober. Chances are they were seeing two of me and didn't know which one to hit. It wasn't hard to get the better of them. It got boring after a while, and then annoying. Then we were always having to call the police and sometimes an ambulance. I saw a bloke hit his girlfriend once. Broke her nose. I quit the day after. That did me in.'

Jess nodded.

'Yeah. That doesn't sound like a good day's work,' she struggled.

'The warehouse job was fun too, but it didn't pay well. And our contract hours kept getting dropped. It was simple. Maybe too simple. My hands started to get itchy.'

'Itchy?'

'Yeah. I guess I got bored.'

Jess smiled and looked back at him.

'You need a job where you're fixing problems.'

Marshall nodded, pulling away from the traffic lights and heading towards Jess's road. No chance of pulling over for a quick kiss then, Jess thought, the feelings of relief and disappointment mixing in her gut.

'Definitely. Being a handyman so far blows all the other jobs out of the water. It's the perfect mixture of using my brain and hands. So, what do you love about marketing?'

'Oh, who knows. I just sort of fell into it. My friend, Erica, is much more professional about it all. I left university, applied for any job I could find and just happened to get offered a marketing one. Ric got a degree in marketing. She works so hard, but she keeps getting held back. When we first met, we talked about starting our own agency. It seemed like the best option then, but…I don't know. I don't think I can stomach the idea now. She'd be amazing. I'd be fed up.'

'You need something else. If she isn't happy either, you could still go into some other sort of business together?'

Jess almost laughed. If only he knew. Should she tell him?

'Well, I would like that. I've been thinking about it a lot, but Ric is, erm, resistant.'

'She wants to stay in marketing?' Marshall pulled his van up to Jess's house.

'Maybe. I think it's more my business ideas that she doesn't approve of.'

Marshall pulled up the handbrake and looked Jess in the eye.

'Like what?'

She hesitated. His brown eyes were soft and inviting. He was so close to her. She could just lean forward and...

'I…don't know.'

Marshall narrowed his eyes.

'You don't want to say?'

Jess grinned and for a moment, the world outside was forgotten.

'Is it embarrassing?' Marshall whispered.

Something inside Jess twisted.

'A little,' she whispered back. 'I'll tell you if it ever happens,' she said. Marshall gave a slow smile.

'I'll leave a bucket of worms by your back gate tonight. For Ruby.'

Jess opened the passenger door and looked back to Marshall.

'Well, I'd hope you wouldn't be leaving them for me.' She jumped out of the van. Marshall walked round to the back to retrieve her shopping. 'Actually, there was something.'

'Yeah?'

Jess reached out to take the bags but Marshall walked past her with them, towards her front door. After a moment, she followed.

'When I bought the house, I wanted to replace the skirting boards. Especially in the living room. They're mostly dented and I have these ideas of these pretty skirting boards.' Jess hesitated, feeling silly. Marshall placed her bags on her door step as she fumbled for her key.

'I can fit skirting boards for you,' said Marshall. She looked up into his eyes.

'That would be great. Thank you.'

'How's the washing machine?' Marshall watched as she opened the front door.

'Perfect. Thank you. You saved me so much time and money. Especially after Paul let us down this weekend. It's a little glimpse of hell, taking a four-year-old shopping for white goods.'

Marshall laughed.

'I'll take your word for that.'

'You don't have kids?' Jess asked carefully.

'No.'

Jess thought quick. How could she ask if he was single without outright asking if he was single.

'No kids, although I always wanted them. But I don't have anyone to have kids with,' Marshall told her, rubbing his hand over his short hair. Again, they caught each other's gaze and there was a tense pause. Jess cleared her throat.

'How much would the skirting boards cost?'

Marshall gave her that lopsided smile.

'That depends on the size of the room. I can

come in and measure it now, if you like? But I really need to finish Mr Horton's garden before I get started.'

'Of course. No rush. Whenever you can. You can come in now. Mind the puppy.' Jess led the way into the house. The puppy, locked in the kitchen, began barking at the sound of them. 'I'd best see to her. The living room is there.' She pointed to the room as she went into the kitchen with her shopping bags. The puppy bounced off her, her large paws pushing Jess back. She placed the shopping on the kitchen counter and bent down to make a proper fuss of the dog. 'What the hell am I doing? Huh? I'm so out of practice,' she murmured, moving to let the puppy out into the garden.

'It'll probably be a couple hundred, depending on the skirting you want,' Marshall said, entering the room. Jess's breath caught in her throat. She took a moment to study him before deciding he hadn't heard her.

'That sounds great. Should I get the skirting?'

'No, no. I'll get some samples so you can choose. It's no problem.'

That time Marshall definitely looked her up and down. Jess breathed in slow. They were so close to the stairs. It wouldn't take much, she thought, to just go up to her bedroom.

They both jumped as loud music filled the room. Jess pulled her phone from her pocket.

'Sorry. It's work. I should take this.' Work. Jess had never hated them more. Marshall gave a quick nod.

'I'll come back later with the samples. And worms.'

'Thank you. I really do appreciate it.'

Jess answered the phone as Marshall left, trying hard to concentrate and stay professional.

Steve

It was coming up to lunchtime when Steve woke with a start. The house was silent, Joe sleeping soundly in his cot. Steve sat up in the rocking chair, his spine complaining. He stretched, his neck and shoulder popping. Blinking, he settled back into the chair and tried to remember his dream. Had there been a dream? There was a memory of his heart pounding, but it was fading fast.

There had been a bang. That was a vivid memory. A bang and, somewhere in the distance, a baby crying. But Joe was quiet.

A knock at the door made Steve jump up to his feet. He froze, staring at the baby. Joe didn't stir. Steve made his way out of the nursery and down the stairs. There came another knock on the door.

'All right, all right, I'm coming,' he grumbled, reaching for the latch. The door opened and Steve took a moment to focus. Time stopped. Steve's chest tightened. He couldn't breathe. He stared, swallowing against his dry mouth, his tongue heavy.

'Steve?'

Steve opened his mouth but no sound would come. The sound of Joe crying began to fill the house.

'Can I come in?'

9

Erica went straight into the shower to wash away work when she got home. The evening sun filtered through the windows at the back of the house. With baggy clothes on and her hair towelled dry, Erica peered out of her bedroom window and looked down onto the family's back garden. There was the herb garden her mother tended, and there was the pond. At the back was a line of large trees. They were the reason her parents had bought the house. Not only did they offer the garden privacy, but Esther loved having mature trees close by. They gave off a particular energy, she said, that brought a sense of calm and peace to the household. In the shade of the trees was a bench her father had installed, and sat on that bench was her grandmother. Minerva sat back, face up to the sun, eyes closed, her hands clasped in her lap. Erica made her way down the stairs and out into the garden.

'Sometimes you just need to warm your bones,' Minerva told her as she sat next to her grandmother on the bench. Erica closed her eyes and faced up to the evening light.

'Especially after being stuck in an office,' she murmured. When she opened her eyes, Minerva was watching her.

'You'll be out of there soon.'

Erica smiled.

'How? I haven't even started applying for jobs yet.'

'Oh, you won't need to do that. Waste of time.' Minerva sniffed and looked over to the pond. 'Have you seen the frogs lately?'

'Yes. How will I be out of the office if I don't have another job to go to?' Erica asked.

Minerva shrugged.

'You'll have another job. Just one you won't have to apply for.'

Erica sighed.

'Did Granddad tell you this?'

'No.'

'The fae?'

Minerva glanced quickly towards the house and then back to Erica.

'I do wish you'd meet them.'

'Mum wouldn't be happy.' Erica didn't know how she felt about meeting the fae folk. Her grandmother had told her so much, but the force with which her mother objected was a cause for concern. It wasn't just that. There was something else, an itch at the back of her head that she couldn't shift whenever the topic was raised. Something that held her back, that stopped her from agreeing. It wasn't that she didn't believe in the fae. It was more that she didn't want to believe. 'Which one knows all about my work, then?' she asked.

When she'd returned from university she'd assumed Minerva was referring to voices in her head whenever she mentioned the fae. When Erica was a teenager, she'd decided that the spirits in her grandmother's house were just that. Voices. Nothing sinister, just the eccentricity of Minerva.

Upon her return in her early twenties, she admitted that the spirits had been real, but the fae? Surely the line had to be drawn somewhere. She'd known the spirits of her grandmother's house, but she'd never met the fae. Yet, still that itch at the back of her mind grew and tingled.

Minerva watched her closely.

'Would you like to meet them?'

Erica squirmed a little, looking back to the house.

'No. But I don't know why.'

Minerva gave a nod.

'That's your mother.'

'No. No, it's something else. But I don't know what it is. Honestly? I want to meet them. There's still a big part of me that thinks you're having me on. If it wasn't for Mum being so adamant about it all... But there's a bigger part of me that really doesn't want to know.'

Minerva considered this.

'You understand why your mum is so against it, don't you?'

'No.' Erica looked at her grandmother. 'Why?'

Minerva shook her head.

'The fae can be tricky folk. Lustful and powerful. Those are the two things that define them. They fall in love quickly and sex is very important to them.' Minerva gave a secret smile that made Erica's cheeks redden. 'But just because they're all about the lust doesn't mean they don't fall deeply in love. They do. Most will love for life, it's just some will love more than one person for life. Monogamy isn't for all. But they have more passion than humans.'

'So why is Mum so against them?'

Minerva looked away a little too quickly for Erica to ignore. 'Gran? Come on. I thought we had no secrets?'

Minerva laughed.

'My dear, I'm a lot older than you. I'm entitled to my secrets. You can't know everything about me when you've only been on this planet for thirty odd years.'

'No?' Erica smiled. 'You've been holding back on me, then?'

Minerva shrugged.

'It's dangerous to tell your sixteen year old granddaughter about the fae. Far too many hormones. But you're an adult now. I should have introduced you years ago, really.'

'Should you? Why is it so important to you that I meet them?'

Again, Minerva looked away, avoiding eye contact. 'Gran!'

'Oh, fine. Your mum met the fae when she was a teenager. In the woods, I seem to recall. She liked going to those woods, the way I like going to the secret garden in the cemetery. That's not my story to tell, it's hers. But she met them again when she was in the early stages of pregnancy with you, and…well…'

'And?' Erica's eyes widened, her mind filling with possibilities. 'And what?'

'And he told her that he looked forward to meeting her daughter. That she would be the one for him.'

Erica reeled, rocking back on the bench.

'Well. That's not creepy at all. Who was he?'

'Oh, he's nothing to worry about. He's a good one. Handsome, too. I used to secretly wonder if your mum was jealous, that he wanted you and not her. But she'd already given her heart to another. Some fae are very particular about that. This one especially.'

'Does he have a name?'

Minerva looked her in the eye.

'Alfie.'

Erica blinked.

'That's a fae name, is it?'

'It's short for Aelfraed.'

'Of course it is.'

Minerva rolled her eyes.

'Erica, this is serious. I've told you now, and maybe I shouldn't have. And I've told you his name because I want to protect you. I shouldn't have done that. He might not be best pleased, although I'm certain he'd forgive me. Anyway, he's the one that told me about your work. Your granddad told me about the promotion, but Alfie told me about your future. The spirits can't see that far. They can only see what has been, but the fae can see what has been, what is and what will be.'

Erica rubbed at the spot between her eyes.

'And this Alfie has seen that I'll give my heart to him, or however you say it?'

'Exactly.'

'What if I don't? Don't I get a choice in this?'

'Of course you do. Just like you get a choice whether you stay in this poxy job or not. Your heart is yours to give to who you want. But you haven't met Alfie yet.' Minerva finished with a sly smile. 'He might change your mind about the fae.'

'I see why Mum isn't happy about it,' Erica muttered. Minerva didn't respond, although she'd obviously heard.

'What's going on with Baby Monitor Man? How did the investigation go?'

Erica told her about the silhouette in the nursery and the blinding light.

'Does that sound like a spirit?'

Minerva rubbed her chin thoughtfully.

'Could be. Could be. Spirits can emit so much energy that they create a bright light. But it can't be his wife.'

'Oh? Why not?'

'She's fresh, Ric. Too fresh and young in the spirit world to have that much power, unless she was particularly powerful in life and died in a rage.'

'What kind of power would she have needed in life?'

'Like me and your mum. And you.' Minerva winked at her granddaughter.

'I don't think she was like you.' Erica frowned. She didn't think many women were like her grandmother. 'No evidence that she was like Mum, either. But she was a mother taken from her newborn. Isn't that a power? I remember when Jess had Ruby. Ruby was a complete accident and yet no power in the universe could have kept Jess from her. Mum's always saying there's a deep connection between a mother and her child, depending on the individual. But couldn't that be powerful enough to help Steve's wife appear and disappear from her own son's nursery?'

Minerva stared into the distance, wide-eyed, and nodded thoughtfully.

'Indeed. That can be a powerful bond. Powerful enough to create a strong spirit. Tell me.' She looked at Erica. 'How was the baby while this figure was standing over him?'

Erica paused to remember.

'Fine, I think. I don't think he made any noise. He certainly didn't sound distressed.'

'Depends on the baby, of course, but I don't think many babies would be happy to have a strange spirit in the room. Whoever it was, sounds like he might have known it. So yes, I suppose it could have been his mother. But she must have been exceptional to have that kind of power. Or she had a secret.'

Erica sagged into the bench.

'Not very conclusive, is it?'

'Nope.'

'Steve said he's heard a voice, too. It won't talk back to him.'

'You could try a séance?' Minerva asked slowly and carefully. Erica turned to look at her as if she were mad.

'I thought they were dangerous?'

'Ridiculously so.' Minerva agreed. 'I've heard of more going wrong than right. You open a portal and anything can come through. Demons, angels, monsters. Anything other than the spirit you're actually looking for.'

'So…no?'

Minerva beamed at her granddaughter.

'Oh, but that's when they do it wrong. With me, my love, we'll do it right.'

'With you? You want to hold a séance?'

Minerva shrugged. Erica was pretty sure she was feigning the hurt expression. 'It might be good if you came to check it out?' Erica suggested. 'No séance. Not yet. But just see if you can feel the spirit?'

'If you can't feel it, I won't be able to,' Minerva

told her. 'Oh, I know!'

'What?'

'Alfie will be able to tell you within five minutes of stepping foot in that house.'

The two women stared at one another.

'And again. No,' said Erica.

'Oh, why not?' Minerva looked crestfallen.

'Because I don't want to go behind Mum's back, because I don't particularly want to meet a so-called man who apparently claimed me before my birth and I certainly don't want to introduce Jess to all that.'

'Jess doesn't have to come.'

'Yes. She does. Steve is her friend, this is her thing.'

'Okay. We can invite your Mum along. You won't be keeping anything from her.'

Erica twisted her lips and Minerva grinned. 'And I'll tell Alfie that you're spoken for. He can't have you. How's that?'

'Won't he know you're lying?'

'Of course he will. But he's very respectful. He'll understand. It's the gentlest way of letting him down.'

Erica glanced around the garden but she'd run out of arguments.

'Fine. I'll go ask Mum and call Jess.'

'Wonderful! I'll let Alfie know.' Minerva went to stand.

'Wait!'

Minerva fell back down onto the bench.

'Not until I've told Mum. Otherwise this could get messy.'

ഇരു

'I'm still not sure about this,' Esther muttered as she pulled the family car into the cemetery car park.

'It'll be fine, love,' Minerva told her, immediately unbuckling her seatbelt and preparing to leap from the car. Esther and Erica exchanged a glance.

'It'll be fine,' Erica told her. 'Trust me. I want nothing to do with a fae man.'

Esther sighed.

'Oh, Ric. You don't know what you're saying. You've never met them. You don't understand.'

Looking at her mother, Erica almost demanded they all get back in the car and drive back home, to forget all about it.

'She's a strong one, Esther,' Minerva told her daughter. 'She'll be fine. Just like I was. Just like you were.'

Esther glared at her mother.

'Like you? You're sleeping with them.' Esther trudged off in the direction of her father's grave. Minerva glanced at Erica before scuttling after her.

Erica hesitated before joining them. By the time she reached them they were standing before her grandfather's grave in silence. Minerva had her eyes closed.

Erica stopped beside them and smiled at the gravestone. Her grandmother reached out and squeezed her hand.

'Let's go.' She lifted her head and moved away in one swift motion.

They followed Minerva through the cemetery and the gate, into the secret garden. There was no one else there. The breeze lifted the grass and leaves, creaking through the branches above their heads. Even the birds were quiet. Erica shivered and moved closer to her mother.

Minerva moved away from them, heading towards the line of trees.

'Eolande?' she called softly into the trees. 'Eolande, are you there?'

Erica risked looking away to glance at her mother. Esther was frowning.

'Do you know Eolande?' Erica whispered.

'I know of her. But only a little.'

'I thought Gran's fae lover was a man.' Erica looked back to the trees and stopped. A woman was walking out, seemingly out of the air from behind a tree trunk. Her chestnut hair was straight and heavy, down to her thighs. She wore a dress the colour of golden autumn leaves that gathered and amplified her cleavage, the hem dropped down to her ankles, and there was a split up to her hip on one side. Her arms and back were bare, revealing brown, soft-looking skin. Erica blinked and tried to look away. Eolande caught her eye and gave a sweet smile.

'Your mouth's open,' Esther whispered. Erica snapped her mouth shut. 'Your gran has a number of lovers. I thought you knew. Eolande has always been her favourite though.'

'I...I...She told me that the fae fall deeply in love.'

'They do. But not always with just one person.'

Minerva and Eolande were talking in gentle, hushed tones. Then Minerva turned back to them and gestured for them to approach. Esther did so without hesitation. Erica held back, glancing around them at the trees, wondering if anyone else was hiding there and watching.

Her gaze landed back on Eolande who gave her a cursory glance.

126

'My granddaughter here would like some help,' Minerva told Eolande. 'A friend of hers believes he's being haunted by his wife who was recently killed in an car accident.'

Eolande raised an eyebrow and looked Erica up and down. Erica resisted the urge to take a step back. She crossed her arms tight against her chest and leaned towards her mother.

'What help can I possibly give?' Eolande's voice was gentle but there was a fierce edge to it. She softened as she looked at Minerva. Her love for Erica's grandmother was obvious and Erica found herself quite glad of that. It was a comfort that Minerva had found love, and, by the looks of it, a powerful love. She glanced at Minerva. Her grandmother's eyes danced as she spoke to the fae woman. Erica relaxed a little.

'Erica can't feel anything in the house,' Minerva told her. 'And she's got the touch. And yet things are happening. She saw a figure and a bright light. It's not making any sense. But she's also got a life to live. A helping hand, someone to walk into the house and say once and for all if there's a spirit there, within seconds, would be a great help.'

Eolande stared at Minerva for a little too long. Erica looked between the two.

'It's okay,' she said, her tongue heavy and dry in her mouth. 'No one has to come. We shouldn't have come here,' she added under her breath to her mother. She turned to leave.

'Don't go,' Eolande said. Erica stopped, keeping her back to the fae woman. 'Aelfraed will want to meet you.'

A shiver ran over Erica's arms. Her mother gripped her wrist.

'No. Erica wants to go, we go.'

Erica turned back to look at Eolande. The fae was smiling gently.

'You don't have to meet him, Erica,' Minerva told her.

'Good. Can you help me or not?' Erica asked Eolande. The fae approached. Erica straightened, standing her ground. The woman was tall, peering down with narrowed eyes.

'Aelfraed can help you.'

'I don't want his help. I was asking for yours.' I deserve a medal for this, Erica thought, her breathing coming quick. 'I appreciate what you and my grandmother have. I respect that. She has love for you, and so I trust you. But only you,' she added quietly, just between her and Eolande. Eolande smiled and bowed her head.

'You can trust Aelfraed. You have my word.'

I don't want to fall in love with a fae, Erica thought.

Eolande cocked her head.

'Your heart is yours to give,' she said. Erica blinked. Had the woman just read her mind? Could the fae do that? 'And your heart won't be given to Aelfraed.'

'No?' Erica forgot her awkwardness, her fear dissipating. She leaned into Eolande. 'How do you know that?'

Eolande turned back to Minerva. She held out her hand and behind Minerva, a man emerged from the trees.

His skin was white but lightly tanned, brown hair curling around his ears. He was as tall as Eolande and wore a loose white shirt, the top two buttons undone, and muddy jeans. He wasn't skinny, but could be described as stocky, and his blue eyes were piercing as he looked straight at Erica.

Erica realised she was holding her breath and tried to exhale slowly instead of all at once in a loud puff.

He smiled, showing off perfect, clean teeth, and Erica swallowed hard.

'Hello Erica. Finally,' he said.

'She is not for you,' Eolande told him matter-of-factly. Alfie didn't seem to mind. He gave a small shrug and then gave Erica a wink.

Esther stepped close to her daughter.

'Right. They've met. That's done. Now, will you help us?' she asked Eolande.

Eolande looked back to Alfie and nodded.

'Yes. We will help you.'

10

'Ruby! Get your bag. Your dad will be here soon,' Jess shouted up the stairs.

A muffled, 'Okay, Mummy,' was called down to her. Jess considered going up to see what her daughter was doing when Marshall appeared in the living room doorway.

'Going to stay with her dad?' he asked. He was rubbing at his hands.

'Yeah. As she couldn't stay with him at the weekend, he's taking her tonight.' Jess turned back up the stairs. 'Ruby! What are you doing?' she shouted.

They waited.

'I'm coming!'

'What's wrong with your hands? Have you hurt them?' Jess asked, nodding at Marshall still rubbing at his palms. He looked down at them and then smiled.

'Just a bit achey.'

'Take a break. I'll make us a cuppa.' Jess led the way into the kitchen and Marshall followed. 'I really appreciate you helping with this,' Jess told him as she filled the kettle. 'But you don't have to.'

'Well, you've got half a room with no skirting now, so I sort of do.'

Jess's smile faded and she turned to glance at

Marshall. Her spirits lifted when she saw him grinning.

'Okay, fair point. But if you want to stop after this room, I'll understand.'

'You realise you're paying me? This is a job,' Marshall pointed out.

'Yeah and I also realise that you're giving me a huge discount. I got quotes for this work before I bought the house.' Jess turned to Marshall, leaning her back against the kitchen worktop as they waited for the kettle to boil. 'I don't think you're making any money out of this.'

Marshall held her gaze for a moment and then looked away with a shrug.

'That's my choice.'

'It is. But I don't want to take advantage,' said Jess, the smile growing on her lips. This wasn't just her, she thought. Could he be feeling this too?

'You're not. Like I said, it's my choice.' He looked up at her and there was a tense silence, broken by the kettle clicking itself off.

'Well. Thank you.' Jess gave him her softest eyes before turning to make the tea. She took a deep breath while her back was turned. It had been such a long time since she'd been in this situation, and even then, Paul had asked her out. How on earth did she move this on? And if she did, what if she was wrong and he turned her down? She'd have to get in someone else to finish the skirting boards, she thought, as if that would be the worst of it.

She gave Marshall his cup and joined him sitting at the table. He opened his mouth to speak when Jess's phone started to sing.

Inwardly cursing all technology, Jess glanced at the name and hesitated. If it had been her parents or the school or Paul or Erica or even Erica's family, she would have answered. But it was Steve.

'Do you need to get that?' Marshall asked.

'I don't know,' Jess grumbled. 'Probably. Yes. No, yes, I should. Hey, Steve,' she answered the phone, trying to avoid looking at Marshall. He sipped at his tea and looked out of the windows at her garden. This had better be good, Jess thought.

'Erm. Hi. I don't know how to say this...'

'What?' Get on with it, Steve.

'She's back.'

Jess blinked.

'What? What are you on about?' Jess snapped, momentarily allowing her frustration to shine through. Marshall looked back at her and she bit her tongue to stop herself saying more.

'Rachel. She's back.'

Jess's stomach twisted. Had it all been a big joke?

'Rachel. Your wife?'

'Yes.'

Oh. Jess realised what was happening. She stood and moved to the other side of the kitchen, turning her back on Marshall.

'Steve, maybe you need to see the doctor again. Rachel died three months ago. Remember? She's not there.'

'Yeah, I know. But she is here, Jess. She's in the living room, right now. Holding the baby.'

Jess scrunched up her eyes and rubbed at her forehead.

'There's a woman in your house who you think is your wife and she's holding your baby?'

'I don't think, Jess. I know. It's her. Who else could it be?'

An imposter, a twin, a cyborg. Jess didn't dare say any of that out loud.

'But…she died.' She fought the urge to scream. 'What's going on, Steve?'

'I don't know. They must have got it wrong. At the morgue.'

'The police, the hospital and you all got it wrong? You ID'ed her. I remember you telling me.'

'I did.' Finally, Steve sounded a little unsure.

'Are you sure this woman you're seeing is real?' Jess snuck a glance over her shoulder at Marshall and was alarmed to find him watching her curiously.

'Very. I know her, Jess. It's my Rachel.'

'You said that when you ID'ed her. You said you knew it was her.'

'I know. I don't know. I can't explain it.'

There was a pause.

'Can she?' Jess asked. 'Have you asked her what this is all about? Where she's been? Have you tested her? Made sure it's really her? You're still grieving, Steve. You might be… I'm sorry, but you might be seeing what you want to see.'

Jess could hear Steve thinking about this.

'You think I should test her?'

'Definitely. Ask her questions only Rachel would know the answers to. And for the love of everything, take Joe away from her until you're a hundred per cent sure.'

'Yes. Right. You're right. I will.'

'And maybe…' Jess pinched the bridge of her nose and sighed. 'Shall I call the police?'

'What? No.'

'I don't feel comfortable you going through this alone,' Jess admitted, sparing another glance to

Marshall. This lovely, attractive man sat in her kitchen. Marshall looked back with concern.

'Well, maybe you could come. Here. To help me.'

Jess stopped.

'You want me to come help you interrogate this woman?'

'Interrogate's a bit strong. I understand if you can't. You couldn't bring Ruby into this situation, I know.'

'Right.' Except Ruby was spending the night at her dad's. Jess chewed on her lip. 'I'll, err, see what I can do. I'll ring you back? Go get Joe off her and talk to her. I'll let you know.'

'Okay. Thank you, Jess.'

'No problem.'

They said their goodbyes. Jess hung up and stared at her phone.

'Is everything okay?' Marshall asked slowly. 'That sounded a bit…weird.'

Jess laughed.

'You could say that. Hang on, I just need to make a call.'

'Of course.' Marshall stood up. 'I'll go carry on with the skirting.'

'No, no,' Jess said too quickly. 'It's okay. This won't take long.' Then I'm all yours, Jess stopped herself from saying. She quickly called Erica.

'Hey,' she said when Erica answered. 'So, I have strange news. Steve just called me.'

'Oh God. What now? Blood writing on the wall?'

'No. He—is that a thing?' Jess asked.

'I don't know. What did he want?'

Jess hesitated.

'Are you okay? You don't sound okay.'

'I'm fine. Just, a bit, no, I'm fine. Actually, I have news too. Gran thought it might be good to get the fae involved. Her…friend…can basically walk right into Steve's house and tell us if it's haunted or not in seconds. It'll save us a lot of time. What do you think?'

'Well, obviously I say yes because I want to meet—' Jess glanced up at Marshall. 'Your Gran's friend,' she continued carefully. 'I don't know how this fits in with that but Steve just called to say his wife has shown up.' There was silence over the phone. 'Ric?'

'His dead wife has turned up? Alive?'

'Sat in his living room, holding his baby. Yes.'

'And it's definitely her?'

'I told him to make sure. Ask her stuff. But yeah, he seems pretty sure.'

Erica sighed.

'What about the dust in the baby monitor? And the silhouette?'

'Maybe the silhouette was her.' Jess had forgotten about the dust. What about the dust?

'And the bright light? What? She was holding a torch while she snuck into her own house after rising from the dead?'

Wow. Jess fell back against the kitchen counter from the force of Erica's voice.

'What happened to get you in this mood?' she asked.

'Sorry. I'm sorry. I can't – I'll tell you later.'

'Okay. Hey, would your Gran's friend be able to tell if Steve's wife really is Steve's wife?'

'Probably. Good thinking. She's there now, right? Let's just go. Get this over with.'

The phone beeped in Jess's ear.

'Okay. Paul's collecting Ruby in a bit. So we can go after that?'

'Great. We'll come pick you up.'

After saying goodbye, Jess hung up and looked straight up into Marshall's eyes.

'That sounded interesting. I didn't mean to pry, but, well, you told me to stay.' A smile played on his lips.

She'd forgotten about him. Jess gave a long sigh.

'Yeah, it's complicated.' She looked at him with narrowed eyes and then shrugged. What the hell. The worst that could happen was that he'd run away and better he did that now rather than later. A voice at the back of Jess's head strongly disagreed, urging her to tell him after she'd gotten him into bed, at least. She ignored that voice. 'An old friend of mine, who I used to work with. His wife died a few months ago. They'd just had a baby.'

Marshall pulled a face.

'And now she's turned up?'

'Apparently so. This is after the friend told me he was going mad because he thought his wife was haunting the house. Me and Ric went to investigate and we saw…things.'

'Things?' Marshall leaned back in his chair. 'You went ghost hunting?'

Jess shrugged, wondering if she'd said too much.

'Ric's family is a little on the hippie side and her grandmother is very,' Jess struggled for the right word. 'Spiritual, you could say.'

Marshall raised an eyebrow.

'And you saw things?'

'Yes. Things even Ric's grandmother couldn't really explain. But now his wife is back, so.' Jess shrugged again. 'It's been a bit weird.'

'Sounds it.'

Jess looked up at Marshall and caught him gazing at her. He snapped out of it as Ruby appeared in the kitchen.

'Mummy? Can Bubbles come with me?' Ruby asked. She was glad to see Marshall was still there. Her mum seemed a little happier when he was around. Actually, Ruby thought, she was quite happy when Marshall was around. She liked Marshall.

'Bubbles?' Marshall looked from Ruby to her mother.

'Oh yes! We finally named the puppy. She's in her bed with a massive Do Not Disturb above her head. You leave her be,' Jess added to Ruby, gesturing to the sleeping puppy curled up on her bed beside the kitchen table.

Ruby pouted and dropped the little backpack she was holding.

'But can't Bubbles come with me?'

'Actually, that might be good. Save me leaving her all alone when I go to Steve's.'

Ruby cocked her head but didn't question her mother. She'd heard Steve's name mentioned and had ascertained upon questioning that, as far as Ruby was concerned, Steve was boring. 'I'll ask your dad when he gets here,' Jess finished. She looked down at her phone and made a noise with her mouth. She didn't think Ruby knew what that meant, but Ruby did know. Her mother had been about to swear. She'd remembered at the last moment that Ruby was there. She hated when adults did that. It was as if her mother was hiding something from her.

'Everything okay?' Marshall asked. Ruby picked up her bag, approached the table and dropped it again next to Marshall. He gave her a warm smile.

'Not really,' Jess muttered.

Something dropped into the pit of Ruby's stomach. She'd heard that tone of voice before, despite her mother trying to hide it. She stared at her mother. 'Hang on. Can Ruby stay in here with you a moment?'

Marshall nodded and Jess quickly left, holding the phone to her ear. Ruby knew what that meant.

'Dad's not coming,' she said, unable to keep the sadness from her voice. Marshall looked shocked. Ruby wasn't shocked.

'What makes you say that?' Marshall asked.

'This is how it happens,' Ruby told him. 'Mum tries to not say bad words. Most of the time she manages it. Then she takes the phone into another room and tells me to stay where I am. It's so she can be angry with him without me hearing it.'

Marshall took a deep breath and sat back in his chair.

'Oh. You're being very mature about it.'

'Am I?'

'Yeah.' Marshall gave her another smile but it was forced. He opened his mouth and closed it, looking over Ruby to where her mother had gone. 'I'm sorry, Ruby,' he said eventually. 'I don't know what to say. I'm sorry you think your dad isn't coming.'

Ruby stared at him. That wasn't the usual grown-up response.

'Do you think he is?' she asked.

Marshall held up his hands in defeat.

'I don't know. You know your dad better than me. I've barely met him.'

Ruby's gaze shifted away from Marshall and onto the large puppy sleeping in her bed behind the table.

'That's why he gave me Bubbles. Because he can't always be with me.'

'He told you that?' Marshall joined her in watching the sleeping puppy. Bubbles opened an eye and watched them back.

'No. But it's obvious.' Ruby sighed.

Jess walked back into the kitchen and they all, including the puppy who lifted her head, turned to look at her. She stopped and stared back.

'Sorry about that,' she said slowly. 'Did I interrupt something?'

'Daddy's not coming, is he?' Ruby asked. A shadow passed over her mother's face, replaced quickly with such sadness that Ruby wanted to cry. Tears sprang up in her eyes.

'Oh, baby.' Jess moved forward with speed, landing on her knees in front of her daughter and wrapping her arms around her. 'I'm sorry. No, he isn't. He has to work.'

Ruby nodded, staring at the floor as her mother let go. When she glanced back up there were tears in her mother's eyes. Ruby couldn't hold them back then and with one blink, her own tears started dripping down her cheeks. Jess wiped them away.

'He loves you so much, you know,' she told her. 'This weekend. He says you can go stay with him. How does that sound?'

Ruby shrugged.

'Can Bubbles come with me?'

Jess glanced at the puppy behind Ruby who was

now sat up, watching them intently.

'I'll ask your dad,' she said.

That means no, thought Ruby.

'I'll go unpack my bag,' she said.

'No. I'll do that. Why don't you go watch cartoons?' Jess offered her a smile.

Cartoons did sound good.

'Marshall's made a mess of the living room,' Ruby pointed out.

'I can go tidy it up,' the big man offered from behind her.

'You can go watch them in your bedroom. Use my tablet. I'll let you know when dinner's ready. What would you like? We'll have your favourite.'

'Fish and chips,' said Ruby without hesitation. Jess laughed.

'That's my girl. No cooking involved.' Jess planted a big kiss on Ruby's cheek and pulled her in for a tight hug. She passed Ruby her tablet, unlocking it and bringing up the cartoons channel. 'Only cartoons, mind. I'll be up to check on it any second now.'

Ruby took the tablet and ran to the stairs before her mother changed her mind. It was only when she reached the top that she realised she'd forgotten about Marshall.

'Bye, Marshall!' she screamed down.

'Bye, Ruby!' Marshall shouted back, grinning. The grin faded as he turned back to Jess. 'I'm sorry.'

'Oh. It's Paul. This is what he does. I want to say it started when we stopped living together but actually he was just the same when we were all under the one roof. What can you do. It's the pain it causes Ruby. I want to inflict that pain right back on him.' Jess realised she was growling and stopped.

'It's okay. It makes me angry too and I'm not her mum.' Marshall offered Jess his lopsided smile and she relented, her shoulders relaxing.

'Well, an evening of fish and chips and my little girl. I can't complain. Do you want to join us? You're more than welcome.' The words were out of Jess's mouth before she could think and she hesitated, wondering how he would react.

'That would be lovely, except—'

Here we go, thought Jess. The excuse. She had misread him after all. She braced herself.

'—what about your friend?'

'Friend?'

'Steve?'

'Oh fuck.' Jess slapped her hand over her mouth and looked up the stairs. Ruby was nowhere to be seen. 'I thought I needed a puppysitter. Turns out I need a babysitter now too.' Jess fell into one of the kitchen chairs and thought quick. Who could she ask? Not Erica's family. Not again. They looked after Ruby so often and she was pretty certain that if they looked after Bubbles again, Erica's dad wouldn't give her back.

Her own parents were away on a six month holiday in Australia. She'd known that would be trouble as soon as they'd announced it. There had to be someone from school who owed her a favour. But no, there wasn't. She hadn't looked after any of their kids since they'd moved into the new house. She'd been relying on Erica's family too heavily. Jess groaned and put her head in her hands.

'I wonder if I can find a professional babysitter with this short notice,' she murmured, dropping her hands into her lap.

'I'll do it.'

Jess glanced at Marshall and laughed.

'You don't have to offer every time I have a problem,' she said kindly. 'And this is hardly fixing something.'

'It is. I'd be fixing your sudden childcare problem.'

'No. I'll just tell Erica she'll have to go without me. That's it.' And I won't get to meet the fae, thought Jess. Or check on Steve. Her shoulders heaved again in another sigh.

'I really don't mind,' Marshall told her. 'I'd be happy to do it. You don't have to pay me. Although those fish and chips afterwards sound good.'

Jess glanced at his soft expression and then looked up the stairs.

'You really wouldn't mind?'

'I wouldn't offer if I did.'

Jess bit her lip.

'Hang on. I'll be right back.' She walked slowly up the stairs. Bubbles sprang up and bounded up after her, leaving Marshall behind in the kitchen. Was she really considering leaving her daughter alone with a man she hardly knew? That was the thing though, it felt like she did know Marshall. He fitted into their house so well. But was it all a trick? Could she trust those instincts? She knocked lightly on Ruby's bedroom door and then poked her head around. Ruby was sat on her bed, legs stuck out, glancing from the tablet to her mother.

Jess sat next to her on the bed and Bubbles snuffled at Ruby's feet. Jess absent-mindedly told the puppy to sit and rubbed her ears.

'Can I ask you something?'

'Yes.' Ruby put the tablet down to stroke the puppy.

'Mr Horton next door is Mr Horrible. Miss Gabby is Miss Crabby. What's Marshall's nickname?'

Ruby thought carefully, looking back down at the tablet on her lap, paused on its cartoon.

'He doesn't have one.'

'Why not?'

'He's not mean.'

Jess smiled.

'If you had to give him a nickname, what would it be?'

'Big Man,' said Ruby with a defiant nod.

Jess laughed.

'That's descriptive. Ruby, what do you think of Marshall?'

'I like him. Why?'

'I have to pop out for an hour or so before dinner and Marshall's offered to stay here with you and Bubbles.' Jess studied Ruby for any sort of reaction and was a little shocked when Ruby's eyes brightened.

'Oh yes, please. I'd like that. Please. Can he?'

'You really like him?'

'Yes. Don't you?'

Jess felt her cheeks reddened.

'Well, yes. But I haven't known him long. I don't know if I should be leaving you alone with him.'

'Mummy, we'll be fine.' Ruby rolled her eyes. 'He's not a stranger.'

'Do you feel safe around him?'

Ruby nodded.

'Yes.'

'Me too,' Jess murmured. They smiled at one another. 'Okay. Okay.' She got off the bed. 'Okay, he'll watch you while I'm gone.'

'Yay!' Ruby leapt off the bed. Bubbles bounded away and hid behind Jess's legs.

Jess shook her head. Was this right? Ruby followed her downstairs.

'All right,' said Jess as they entered the kitchen. Marshall looked up at the three of them. 'That would be wonderful, if you could watch them both. Please. I mean, if that's still okay?'

'Of course.' Marshall grinned and looked down at the bouncing Ruby. Bubbles bounded after Ruby and gave a couple of barks. Jess ushered her outside to the garden.

'Okay, but there are ground rules,' Jess told them as Ruby jumped over to Marshall. Ruby stopped bouncing. Jess stood in the open door so she could watch both her daughter and the puppy, who was squatting in the corner of the lawn, soon to be lost in the dusky evening.

There was a knock at the door. Jess jumped and Ruby began bouncing again.

'There are ground rules, which I'll go over in a minute. Ruby! Don't you dare open that door.' The door might have a fae behind it. Jess's heart pounded. 'And you're to call me whenever,' she added to Marshall. 'No question is silly.'

Marshall gave a mock salute which Ruby mirrored. Jess smiled. This had to be the right thing. Jess brought the puppy back in and went to open the front door. Erica didn't smile. Behind her was a tall, handsome but ordinary looking man. Jess studied him as best she could without staring.

'Be right with you. Paul bailed again.'

Steve

Steve took the woman sat on his sofa a cup of tea and placed it on the table near her.

'Three sugars. Just how you like it,' he murmured, watching her.

'Sweet. Just like me.' Rachel smiled and cooed at the baby in her arms. Steve nodded. Yes, that's what he always used to say.

'Where have you been, Rachel?'

Rachel didn't answer. She blew kisses to the baby, making Joe gurgle happily.

'I can't tell you,' she said eventually.

'Why not?'

Rachel looked up at her husband.

'It's not safe.'

Steve blinked, his vision blurring. He was so tired. He moved closer, sitting on the sofa beside her.

'What? Why isn't it safe? What's going on?'

Rachel took a sip from her tea.

'Mmm, perfect.'

'Please,' said Steve, leaning closer. He reached out and stroked Joe's feet. 'Please. Do you remember? We said we'd have no secrets?'

Rachel shook her head, her short brown hair bouncing. She didn't have a scratch on her face, which seemed strange because Steve vividly remembered the blood and cuts over her skin when he'd had to identify her. Then again, with make-up covering the careful stitches, at the funeral home. 'Please, Rachel. You're scaring me.'

Rachel met his gaze.

'I love you, Steve. And I love Joe. And I don't want to put either of you in danger. I shouldn't have come.' She looked down at her baby. 'I don't know why I thought I could stay away. I just needed to hold him again. And see you again.' She looked back up at Steve, leaned forward and kissed his lips. Steve let her.

'I miss you,' he breathed, not opening his eyes as the kiss broke.

'I miss you too.' Rachel leaned her forehead against his, Joe cradled in her arms between them.

11

Erica let Jess go first but Alfie stayed behind her, as much as she tried to hang back and let him go in front. There was something about him that made her feel wobbly. Her world seemed to dip when he was close to her, and he was always close to her. Too close. Erica had to wonder if personal space was more of a human thing than a fae thing. Maybe he'd never heard of the concept.

Minerva and Eolande had dropped back, standing behind Alfie. They didn't want to intimidate Steve when he got round to answering the door.

Jess knocked again.

She was just turning back to them, presumably to suggest that maybe he was out, when the door opened and Steve appeared, bleary-eyed.

'Steve? Are you okay?' Jess asked gently.

Steve looked behind her to Erica and then Alfie, then behind them to Minerva and Eolande.

'What's going on?' he asked.

'I called you and told you, remember? I said we'd bring some friends, to see if there's a spirit in the house? And to meet this woman who says she's your wife?'

'Oh. Yes. There's no ghost. Rachel's back now. It was all a big mistake. Sorry to have wasted your time.'

Steve shut the door.

'What?' Jess nearly screeched. She turned to face the others and Erica flinched back involuntarily. 'What the hell? I've left a gorgeous man in my house and my daughter who's been let down by her dad yet again and for what?' Jess stomped back towards the car, squeezing past Erica and Alfie. Erica looked over her shoulder, ignoring Alfie and catching Minerva's eye. Her grandmother raised an eyebrow and gave a subtle nod. As Erica turned back, Alfie stared up at the house.

'Can you feel anything?' she asked.

'No.' Alfie looked at her. 'Can you?'

The way he asked it made Erica not want to answer. Instead, she stepped up and knocked on the door, loud and hard.

After a moment, Steve opened it.

'Please. I'm sorry I wasted your time. Please, go away.'

'No. You owe us at least an explanation,' said Erica, preparing to block the door should he try to close it again.

'My wife came back. I was wrong. That's all there is to it.'

Steve went to shut the door and Erica slammed her palms against it.

'What about the dust, Steve? In the baby monitor?'

'And the silhouette. And the bright light?' Jess called from where she now stood behind Minerva.

'I didn't see those,' said Steve.

'But you heard her voice.'

Steve looked Erica in the eye.

'Because she's alive.'

150

'And the baby monitor?'

Steve opened his mouth then closed it. He didn't have an answer.

'It doesn't matter anymore,' he said, although he didn't sound sure. Erica gave him a questioning look. 'It doesn't,' he repeated, and went to close the door.

In one swift motion, Alfie moved around Erica, easily forced the door open and stepped inside.

'Oi!' Steve fell back a step. What Erica found curious was that Steve didn't move to stop Alfie. He just stepped back and allowed the fae inside his house. Erica followed Alfie in.

'I'm pretty sure this is close to breaking and entering,' she whispered to him. Alfie gave her a sly smile before turning his face up to the ceiling and closing his eyes.

They all waited.

'There is no spirit here,' Alfie announced.

There was a pause as they looked between each other.

'See. I told you. Now, please leave.' Steve gestured to the open door.

'So how do we explain the dust? Hmm?' came Minerva's voice from outside. She stepped into the house. 'Sorry, love, but it's getting chilly out there. You wouldn't force an old woman to stand outside in the cold.'

Steve went to protest, but what could he say?

Minerva stood beside Alfie, gazing around the hallway.

'Nothing,' she said after a moment. She looked at the fae man and then back to Eolande, still standing on the doorstep with Jess. 'If his wife's alive and there's no spirit, what blew the batteries in the baby monitor?' Minerva looked at Steve. 'And I suppose it was your wife that Ric saw standing over the cot? She disappeared in a flash of bright light?' She raised an eyebrow, as if the very idea was preposterous. 'I don't suppose we can meet this wife of yours?'

'She's resting.'

'Well, yes. Coming back from the dead is exhausting.' Minerva gave a loud sniff and exchanged another look with Eolande. 'Just a little hello wouldn't be out of the question, though. Would it?'

'Please, just go.' Steve tried to wave them out of the door but Minerva wasn't moving. Alfie watched with a smirk on his face. Erica allowed herself a glance at him before looking away. Attractive he might be, but she wasn't going to fall for any fae tricks.

'Please, Steve,' said Jess, still standing out on the front door step. 'I just need to make sure you're okay. That you and Joe are safe. Then we'll go. I promise.'

'I'm fine. We're fine. Please.'

'Oh,' whined Minerva. 'I do feel a bit faint.'

Erica snapped up to look at her grandmother and immediately relaxed. Minerva wasn't the best of actresses. Erica jumped into action as her grandmother gave her a warning look.

'Gran! Are you okay? You look very pale. Maybe you should sit down. Is there anywhere she can sit down?' Erica leapt forward and took her grandmother's elbow, helping her further into the house.

'Oh. The world's gone wobbly. My knees.' Minerva stumbled.

'Careful, Gran,' Erica murmured under her breath as she fought to keep Minerva upright. Steve hurriedly followed them in.

'Of course. Here, in here, take the sofa. Shall I get you some water? Should I get her some water?'

Minerva sat down where Steve had offered and Erica stood over her, pretending to study her face. Behind them, Alfie, Eolande and Jess followed. The living room was empty.

'Yes, please, if you don't mind.' Minerva smacked her lips as if she was parched. Steve rushed out of the room and into the kitchen. Minerva straightened and looked around.

'Where is she?' she hissed.

Alfie and Eolande were already studying the furniture, the walls, the pictures in frames. Jess crossed her arms, frowning.

'Where's Joe, Steve?' she called into the kitchen. Steve reappeared with a glass full of water which he gingerly passed to Minerva.

'Hmm? Oh, with Rachel.'

'And where's Rachel?'

Steve finally looked around the room and faltered.

'Upstairs. She must be upstairs.' His worried eyes landed on Jess for a moment too long and a ball of fear dropped into Erica's stomach.

'Maybe you should check,' she suggested gently.

Steve, wringing his hands, left the room and they heard him calling, 'Rachel? Rachel, are you up there?'

There was no response.

'Rachel?'

Jess swore and followed him out. Soon, the sound of footsteps on the stairs could be heard.

'She's left with the baby,' said Minerva. 'I do hope it was his wife and not an imposter.'

Erica blinked at her grandmother.

'Maybe we should call the police,' she wondered out loud.

'No.'

They all turned to the door. A woman with short brown hair, wearing shoes and a light coat, and holding a baby, stood in the doorway. 'Steve? I'm here. What's all the fuss about?'

Steve and Jess jogged down the stairs and Steve took the baby from Rachel's arms as the woman glanced at each visitor in turn. 'Who are all these people?'

'Where did you go?' Steve demanded after checking the baby over.

'Out into the garden. For a bit of fresh air.' Rachel looked down at Minerva still sitting on the sofa. 'Who are you people?'

'Hmm,' said Alfie. Erica inadvertently glanced at him. What did that mean?

'I'm Jess.' Jess stepped forward, holding out her hand. 'A friend of Steve's. I've been giving him a helping hand where I can, since your passing. You understand that this is a bit confusing for us. We just wanted to check that Steve and Joe are okay.'

'This lady had a funny turn,' Steve said weakly, gesturing to Minerva.

'Oh.' Rachel looked Jess up and down and then did the same to Erica, Alfie and Eolande. 'Well, that's good of you. But as you can see, I'm here. Alive and well. And everything's fine. Thank you for your concern. Now, if you don't mind, I'm tired. It would be nice to be able to catch up with my family in peace.'

The silence that followed was heavy. No one moved.

'But, where have you been?' Jess asked.

'I don't believe that's any of your business,' snapped Rachel. She looked down at Minerva. 'Are you feeling better yet?'

Minerva raised both eyebrows and proffered her arms to Erica to help her up.

'Well. How rude. We'll be on our way then.' Erica couldn't miss the pointed look Minerva gave Eolande. She doubted anyone missed it.

The group filed out until only Jess remained, talking quietly to Steve before Rachel's glaring finally pushed her out.

They waited next to the car.

'Well. That wasn't as fun as it should have been,' said Minerva. 'I'd like to go home now.' She looked up at Eolande and Alfie. 'Anything exciting you can tell us?'

'I think so.' Alfie smiled. It was a charming smile, one that could melt hearts. Except Erica's heart wasn't for melting. She bit the inside of her cheek. 'There's no spirit in that house.'

'You said that already. That's not exciting,' Minerva told him. Alfie's charming smile turned into a boyish grin.

'No. There's no spirit. But that woman isn't from this world.'

Erica's eyes widened as she was forced to look at him. On the other side of him, Jess gasped and then began to smile.

'No.' Erica told her, pointing a finger. 'No being happy about that. We don't even know what that means. What does that mean?' she asked Alfie. Alfie's gaze softened at he looked at her, the grin now playing on his lips. Erica snapped her mouth shut.

'He means that she is not of this present world. She does not fit in with our current timeline,' said Eolande.

Minerva rubbed her head.

'Sounds an awful lot like you just suggested time travel was an option here.'

'Perhaps not time travel in the way that you mean it,' Eolande told her. 'There are many ways to end up in a world or time that is not your own. That woman is theoretically of this world but not of this time.'

'How can you tell?' asked Jess.

Eolande shrugged.

'There are ways.'

'We can sense it,' said Alfie, giving Jess a wink. Erica gritted her teeth. No. She forced herself to relax. She certainly was not jealous of Alfie winking at her friend. What did she care who Alfie winked at. 'After all, we are not always from this world. There are a number of ways to cross over into different times, dimensions and worlds.'

'Can you tell where she came from?' asked Minerva.

'Unfortunately not,' said Eolande.

'We'd need more time with her,' explained Alfie. 'I'm happy to work with you on it, though,' he said to Erica. Erica stiffened. She'd rather work with Eolande. She looked up at Jess to find her friend grinning at her, her eyes shining.

'Maybe you should work with Jess on it. This is more her thing.'

Jess narrowed her eyes at Erica. Alfie gave a disappointed shrug and dug his hands into his

156

pockets.

'Yes, well. We can decide that later. Obviously they don't want us around and that fella and the baby seem fine.' Minerva gave Jess a nod. 'Time to go home, I feel. Come on, we'll drop Jess off first, and then Eolande and Alfie.'

Erica took out her car keys and blew out her cheeks.

12

It was only when she squeezed into Erica's car, pushed up against Eolande on the back seat, that Jess remembered Ruby and Bubbles left home with Marshall. Her stomach twisted and she was overcome with a sudden and violent need to get home right that second. She didn't join in with the conversation, as Minerva and Eolande discussed how it might be possible for Rachel to have crossed between times and worlds, or even across the veil and resurrected without a scratch on her. Witchcraft was mentioned but both fae dismissed the idea. Something about it not smelling right.

Please let everything be all right, thought Jess. It was all she could think. Her little personal mantra repeated over and over until Erica pulled up outside her house.

'Call me later?' she said as she got out. Erica agreed, saying they'd speak in the morning. Jess didn't wait for the car to pull away. She strode up her driveway to the front door and shoved her key into the lock.

The sound of high pitched giggles and deep laughter met her as she opened the door and Jess smiled.

All was right with the world.

She followed the sounds into the kitchen where

Marshall and Ruby both sat. The table was covered with pieces of paper and crayons. They were drawing. Behind them, Bubbles was flat out on her bed, her paws twitching in a deep sleep. The large puppy gave a snort and woke up, looking bleary-eyed at Jess before her tail started pounding and she gave a short, muffled bark.

'Oh yeah, you're gonna be a great guard dog,' said Jess, blowing the puppy a kiss. Marshall and Ruby looked up at her. Ruby kicked her legs.

'Hello, Mummy. Did you have fun?'

'Fun isn't the word I would use.' Jess kissed the top of her daughter's head, looking down at her creations scrawled across the paper. 'It looks like you've been having more fun.' Her eyes travelled over to Marshall's side of the table. The big man sat back, revealing a piece of paper with the rough outline of a castle drawn in pink crayon. Jess raised an eyebrow at him.

'I asked Ruby what I should draw. She said a pink castle. And here it is.' He brandished his artwork proudly. Jess laughed.

'Very good. So you have had fun?'

Ruby nodded, lifting her drawing and giving it to her mother. Jess took it, her mind rushing into the blind panic it always did when Ruby handed her a drawing. It was that trickiest of all questions; what was it? 'Oh, it's lovely Ruby,' she tried.

Ruby looked up at her.

'It's a dragon.'

'I know it is,' Jess told her. 'See, there's the head and the wings.' She pointed, the shape becoming more recognisable. Ruby beamed up at her. 'Is it to go with Marshall's castle?'

'Yes. There's a princess here too.' Ruby shuffled

through the papers. 'And look, here's you, me, Marshall and Bubbles.'

Jess hadn't expected the tears, never mind for the tears to come so fiercely. She looked down at the stereotypical family drawing Ruby had created. There she was in the middle, Bubbles, a little brown ball, beside her, and Jess and Marshall side by side, their hands almost touching. Ruby had never drawn a picture like that of her, Jess and Paul. Jess wiped at her eyes quickly before Ruby could see, but Marshall had seen, she realised as he gazed at her with soft concern.

'That's beautiful, Rubes,' Jess told her daughter, kissing her head again. 'Do you want to pick one to go on the fridge?'

Ruby jumped up.

'Yes! Can one of Marshall's go up too?'

Jess did a double take at Marshall.

'There's more than one?'

Marshall had the decency to look a little embarrassed. He used his drawing of a castle to cover up other papers.

'No.'

'Yes there is.' Ruby, like all good little girls, walked over and pulled out Marshall's other hidden drawings. 'He's rubbish at coming up with his own ideas,' she told her mother. 'I had to tell him what to draw every time.' She handed the papers to Jess. 'Look, there's me. And there's you.'

'Very good. Which one should go up on the fridge?' asked Jess, carefully avoiding looking at the drawings.

'Oh, I don't think any of them should.' Marshall stood up, scraping his chair back. Bubbles, excited by the fact that everyone was now standing, jumped up and began barking. 'Sorry. My fault. I'll take her out.' Marshall, perhaps too keen to leave the conversation, hurried Bubbles out into the garden.

As soon as he was outside, Jess allowed herself a glimpse at his drawings. There was Ruby, a crude stick figure of a small girl with dark hair and wearing a blue dress. Jess smiled, wondering if Ruby had demanded the blue dress. And there, on the next page, was a woman drawn in long, curved strokes. Jess held her breath. She had wondered if there would be clues in his drawing of her, but from first glimpse it seemed to her that the whole thing was a clue.

'How about we put this one of you up on the fridge? I like that one,' Jess offered, hiding the picture of her behind the crude castle.

'Yes. Me too,' agreed Ruby.

'Okay. You go put them up. Remember to take down two. You know the rules.'

'Yup.' Ruby took Marshall's drawing and the one she'd created of her, Jess, Marshall and Bubbles and began staring at the drawings already up on the fridge. Gently, she took down two and replaced them with the new ones. 'There.' She straightened Marshall's drawing and stepped back.

'Lovely. Now, go wash up. Marshall can clear up the table,' Jess said pointedly as Marshall and Bubbles returned from the garden. 'And I'll sort out the food. Deal?'

'Deal!' Ruby shouted, running out and up the stairs. Jess smiled and shook her head.

'You're a famous artist in this house now.' She nodded to Marshall's drawing on the fridge. He studied them as he began collecting the crayons.

'Oh, good, you chose that one. I liked that one

too.'

'Oh, I don't know. I quite like the one of me,' Jess murmured.

'Yeah. Me too.'

Jess turned at Marshall's soft voice to find that he'd paused, gazing at her.

'You're still staying for food, right?' she breathed. Marshall nodded. 'Good. I mean, Ruby will be pleased. I'll go out and get it in a bit.'

'How did it go? How's your friend and his wife? Is she her?'

'Apparently so. Sort of.'

'Sort of?'

'It's complicated. But it does seem that his wife is alive and well, and wasn't happy about us being there. We got kicked out.'

Marshall scratched his head.

'Is your life always this weird?'

Jess smiled.

'No. Unfortunately. Thank you, for looking after Ruby. Even though we got kicked out, I'm glad I went. I needed to see all that. So, thank you. I should pay you babysitting rates, really.' Jess moved towards her purse.

'Don't you dare.' Marshall held up a crayon threateningly. 'I had fun. Ruby's great. She's so quick-thinking.'

'Yeah. That's not always as great as you think it is.'

They smiled at one another and Marshall brought the paper and crayons over to her, placing them on the worktop. He stood closer than he had to, his eyes on hers. Jess reminded herself to breath as he towered over her, so close they almost touched.

Marshall slowly began to lean down. Jess was

quite proud that she didn't leap at him, instead reaching slowly up on tiptoe. Marshall's arm snaked around her waist and then he hesitated. Jess stretched up further but there was only so far she could go. They stared into one another's eyes for a moment and then he kissed her.

She had expected a short peck on the lips, but at the point where one of them should have pulled away, they moved closer instead. Jess wrapped her arms around his neck, holding him in place as his grip on her waist tightened, but the kiss remained soft. The tips of their tongues met and in that moment the kiss deepened. Marshall's arms moved lower and he easily picked her up, her legs automatically wrapping around him as he sat her on the worktop.

Bubbles barked and Jess remembered herself. She pushed Marshall away but only a little, breaking the kiss. They remained close, their foreheads touching, breaths mingling.

'If Ruby comes downstairs,' Jess murmured.

Marshall lifted Jess down. Her hands lingered on him as he let go of her.

'I'm sorry. I shouldn't have done that,' Marshall said, unable to look away from her.

'Why not?'

He gave her his lopsided smile.

'I don't want to take advantage.'

Jess laughed.

'You're not.' Jess jumped away as Ruby ran down the stairs. 'Walk down the stairs, Rubes. Don't run,' she said, turning away from Marshall and pushing her hair back. 'Right. I'll go get the food, shall I?'

A few hours later, Jess walked down the stairs after putting Ruby to bed, and made her way into the living room. Marshall, sitting on the sofa, looked up at her.

'She's okay?'

Jess nodded.

'Fast asleep. I think all the fun she had drawing with you tired her out.'

Marshall gave a nod and stood up.

'I'll get going then.'

'Oh.'

'Oh?'

Jess studied his face. Didn't he want to go back to that kiss? Didn't he want to continue it?

'Only, I've got a bottle of wine in the fridge that needs drinking. Going past its drink by date. You'd be doing me a favour.'

Marshall grinned.

'I didn't know wine had a drink by date.'

'Semantics.' Jess waved the words away.

'Well, if it needs drinking, who am I to say no?' Marshall sat back down. Jess went into the kitchen for the bottle and couple of glasses before he could change his mind.

'Here we go. It's cheap stuff, sorry about that.'

'You're not talking to a wine connoisseur. Wine's wine.' Marshall took the glasses from her as Jess opened the bottle.

'So, can you tell me about your friend's wife? What happened? A mistake at the morgue?' Marshall asked as Jess poured the wine.

'I don't know. She wouldn't tell us where she'd been or what happened. Steve identified her after the accident and saw her before the funeral. He never mentioned any doubt about it not being her. She was definitely dead.'

'Except that now she's alive.'

'And Steve doesn't seem convinced.' Jess frowned thoughtfully, sipping at her wine. 'He panicked a bit when he couldn't find her. There was a brief moment when we thought she'd done a runner with the baby.'

Marshall pulled a face.

'Has he told the police she's back?'

'I don't think so. Is that what you have to do? When someone comes back from the dead?'

Marshall shrugged.

'Can't say I've ever heard of it.'

'Well, it happens though, doesn't it. There was that case in the papers a while back. That millionaire who fell on hard times and… ' Jess drifted off, her eyes glazing over.

'And?'

'Faked his own death.' Jess slowly turned to look at Marshall. 'Maybe she faked her own death.'

'Why? For the insurance?'

'No. I don't think they had any. Steve was really worried about the finances.' Jess frowned again. 'And why would you fake your own death when you have a husband and brand new baby.' Her expression lightened. 'I'll tell you why. Because of the overwhelm.' She looked back at Marshall. 'Maybe she had postnatal depression.' Marshall nodded. 'Except…'

'What?'

Jess shuffled her position, moving her legs under her on the sofa and in the process, moving closer to Marshall.

'I can't tell you.'

Marshall feigned a glare.

'What? You have to tell me now. You can't just leave it like that.'

'You'll think I'm crazy and then you won't kiss me again.' Jess looked at her empty wine glass. That hadn't taken much.

'Oh, I definitely want to kiss you again,' Marshall told her gently. Their eyes locked for a moment.

'Okay.'

'No, you have to tell me first. Otherwise you'll forget.' Marshall leaned forward to refill their glasses.

'You promise not to tell anyone? Especially Ruby? What am I saying, you probably won't believe me anyway.'

'I promise.' Marshall put his hand over his heart. 'I won't even tell Ruby.'

'Okay. But don't laugh. There's a small chance that Steve's wife isn't from our time.'

Marshall stared at Jess and blinked.

'You mean, she's a lot younger than us?'

'No. I mean she's from another dimension or world or a time traveller, or something.'

Jess instantly regretted saying that. Marshall leaned away, if only for a second, and their second kiss suddenly seemed hours away rather than minutes.

'Just because she's alive when she was dead?'

Jess clenched her eyes shut. She could end this here. Right now. Instead, she said, 'No. Because Minerva's supernatural fae girlfriend told us so.'

Slowly, one at a time, Jess opened her eyes. Marshall was expressionless but he smiled when he saw her looking.

'Naturally,' he said.

Jess laughed.

'Really? You don't want me to explain any of that?'

'Just one thing.'

'What?'

'Who's Minerva?'

'My friend Ric's grandmother. She's a witch.'

Marshall nodded.

'Thought as much.'

He placed his wine glass down on the table. Then he took Jess's glass and placed it beside his own, before leaning forward and kissing her.

Steve

'Everything okay?'

'Yes, Steve. Will you please stop asking that.'

'I meant with the food.'

'Oh.' Rachel looked down at her half-finished dinner. She'd spent the last ten minutes pushing it around the plate, staring wide-eyed at nothing in particular. 'Yes. Thank you. It was lovely.' She pushed the plate away.

Steve sighed and picked up the plate, taking it with his to the sink. Silently, he began loading the dishwasher, scraping her uneaten food into the bin.

'I should go check on Joe.' Rachel's chair scraped back.

'He's fine. I checked on him before we ate. The baby monitor is right there.' Steve gestured with his head to the monitor in the centre of the dining table. Rachel glanced at it.

'Still, I'll just go check on him. Pour me a glass of wine, will you?'

Steve didn't respond. He kept his back turned to the room as Rachel left, listening as she climbed the stairs.

It wasn't how it used to be. It was a stupid thing to think. Of course things weren't how they used to be. How could they be? But Steve wondered if they would ever go back to how it was, or had Rachel's supposed and still-unexplained death changed everything? It wasn't just that things were awkward, she had become cold with him. If she could, Steve was sure, she would spend every second in that nursery with Joe. She would rather be with the baby than with him. Steve's chest ached at the thought.

He closed the dishwasher and set it going. Finding a bottle of Rachel's favourite wine, he poured her a glass and sat at the table to wait for her return.

The phone ringing woke him up. Steve lifted his head, his eyes opening but his vision blurry as he sought the source of the noise.

'Are you not going to get that?' Rachel strode into the room and stopped by the table, her arms crossed. 'Oh, thank you.' She picked up the untouched wine glass and sipped at it.

Was it Steve's imagination or did the light above their heads flicker? He dismissed it. His vision still hadn't cleared.

'What time is it?' Steve croaked, standing to reach for the phone.

'It's only nine. Why?'

It had been half seven when they'd finished eating. She'd been upstairs for over an hour.

Steve answered the phone.

'Hello?'

'Hello, Mr Green. Are you with your wife?'

Steve frowned. He didn't recognise the man's voice. He blinked a few times.

'Sorry, who is this?'

'A friend, Mr Green. I'm a friend. She's in the room with you, isn't she? I need you to go to an empty room, please. I must talk to you.'

'What?'

'Who is it?' Rachel asked. Steve shrugged. He honestly had no idea.

'Probably a scam or sales call,' he said quietly, placing his hand over the receiver. She nodded and walked out of the kitchen.

'I'll be in the nursery, then.'

She took her glass of wine, Steve noted.

'Has she gone?' asked the voice on the other end of the phone.

'Who is this?' Steve was waking up now and this was certainly not a scam or sales call.

'Has she gone?'

'Yes. Who are you?'

'Good. My name is Detective Sergeant Rick Cavanagh, Mr Green. I need to tell you not to put so much trust in your wife. She's not who she claims to be.'

'You don't say,' Steve murmured, looking towards the door where his wife had disappeared. 'She's been through a lot. How do you know her?'

'I'm the detective charged with arresting her, Mr Green.'

Steve didn't respond. His bowels loosened, his dinner threatening to come back up.

'Arrest?' he repeated in a hushed tone, just in case his wife could hear him. 'Don't be ridiculous. What for?'

'Murder. I'm sorry. You should never have been involved in this. If it were up to me, you wouldn't have been.'

Murder. The kitchen span around Steve. This was a joke. It had to be.

'This is a joke. Some stupid prank. If you call this place again, I'll call the police.' Steve hung up the phone and dropped it on the table with a slam.

'Who was that?'

Steve jumped and span round to face Rachel standing in the doorway, wine glass still in her hand. Had she ever really left?

'No one,' Steve told her, brushing his hands and turning to tidy the kitchen. 'A prank call. I shouldn't have answered it. But you never know at this time of night.' He was rambling. It had just been a prank call. Why had it affected him so much?

'Okay.' Rachel nodded. 'Good.' She spent a moment staring at him but not with any affection.

His body sagged as she left the room again and made her way into the living room. Steve stared at the kitchen worktop for a moment before swiftly making his way up the stairs and into the nursery.

13

Erica sucked on her lower lip. She wasn't going to cry. She was determined. Keeping her fingers busy, she opened a new document and started typing.

Half an hour later, she had an essay worth of her feelings, honest opinions about the agency and her manager, and a detailed description about what they could do with their job. She highlighted all of it and hit delete. Sitting back, she took a deep breath and glanced to her left at Jess's empty desk. Of all the days for her to call in sick. Not that she was sick. Jess had messaged her that morning to tell her about her evening, and night, with Marshall the handyman, finished with the fact that she wouldn't be in today. While Ruby was at school, Jess had no intention of letting Marshall out of her sight.

Tears burned at Erica's eyes, desperate to fall. She held them back, the tip of her nose stinging with the effort. Hurriedly, she brushed her eyes and took another deep, shaky breath.

Of all the days, Jess, she thought, staring at the blank document on her screen. Her right eye gave a small twitch as laughter filtered out of the meeting room nearby. Her manager and the agency's new senior account manager. She should be in that meeting room, laughing, getting to grips with new accounts. That was her job.

Erica squeezed her hands into fists as the men laughed again. Andy had gotten the job. They'd announced it that morning. He'd been with the agency for three months, but he was an old friend of the director. Jess squeezed her fists again, turning her knuckles white. She was pretty sure she could sue them. Work discrimination, or something. But that would mean legal proceedings, which would mean having to see their faces over and over for months, maybe even years. Whereas she could quit today. She'd have to work out her notice, but—hang on.

Erica sat back. Did she have to work out her notice? She could go to the doctors, get signed off sick. Erica pulled a face. She needed a good reference off them, in order to get her next job.

Erica tapped her fingernails on the desk. Without thinking, her mind just a whir of white noise, Erica picked up her mobile phone and hit the call button.

It rang for longer than usual.

'Hey, Ric. Everything okay?'

'Do you want to start our own agency?'

'What?'

That had got Jess's attention. Erica could almost see her turning away from whatever she'd been doing. Probably Marshall. Erica didn't care.

'Our own agency. Let's start one.'

'What's happened?' Jess asked, her tone low and serious. 'What am I missing?'

'Andy got the job,' Erica said. There was a pause on the other end of the phone. 'If we start our own agency, I don't need a good reference from them. I can leave, right now, and never see this place again.'

'That's not a good reason to go self-employed,

Ric.'

Erica sighed and placed her head on her desk.

'I know,' she mumbled into the phone. 'I don't know what to do. Well, I do know what to do, but I don't want to do it.'

Jess sighed.

'Tell them you're ill. You must have whatever I have. Go home sick.'

'I hope I don't have what you have.'

'Oh, but Ric. You're missing out.' Erica could hear Jess's grin.

'I don't want to know. But I'm glad you're having fun.'

'It'll be more fun later. Paul's picking up Ruby for the weekend and then it'll just be me, Marshall and Bubbles.'

'Won't Bubbles cramp your style?'

'You'd think, but Marshall is great with her. And she's sleeping a lot. We'll be fine. And so will you. Go home sick. Trust me. Take a bit of time, and we'll talk about this agency thing over the weekend. Okay? Don't make any rash decisions.'

'Okay.' Erica looked up towards the meeting room, spotting movement behind the door. 'Okay. I'll speak to you later. Have fun. Be safe.'

Jess gave a dirty cackle and they hung up.

Erica's manager and Andy filed out of the meeting room, grinning and chuckling together. Erica straightened out her twisted mouth and stood up, placing a hand on her stomach.

'Mark? Can I have a quick word?'

Her manager's grin faded as he looked at her and then down at the hand over her stomach.

'Your grandmother hasn't gone missing again, has she?'

'Not that I know of.'

His eyes flittered down to her hand again.

'Good.' He turned and led her back into the meeting room. She followed, only taking a step in and closing the door behind her. Mark didn't bother to sit down either.

'I feel awful. The room started spinning. I have a feeling I've caught whatever Jess has. I'd hate to spread it further round the office.'

Mark nodded.

'You don't look well.'

Erica bit her tongue at that.

'I hope you don't mind if I go home sick.' She stopped herself from offering to take work home.

'Sure. Leave your phone on, in case we need you.'

Erica left the meeting room without another word. Like hell she'd leave her phone on. She packed her bag quickly and left the office without making eye contact with anyone.

Once outside, Erica stopped and breathed in the not-so-fresh air. It tasted a little of freedom. She was so close, and the idea of coming back to this office really did make her nauseous. But, as Jess had said, that might change after a good night's rest. Erica made her way to her Mini and sat in the driver's seat. She didn't want to go home. She'd have to talk about it. She couldn't go to Jess, she didn't want to interrupt what they were up to. She could go to a coffee shop, or the bookshop. Erica pulled a face. She didn't want to be around people and reminded of what she was considering doing. Leaving a good, well paid, steady job for the idea and hope of freedom and something better. That thought made her smile. Only a week ago, it would have scared her, now there was a bubble of excitement brewing.

Erica started the engine and pulled out of the car park, onto the road, heading towards the only place where she knew she would be able to clear her head.

In the cemetery, Erica crouched in front of her grandfather's gravestone.

'Hi, Grandad,' she murmured, brushing the grass that grew around the stone with her fingers. 'It's just me. Gran's not here. She doesn't know I'm here. Well, she probably does, but I haven't told her.' Erica frowned. 'She says you talk to her, about what's going on. That you give her advice, maybe. And I need that help. I don't know what to do.' She paused as a breeze lifted her hair. 'I don't really know how this works.' She looked down at the earth. 'Are you there? Can you hear me?'

'He's here.'

Erica jumped up straight with a squeal and span around. Alfie watched her, his eyes dancing. His arms were crossed against his wide chest and he leaned against a thick tree trunk.

Shit, thought Erica. She thought she could avoid the fae if she stayed clear of the secret garden.

'Is it too much to ask that I talk to my grandad in peace?' she asked, turning away to catch her breath as much as to avoid looking at Alfie.

The fae shrugged.

'He is talking to you. You can't hear him. Maybe you need an interpreter.'

Erica looked around the grave.

'He's here? Where?'

'He's sitting on the gravestone.'

Erica looked at the empty space above the grave.

'Why can't I see him?'

Again, Alfie shrugged.

'Maybe you don't want to.'

Erica sagged.

'I want to talk to him, though.'

Alfie straightened and dropped his arms, moving to stand beside her. He was looking at the space above the gravestone. Erica jumped and looked away as he turned to her.

'Well, something's holding you back.'

'What?'

'I don't know. Only you know that. What did you want to talk to him about?'

'I don't think a fae would understand.' Erica regretted those words as soon as she'd said them but Alfie didn't seem bothered.

'Try me.'

'It's about work. And my life. You don't know me and you don't work.'

Alfie cocked his head.

'You know, there are some fae who have integrated into the human world. They work. They love. They start families. They get mortgages. Try me.' As if realising what he'd said, Alfie grinned and winked at her. Erica struggled to keep the smile from her face.

'Okay. I guess talking it through with someone impartial might help anyway.'

'That's the spirit.'

Erica looked at where she supposed her grandfather was.

'I want to quit my job,' she told him. 'I'm sick of it. They passed me over for promotion again and hired this bloke the agency director is friends with. It's just a massive clique that me and Jess aren't a part of, and I'm done.'

There was a pause and Erica looked to Alfie. His eyes were distant and then he gave a small nod.

'Your grandfather tells me that's quite something from you.' Alfie's eyes flashed. 'Sounds like you had big dreams for this job.'

'Me and Jess could start our own agency. That was what she's wanted to do for a while. We could do it.'

Alfie looked her up and down.

'So, why the hesitation?'

'I don't think she wants to anymore.'

'Set it up yourself then.'

'Go it alone?' Erica gave a small shiver but her mind started whirring with the possibilities. Could she do that? It would be difficult and hard work, but she'd have complete control. It was tempting.

'Your grandfather would like to know what you think Jess wants to do instead?' Alfie told her.

Erica blinked away her thoughts.

'I don't know. I'm not sure she knows. She's a bit distracted at the moment.'

Alfie smirked.

'She is.'

Erica did a double take at him, narrowing her eyes. There was a moment of silence and then Alfie sighed.

'You should quit your job,' he said with a note of finality.

'What?' Erica looked between him and the gravestone.

'That's what your grandfather suggests and I agree. Quit.'

'And do what?'

'Take a break. Relax. The future will become clear. In the meantime, have some fun.'

Erica studied Alfie's face.

'Is that my grandfather's suggestion or yours?'

Again, Alfie smirked and gave a shrug.

'You deserve a little fun. Before it all becomes serious.'

'Serious? What's going to become serious? Work?'

'You'll see.'

'That's not helpful. If you can see the future, can't you be a little clearer?'

'I think we've been plenty clear,' said Alfie. 'Quit.'

Erica stared at the space above the gravestone and told her mind she was going to quit. Her stomach didn't twist, there was no fear or resistance there. Instead, her shoulders relaxed, her stomach settling.

'Okay. I will.'

'Excellent. Now, how will you be spending the rest of the day?'

Erica looked up at Alfie.

'I should probably tell Jess. And figure out what I'm going to do.'

'And what happened to relaxing and having a bit of fun? Come with me, let's get a coffee. I know a lovely place down by the harbour. We can get to know each other a bit.'

Erica hesitated, mulling the situation over.

'Down by the harbour?'

'Yes. I'll buy.'

'You have money?'

Alfie gave her a withering look.

'You want a coffee in a lovely setting or not?'

This time Erica shrugged.

'Okay.'

As Alfie led her to her Mini, Erica glanced back to her grandfather's grave over her shoulder. There was no one there.

Alfie wasn't wrong about the café by the harbour being lovely. It was busy but they were served quickly. They managed to find a table overlooking the water, just as the previous occupants left, and ordered their coffee. Erica took a moment to stare out at the boats and the reflections on the water, blocking out the noise and proximity of Alfie, so that it was just her in this world. A weight started to lift.

'Your grandmother is something,' said Alfie, shattering Erica's peace. She gave him a smile and sipped at her hot coffee. 'You've inherited some of her gifts.'

'Have I?'

Alfie nodded.

'You could sense that there wasn't a spirit in that house, for one thing.'

'That's not a gift. It's just experience. If you were human and had grown up with my gran, you'd be able to do that too.' Erica's voice dropped, trying to make sure those around couldn't hear. Alfie didn't take the same care.

'That's not true. Your mother can't do it.'

'She can. It's just different for her.' Erica narrowed her eyes against Alfie's easy smile. 'And what do you know about my mum?'

'I met her, when you were growing in her belly.'

Erica cocked her head at Alfie.

'How old are you?'

Alfie grinned.

'You know, I'm not sure. You lose count after a while. Who cares how old you are when there's so much life to be lived? I think that's a lesson you need to learn. Somewhere, Erica Murray, you've lost your grandmother's spirit. It's in there somewhere, deep in your blood. We just have to find it again. I think quitting this job you have will be the perfect catalyst.'

Erica wanted to disagree, she really did, but there was a good chance that he was right.

'There is so much I haven't done,' she murmured in agreement. 'Maybe I should go travelling. I have enough saved up.'

Alfie barked a laugh and Erica snapped her head up to him. 'What?'

'Travelling the world isn't what I had in mind.'

'I can guess what you had in mind,' Erica muttered. 'Anyway, so you met my mum before I was born. That doesn't mean you know us.'

'Minerva speaks highly of both of you. She's proud of you both.'

'Well, that's nice.' Erica smiled down into her coffee. 'She tells you about us, then?'

Alfie looked out onto the water.

'There are things that we are told and things that we know. It depends on the person, of course. Your mother is hard to read. She got that from her father. But you, you I can read the same way I can read Minerva. Which is different, of course, to the way that Eolande reads Minerva. Or you.'

'Makes sense,' said Erica, wondering if it did. She gave Alfie a sideways look. 'I've been warned away from you, you know.'

Alfie grinned.

'Oh, I know. By your mother.'

'And Gran. Something about you being inappropriate when mum was pregnant with me.'

'Yes. I regret that.' Alfie's grin was gone in a second and he looked seriously down at the table, a fingernail scraping against a notch in the wood. 'I shouldn't have said those things. I lost your mother's trust. I shouldn't have done that. We could have had more time if it wasn't for my stupid mouth.'

Erica raised an eyebrow.

'More time?'

The corners of Alfie's mouth lifted again.

'You are not for me, Erica Murray. But a part of you is.'

Erica sat back, putting a bit of distance between them.

'That's for me to decide, not you.'

'I didn't decide it. I just saw it. When your mother visited with you in her belly. Each of us saw you in different ways. I don't know what others saw. Your hopes or your accomplishments or your fears, maybe. But I saw us.'

Erica didn't respond for a while, allowing that to sink in so she could judge how she felt about it.

'You're suggesting that everything is pre-determined. That we actually don't get a choice.'

'We all get a choice. Of course we do. As you now know, this isn't the only world, nor is it the only world with you in it. And of course, maybe I'm wrong.' Alfie lifted his hands in defeat. 'Maybe I saw a different Erica Murray or a different Alfie. But what if I didn't?'

'How would we know unless we kissed,' Erica

mocked. Alfie grinned.

'Exactly.'

'I wasn't being serious.'

The fae shrugged.

'You have a choice. But you don't have much time.'

'What's that supposed to mean?'

Alfie's smile dropped again.

'As I say, I regret losing your mother's trust in me.'

Erica frowned.

'Why don't I have much time? Time for what?'

'For us.'

Erica sighed and rubbed at her forehead. This was getting too complicated.

'Okay. Fine. Whatever. So, Steve's wife is from another time. Are you and Eolande going to do anything about that?'

'It's not our place to,' Alfie told her, downing the remainder of his cooling coffee. 'Why do you have an objection to kissing me?'

Erica bit down on her tongue, her cheeks beginning to burn.

'Because you claimed me before I was born.'

Alfie laughed so loud that those around them stopped and turned to look. Erica, feeling the heat from her cheeks travelling down her chest, sunk down in her seat.

'Is that what your mother told you? It wasn't as bad as that. I'm not claiming you. And I didn't back then. I just stupidly told your mother that we would have a relationship one day. That's all. And she took offence. I don't blame her. It was foolish of me.' His smile made his eyes sparkle. 'You don't have to kiss me. You don't have to have sex with

184

me. In some world, an Alfie and an Erica do get naked, but maybe I'm wrong about it being us. I would never force anything upon you, that's not our way. But it's nice to know why I'm being rejected.'

'I'm not rejecting you,' said Erica without thinking. She snapped her mouth shut. Alfie's expression turned from playful to knowing, and there was something both charming and irresistible about it. Erica looked back out onto the water.

'Go for a walk with me. Around the harbour.' Alfie stood up, scraping his chair back. 'Talk to me about happy things. Tell me about how you and your friend Jess met.' He tilted his head, gesturing for her to follow. Erica downed the last of her coffee and stood up.

'Okay.'

14

'Woah.'

'What?' Marshall pulled up his jeans.

'Ric's quitting.'

'What?' Marshall sat on the bed behind Jess and put an arm around her waist. Instinctively, she leaned back into him. His hand was warm against her bare skin and, with a smile, she put her phone down and turned to him. Kneeling up, she kissed him, running her hands down his still naked chest. He smiled into the kiss. 'I thought we had to get dressed?'

Jess groaned and moved away from him, finding her phone again and checking the time.

'We've got maybe ten minutes.' She glanced back at him, her gaze landing on his wide chest and large arms. 'Ten minutes will do.' She climbed on top of him, pushing him back. Laughing, he stopped her.

'What about that message?'

'Oh, yeah.' Jess sat back on him. 'Ric's quitting her job. I never thought she'd actually do it. I mean, when she called earlier to say she wanted to quit I thought she was just angry. But she says she's handing her notice in on Monday.'

'So, you can start an agency with her?'

Jess smiled at the man beneath her.

'This is a real waste of our ten minutes.'

'It's probably more like nine minutes now,' said Marshall, his fingers brushing over her stomach, his eyes dropping down to her breasts. Jess took his hands and moved them up.

'We'll talk after.' She leaned down and kissed him.

'So?' asked Marshall, nine and half minutes later as Jess yanked on a top and gave her reflection a disgusted look. She turned, searching for a hairbrush.

'Look what you've done to my hair.'

Marshall beamed.

'I like it like that.'

Jess began pulling the knots out. 'I'll say it again. So?' Marshall asked, putting on his shoes.

'So what?'

'Are you going to start up an agency with Ric?'

'Oh.' Jess stopped brushing her hair to think. 'I don't know. I don't think I want to. But it might be different with her, mightn't it? I mean, we could do things our way. But I'd still have to put up with clients wanting stupid things. Although I would also have the power to say no to them if I wanted to. Unless Ric said I couldn't. She'd be in charge. She's always wanted to be the top boss of an agency. I don't know what that would make me.'

'Joint founder?'

'Maybe.'

'And you could delegate all the client stuff to those below you.'

Jess smiled at Marshall, who sat on the bed watching her. Just looking at him, despite now being fully clothed, sent a tingle through her. Her body remembering the touch of him, the smell of him, the feel of him.

'We'd need to get to a stage where we could afford those below us.' Her smile faded as her thoughts moved on. 'It would be nice to find something fun that we could do just the two of us that paid the bills.'

'Like what?'

'I don't know. If I knew, I'd suggest it.' Jess gave herself one last check in the mirror. She was wearing clothes, they were done up properly and her hair and make-up were neat. It would do. 'Right. You act like you've been working on the skirting boards and I'll go pick up Ruby from school.'

Marshall wrapped his arms around her, pulling her in for a kiss.

'Nope.' Jess allowed the kiss to happen but pushed him away after a moment. 'We all know where that leads us and I can't be late.'

Grinning, Marshall smacked her bottom as he walked out of the bedroom. Jess followed him, tracing her fingers down his back. Not allowing herself to look at him, she pulled on her shoes, grabbed her bag and keys, and headed out of the door.

'See you in a bit!' she called behind her.

ℰꙷℛ

'You haven't done much.'

Marshall turned to look at Ruby standing in the living room doorway.

'Well, hello to you too.' He stretched. 'Are you suggesting I haven't been very productive?'

Ruby wasn't entirely sure what he meant by that but decided to go with it.

'Exactly.' She nodded. Her mood lifted as he laughed.

There was something warm about Marshall. When her mother had asked her whether she liked him, Ruby couldn't think of a single thing she didn't like about Marshall. Although she knew there would be things. There was always something about a person that she wouldn't like. She'd learned that in school.

'How was school?' Marshall asked her, putting down his tools. Ruby moved to sit on the edge of the sofa, taking care not to stand on anything that might get her into trouble.

'We're learning about the Victorians,' she told him. 'Queen Victoria always wore black.'

'Did she? Why was that?'

'I don't know. Nadia said it's probably because she looked good in black.'

'Oh. Well, I think it was more to do with her husband's death. She was grieving him.'

'Oh. That makes more sense, I guess. Although why would you spend all your life wearing black clothes because of your dead husband?'

Marshall laughed again, although this time Ruby wasn't sure why.

'It's because she loved him that much.'

Ruby raised an eyebrow.

'Are you sure?'

'Very.' Marshall nodded. 'Ask your mum if you don't believe me.'

'Ask me what?' Jess appeared in the doorway. She looked different, thought Ruby. Something about her had changed although Ruby couldn't tell what. She looked back at Marshall and narrowed her eyes.

'Mummy? Can a woman love a man so much that she only wears black after he's dead?'

'Oh. Is this about Queen Victoria?'

'See, told you.' Marshall smiled at Ruby. Ruby stuck her tongue out at him and then pulled back, waiting to get told off. Instead, her mother was smiling at her. There was a pause as the two adults exchanged distant looks. It was all getting a bit weird.

'I'm hungry, Mummy.' Ruby declared, standing up and moving towards Jess.

'Right. Yeah. I'll make you a sandwich. Then you need to get changed and pack your bag. Your dad will be here to pick you up and.' Jess held up a finger. 'He *will* be picking you up.' She bent to catch Bubbles' collar before the puppy could bounce into the room behind her.

Ruby's stomach rolled. She hoped her dad would pick her up, but at the same time there was a large part of her that wanted to stay with her mum, Marshall and Bubbles. What fun would they get up to when she was away? Her mum would argue that she'd have fun at her dad's, and sometimes she did. When they first lived apart, Ruby would spend evenings with her dad, staying up past her bedtime and cuddling on the sofa to watch a film. It was a big, plush sofa that he'd treated himself to when he'd moved out, and Ruby loved cuddling and falling asleep on it. Paul's girlfriend had made him get rid of the sofa when she'd moved in to be replaced with her own, much stiffer piece of furniture. Apparently it was made by someone famous. She was the problem, Ruby thought. She made sure Ruby went to bed on time and she'd even said no to Ruby's request for ice cream last time she'd stayed. Ruby didn't feel like her dad's girlfriend liked her much. Ruby didn't like her either, but she got the feeling that it was easier to not like each other as adults. When you're the child, you just get pushed around by the adult who doesn't like you.

Ruby sighed and moved to stroke Bubbles' head. The puppy licked at her fingers.

'Oh, Bubs,' Jess chastised. 'Now you'll have to go wash your hands, Rubes. Otherwise you'll be eating Bubbles' spit and that's revolting.'

Ruby went to lick her fingers. 'Don't! You dare.' Jess screeched, making Ruby stop with her fingers near her mouth. 'Go wash up. Now. Quickly. Otherwise your sandwich will get eaten.'

Ruby rolled her eyes. But then Jess moved to go into the kitchen. She'd eaten Ruby's sandwich before. This was no idle threat. Sure, she'd make her another sandwich, but she'd have to wait longer. Ruby ran up the stairs.

Jess called to Bubbles not to follow Ruby upstairs. The puppy barked and wheeled round, sitting beside Jess and looking up with big eyes.

'She's learned that quick,' said Marshall, following her into the kitchen and wiping his hands on his jeans. He checked Ruby was upstairs and not peeking, and gave Jess a long kiss. Jess smiled into it. Everything about the day had gone so well. She wanted to say it had been so long since she'd had nearly a whole day in bed with a man, but in reality she'd never had it. She gazed affectionately at Marshall. This one was different, she thought. This one was special.

'She's a clever one.' Jess popped a bit of cheese into Bubbles' waiting open mouth. The puppy swallowed without chewing and gave her another hopeful look. Jess pulled a face at her.

'You're gonna eat me out of house and home, Pup.'

'Here, Bubbles, come over here.' Marshall sat at the dining table and tempted the puppy over, making her lie down and rubbing her fluffy belly. Bubbles gave in, rolling around on her back.

Jess started making her daughter's sandwich, turning her back on the big man and puppy.

'Why are you looking up time travel? Is this about your friend's wife?'

Jess looked back to them. She'd left her laptop open on the kitchen table and Marshall was reading the screen as Bubbles started nibbling on his hands.

'Yeah.'

'I thought that was over.'

'She's from a different time, how can it be over?'

Marshall glanced at her.

'You think it's all true?'

Jess turned back to the sandwich.

'There were things going on in that house that I can't explain. And you know the biggest thing?' She placed the sandwich on a plate and the plate on the table, ready for Ruby's return.

'What's that?'

'Ric got freaked out at one point. Ric's grandmother talks to spirits. And Ric spent a lot of her childhood in her grandmother's house talking to the spirits that visited, so I'm told.'

'Who told you that?'

'Her whole family.'

'Fair enough.'

'Right. But despite all that, Ric is a sceptic. She'll see a story about a ghost and she'll laugh it off. She'll find the reasonable explanation. As far as she's concerned, it's not paranormal until proven otherwise. And she doesn't think many people do much to really prove it. She says that people want to believe so they put up with lousy proof.'

'But she knows what's real and how to prove it.'

Jess stared at Marshall.

'Exactly.'

'She's a good paranormal barometer.'

Jess blinked.

'Right. And in Steve's house, time after time we experienced strange things but Ric stayed sceptical. Then, when we're on the landing outside the nursery, we saw a figure by the cot. Then there was this blinding flash of light and boom, the figure's gone. And Ric didn't brush it off. She was genuinely thrown by it.'

'So you think it's something big.'

'Time travel. What if that flash of light was Steve's wife disappearing not just from the nursery, but from our time? What if she's, maybe, ping-ponging between times?'

'Is that possible?' Marshall glanced back at Jess's laptop screen.

'I don't know. Are you really taking this seriously?'

Marshall looked into Jess's eyes.

'Yeah. You know why?' Jess raised her eyebrows questioningly. 'Because you're excited about it. I ask you about your job, and it brings you down. I ask you whether you want to start an agency with Erica, and it brings you down. But I ask you about this and you're talking ten to the dozen. This is what you should be doing.'

Jess frowned.

'Time travel? We don't know enough.'

'No. I'm saying you and Erica should set up an agency. A paranormal investigation agency.'

Jess thought mouths dropping open only happened in Ruby's cartoons, but as the ideas started to form in her mind, her mouth fell open, her eyes glazing over as she stared behind Marshall into the distance.

She had to message Erica, right away.

∞∝

'Where's Mummy?'

Marshall put down his wine glass as Ruby walked into the kitchen.

'She's just calling someone. She'll be right back. Are you all ready to go?'

Ruby nodded but she wasn't smiling. Marshall's own smile fell at the sight.

'What's up?'

'Nothing.'

'Shall I get your mummy? Do you want to talk to her?'

Ruby shook her head and sat at the table.

'Daddy might cancel again.'

Marshall's chest ached.

'He won't. He loves you.'

Ruby gave him a withering look that made his shoulders sag while her heart pounded. That look was the perfect combination of pure sadness and something she'd definitely inherited from Jess.

'Are you finished working?' Ruby asked.

'For today, yes.'

'Aren't you going home?'

Marshall gave a small smile.

'I will do, later on.'

Ruby narrowed her eyes at him. Her hair wasn't the fair shade of Jess's but in facial expressions they were almost identical. Marshall fancied she got her intelligence from Jess too, as well as that curiosity tinged with cynicism. Marshall smiled to himself. He couldn't help but mentally pick Jess apart. The more he got to know her, the more he expected to find something he didn't like. So far, the only thing he didn't like was the ex who was going to knock on the door at any moment. Marshall didn't want him there, and yet at the same time if Paul let Ruby down again, Marshall knew he'd have to resist the urge to hunt the man down.

'Why are you staying? For me?' Ruby knew that wasn't the reason, he could tell from her tone. He tried to think quickly while keeping a calm exterior.

'Your mum wants to talk to me about what she wants doing next in the house.' He reminded himself to breathe as Ruby considered this. Finally, she gave a nod, accepting it.

'Can you tell her I'd like my room doing next.'

'I thought she did your room first?'

'She did. But there are some changes I'd like to make.'

'Oh yeah?' Marshall grinned at the girl.

There was a knock at the front door. Bubbles leapt out of her bed and barked.

'Getting better,' Jess called to the dog from the other room. 'Can you get that Marshall? I'll be right there.'

Marshall's gut twisted.

'You'll have to tell me what you want doing later. Sounds like your dad's here.' Marshall stood as Ruby jumped up, grabbing her bag. She led him to the front door, but waited for Marshall to open it, which Marshall found a little strange. Maybe she was still worried that it wouldn't be him, or that it would be him but with an excuse.

The man on the other side of the door stared at Marshall with wide eyes. Marshall didn't blame him. If he was going to pick up his daughter and a strange man so much taller and broader than him opened the door, he'd be worried too.

'Hey, Rubes.' Paul broke his stare from Marshall and smiled down at his daughter. He's where she gets her hair colour from, thought Marshall. He wondered what else she'd inherited from him.

Ruby smiled up at her dad and handed him her bag. He took it and looked back up at Marshall.

'Aren't you, erm, Jess's handyman?'

You could say that, Marshall thought.

'Yes. Marshall.' Marshall offered Paul his hand. Paul took it gingerly and they shook once.

'You're working late. And opening the door.' Paul tried to look behind Marshall, into the house. 'Jess is home, right?'

'Of course. She's just finishing up on the phone, so asked me to get the door.'

'Good.'

The men stood in awkward silence for a moment. Just as Paul looked ready to interrogate Marshall, Ruby said, 'Do you want to see Bubbles? She's in the kitchen.'

'Bubbles? Oh, the puppy. No, love. We should really be going.'

'Big plans for the weekend?' Jess appeared behind Marshall and Marshall felt the secret stroke of her hand against his back. He relaxed and stepped away, allowing her through.

'Oh, there you are. Important phone call, was it?'

'It was.' Marshall half expected a snide remark but Jess held back. 'So, what are you two up to this weekend?'

Careful, Marshall thought. They might return the question.

'I thought we'd go catch a movie. What do you think Rubes?'

Ruby nodded.

'What about that animal park that's opened up?' Jess suggested. 'A little petting farm, I think. Donkeys and ponies and goats and chickens. Ruby wanted to check it out. The weather's supposed to be good for it.'

Paul looked down into his daughter's large eyes.

'Oh. Yeah. Maybe. We'll see.'

'Well, you could do both. A movie will only take a couple of hours, won't it.' Jess crouched to give her daughter a tight hug and kiss. As she dipped down, Marshall and Paul's eyes met.

'Any weekend plans?' Paul asked.

Marshall gave him a small smile without thinking. Was that an instinctual thing? He was marking Jess as his territory with one look. He wanted to feel ashamed but it gave him a small, pleasurable rush. Paul's expression darkened.

'Not really. I've got a lot of work to do. Work and puppy stuff. Not fun puppy stuff,' Jess added quickly as Ruby went to complain. 'Boring puppy stuff. Okay? So, have fun, have a lovely weekend,' she told Ruby. 'And have fun,' she repeated pointedly to Paul who gave a distracted nod. 'See you Monday after school.' Jess gave Ruby another kiss. 'I love you.'

'Love you too, Mummy. Bye, Marshall.'

'Bye, kid. Have a good one.'

'Bye Bubbles!' Ruby shouted at the top of her voice. Jess must have given her a scolding look because Ruby giggled and skipped down the driveway, leading Paul back to his car.

Jess and Marshall watched them go.

'Lots of work to do, huh?' He ran his fingers up her back. She leaned against him and he breathed in her hair.

'Actually, a bit, yes. Which is your fault. You and your great ideas. Which I really should thank you for.' Jess shut the door as Paul's car pulled away, and turned to face Marshall, running a hand down his chest and pulling him down to kiss her.

Steve

Steve came down the stairs, treading lightly, as much for his failing vision as to not wake the baby. He hadn't slept the previous night, instead lying there listening to Rachel breathing. Part of him was scared that if he closed his eyes, she'd be gone when he woke.

As he reached the bottom of the stairs, he made his way into the living room and found her standing by the window. It was what she'd been doing for most of the day. Staring out of the windows, peering up and down the road, scanning the garden, watching the neighbours.

'Joe's asleep. I'll go put dinner on,' said Steve wearily. Rachel made a noise that he assumed was agreement, or at least acknowledgment. Steve didn't move. 'What are you looking for?'

Rachel didn't respond. She kept her back to him, peering out onto the garden. 'Is this about a man? Are you in some sort of trouble?'

Rachel turned to face him so quickly that Steve took a step back.

'Why do you ask about a man?'

Steve opened and closed his mouth. He should tell her about the phone call. This was his wife, the woman he loved, who he had created a child with and promised to share his life with, but still for some reason he held back.

'You look like you're looking for someone.' He shrugged, turning to go to the kitchen. Rachel followed him.

'You specifically asked about a man, though.'

'Whatever. A woman, a man. You're looking for someone. Or waiting for someone.' Once in the kitchen, Steve looked back at his wife. 'Where were you, Rachel? You still haven't told me.'

Rachel relented, moving to look out of the kitchen window before sitting at the dining table.

'I can't tell you where I was. I don't know how to tell you.'

'You could try.' After a moment, Steve sat opposite her at the table. 'Please. I can't do this, Rachel. I need you to talk to me.'

Rachel wouldn't look up at him. Her gaze remained fixed on the table.

'I don't know what to tell you,' she said eventually. 'I was crossing the road when a car hit me. I came back as soon as I could. And I'm here now. Isn't that enough?'

No. No, it wasn't enough for Steve. He'd tried to make it enough but things were so different now.

'I saw you in the mortuary. I saw you before the funeral. Your funeral. You were dead.' Rachel didn't move. 'I grieved for you. It's tough, Rach, to grieve for someone and then they walk back into your life. So, I don't think it can be enough. A man called. He knew you. He's who you're looking for, isn't he? Are you in trouble?'

Rachel had looked up at the mention of the man. She stared into Steve's eyes.

'Why didn't you tell me?'

'I don't know. I thought it was a prank call. I just

wanted things to go back to how they were. But they won't, will they? We can't get that back now.'

The old Rachel would have moved to hold him then, but this Rachel stayed where she was. She fidgeted, her fingers tapping against the table as she swiveled, trying to decide what to do. Steve wondered if the idea of hugging her husband had even crossed her mind.

15

Erica couldn't help looking around Jess's house as she entered. Jess took her coat and led her through to the kitchen. The only sign that there was any work going on seemed to be in the living room, where long lines of skirting were being stored against the wall.

'Coffee or tea?' Jess asked. Erica took a seat at the kitchen table. Bubbles, who had followed them in, immediately plonked herself between Erica's legs and rested her head on Erica's knee. Erica stroked the puppy's ears and then began to rub them. Bubbles gave a satisfied sigh.

'Marshall's not here then?' Erica asked innocently.

'No.' Jess busied herself putting the kettle on. 'He had to go out to a job.' She turned, a smile plastered to her face. Erica couldn't help but smile back.

'It's nice to see you so happy. Did you just need the sex?'

'No. It's more than that. He's different. He's…' Jess searched for the right words. 'Thoughtful and clever. He's so good with Ruby, and with Bubbles. And he can fix things.' Jess looked at Erica. 'I've never been with a man who can actually fix things. Properly. Not just botch it to save money.'

'Handy to have around,' Erica agreed.

'And I'm sure he'll be happy to help if you or your family need anything doing.'

'Mate's rates?'

Jess grinned and turned back to make the tea.

'We're going on a real date tonight. I'm actually a little nervous.'

'Nervous? You've done it all the wrong way round, you know. You're supposed to go on the date and then have the day off sick to spend in bed with him. What's there to be nervous about? He's already seen you naked.'

'I don't know. I hate dating. I'd rather sit on the sofa and chat.'

'Rather than go out for a meal and chat?'

Jess gave Erica a look, handing her a cup of tea.

'All right. I get your point. I guess it's just that thing of having sex too quick. What if he's gotten everything he wanted and that's it?'

Erica sipped her drink.

'Does it feel like that? Like he'll stand you up?'

'No.' Jess grinned again.

'Well, there you go.'

'He's taken such an interest in me. I don't know if that's good or bad. This ghost hunting agency business was even his idea.'

Ah. Erica had wondered how quickly the conversation would move onto that.

Jess sipped at her own drink and pulled a face.

'I need to buy a coffee machine. Sorry we couldn't go to a coffee shop, but...' She gestured with her head to Bubbles who was still enjoying Erica rubbing her ears. 'I can't leave her again. I feel so guilty when I do go out. Or when we disappear upstairs.'

'It's okay. This is cheaper, which is important to me now that I'm unemployed.' Erica held her cup up and clinked it against Jess's.

'You're not going to work your notice?'

'I will,' Erica told her, miserably. She'd considered all of her options when it came to working her notice. Minerva had suggested she get signed off work for the month. Erica was toying with the idea but other than the annoyance and discomfort of going into the office, she couldn't think of a good reason why the doctor would sign her off. Not without her lying, and she couldn't do that. 'But I won't be happy about it.'

Jess gave her a mischievous smile.

'So? What do you think about Marshall's idea?'

Erica sighed and looked down at Bubbles. The puppy glanced up at her and wagged her tail.

'This isn't a movie, Jess. You can't just start a paranormal investigation agency and make a living from it. You know, I'm not even sure they make a living from it in the movies. Most paranormal investigation groups do it for fun, or as volunteers. People don't pay for this stuff.'

'We could ask. I'll ask Steve if he would have paid for us to come and check out his house.'

'I'm not sure that's a good example. We didn't exactly fix a problem. We didn't even give him a definitive answer before his wife showed up.' Erica looked up at Jess. 'How's that going? Have you heard anything?'

'Nope. All quiet on the Steve front. Which annoys me, if I'm honest. After all that, all the trouble we went too, he's not been in touch at all.'

'Well, he's busy. His wife just came back from the dead.' Erica gave a hollow laugh. 'I wonder where she's been all this time. And how did they manage to do a funeral and everything without a death certificate? Don't you need a death cert-ificate?'

Jess nodded.

'Steve saw her in the morgue and everything.'

'How does that work?'

The two women stared into space for a moment, trying to put the pieces together.

'Not a clue,' said Jess eventually. She pulled her closed laptop over, opened it and booted it up. 'Maybe Google knows. Or, you know, you could ask your fae friends to elaborate.'

'They're quite hazy on it all. Turns out fae are quite good at avoiding questions they don't want to answer. And don't ask me why they don't want to answer them. Right now, my only guess is that they're too pre-occupied with the present and what they can get out of it for themselves.'

Jess gave Erica a sideways glance.

'Been talking to Eolande, have you?'

Erica looked away, but she knew the burning of her cheeks gave her away. She ran her hand over her right cheek, as if that would hide it. When she peeked over, Jess was smiling knowingly at her laptop screen. 'I don't blame you,' she murmured, clicking and typing. 'That Alfie's very attractive. And why not? You deserve to have a bit of fun.'

'Hmm.' Erica's mind drifted off to Alfie. He was a strange one. Her head was screaming at her to stay away from him. No good could come from relations with a fae, she was sure of it, despite what her grandmother was up to. Plus, her mother wouldn't be happy. But her heart and body pulled her to him. That was one reason why she wanted to work her notice at the agency. If she had a month at home, she'd inevitably spend it at the cemetery and, sooner or later, in bed with Alfie. She wasn't sure she wanted that yet, or at all. Probably at all.

Erica sighed.

'Nothing's happened. But I have been talking to him.'

'Will something happen?'

Erica gave Jess a smile.

'Why is it that when one person is having great sex, they think all their friends should be too? I'm perfectly happy the way I am. I don't need to jump into bed with a weird, fae man. No matter how attractive.'

'You're right. Sorry. Although, just to be clear, I think you should be having great sex because it's great. But that's it, I won't say any more on the subject.' Jess beamed at her friend before returning her attention to her laptop screen. 'Except that you do find him attractive.' Jess avoided looking at Erica as Erica glared at her.

'Did Steve get a death certificate for his wife?' Erica asked after a moment's thought. Jess stopped typing.

'I assume so.' They looked at one another. 'I don't suppose they have those things online?'

'I doubt it would be available so soon.' Erica shook her head. 'And I doubt Steve will show us now.'

Jess was busy tapping away at her keyboard again.

'Looks like the person needs to be dead at least six months before you can order their death certificate, and even then it's difficult. Rachel was only dead for a few months.'

Erica frowned, letting go of Bubbles' ears as the puppy moved away to snuffle hopefully at the floor beneath the kitchen counters.

'Where do you order them from?'

'Err, the General Register Office.' Jess squinted at her screen before glancing up at Erica and then watching Bubbles. 'Why?'

'I wonder what would happen if we called them up. Just to check the records. We don't necessarily need to see a death certificate, just talk to someone who can see the official records.'

Jess pulled a face.

'It's the Government, Ric. I'm not sure what you're expecting.'

Erica shrugged.

'Worth a shot. I'll do it, if you like. It'll give me something to do.'

The shock in Jess's eyes was evident and Erica didn't blame her.

'Really?' Jess asked. 'I thought you wouldn't want anything more to do with Steve. I mean, it's not a spirit and even if she is a time traveller, so what? Other than being interesting, no one's at risk.'

'I guess. It's just…something doesn't feel right.'

Jess stared blankly.

'Well, no. What we thought might be a regular haunting has turned out to be time traveller who was dead but now isn't and we only found that out because of fairy people.'

Erica grimaced.

'Never call them that to their face.'

Jess leaned across the table.

'Why? What will they do?'

Erica gave her a small smile.

'I know you think some of this is fun and games, but it's serious, Jess. Ghosts aren't just scary, they're sad. And fae aren't just charming people trying to seduce you into their bed, they're magical and powerful. They're scarier than the ghosts.'

Jess considered this.

'Then I don't recommend shacking up with Alfie.'

'Finally, you see my point.' Erica put her attention onto Bubbles, who had come to the conclusion that the floor was clean and was now attempting to chew the cushion Jess was sat on. 'Why do you want to find out more about Steve's wife? Is it just the time traveller stuff?'

'No. You're right, something feels off. I met her once, when they first got married. She was nice, sweet. She didn't seem like the same person when we visited. She seemed...'

'Jumpy.'

'Yeah. I guess, after all this, I just need to make sure Steve and the baby are safe.' Jess pushed Bubbles away but the puppy bounced back. With a sigh, Jess moved over to a high kitchen cupboard and pulled out a new toy. She unwrapped it and handed it to the expectant puppy, sitting watching her with a wagging tail. 'Maybe we should call the police. They might actually be very interested to find out a woman has come back from the dead.' Jess sat back down. 'I have wondered if they had life insurance.'

'What, you think she faked her own death for the money but forgot to tell her husband and so came back?'

'Stupider things have happened. And she didn't come back for Steve, she came back for Joe. That's

why all this stuff has centred around the nursery.'
Jess's eyes gleamed as she spoke.

Erica's heart pounded. Yes, it was starting to
make sense, even though they were no closer to the
big answers.

Jess began furiously typing and hit return with a
little too much force. The sound of Bubbles' teeth
ripping into the thick rubber toy filled the room.

'Apparently it's not that hard to fake your own
death.' Jess's eyes flickered as she read the screen.

'But you said Steve saw her body.'

'True. Maybe the morgue was in on it? Maybe
she took a drug to make herself look dead?'

'There are easier ways, I'm sure,' Erica pointed
out.

'Yeah. Says here you can buy a dead body in
some countries. Cremate it, ship it over and bam,
they think it's you.'

'Don't they do DNA tests?'

'Doesn't say. Anyway, that's not what happened
here.' Jess glanced up at Erica. 'Might be good to
see if there is a death certificate.'

'There must be one, unless Steve has been lying.
What hospital was she taken to after the accident?'

'The BRI, I think. Pronounced dead on arrival.'

Erica pulled out her phone and brought up the
search engine.

'It'll be A&E won't it. They'll be too busy to
help, surely. Maybe the city registrar. They'll have
sorted the death certificate, won't they.' She began
typing into her phone.

'You're really going to call them?'

'What's their surname? She's Rachel what?'

'Green.' Out of the corner of her eye, Erica saw
Jess give a smile. 'So, should we do this paranormal

investigation agency thing?'

Erica hesitated. It would be something different, and technically it matched all of her skills and knowledge. She had more experience with spirits than she did with marketing, so in theory a paranormal investigation agency would be easier to run than a marketing agency. But in Erica's experience, theories hardly ever panned out. On the other hand, neither did her plans. She was tempted to just let Jess figure it out, to go along with whatever she said.

'Call Steve. Ask how things are. Ask if he'd have paid us for our services. Find out if there's any money involved. Then, maybe.'

Jess clapped her hands and jumped up, grabbing her phone and moving out of the kitchen to make the call.

Erica held off on making her own phone call. Instead, she listened to the tone of Jess's voice as she started talking to, presumably, Steve. Part of her expected to hear Jess become worried, to rush in and tell Erica that they needed to leave right then. But Jess didn't run in, her tone stayed low and calm. Beside her, Bubbles paused in her chewing to listen to Jess, glancing up at Erica. Erica looked down at her phone. Maybe she should make that call now. Her stomach twisted with nerves. What would she say? She wasn't even sure who she should speak to. She'd sound silly asking for the death certificate, or at least confirmation of death, of someone she didn't even know. She could hardly say they were related. She wouldn't lie.

Erica's lips twisted at the thought.

They did this in America, though, didn't they? At least, they did on TV. Bounty hunters calling up, or Private Investigators, ringing official departments to ask about this kind of stuff. Insurance companies certainly would. Maybe this call would be easier if they were part of an agency.

Erica made a mental note. Perhaps their agency shouldn't have too laughable a name.

Erica jumped as Jess walked back into the kitchen. Bubbles jumped up and took her toy to Jess.

'No,' said Jess calmly to the dog. 'No, don't get up. I'll see myself in.' She sat back at the table and gave Erica a large, hopeful smile. 'Steve said he would have paid us. Gladly. He even gave me a price range. Five hundred at most, he said. Can you believe that?' Jess beamed and Erica couldn't help but mirror it.

'Wow. Okay. Maybe we should draw up a business plan then.'

Jess clapped her hands again and this time Bubbles jumped up, tail wagging, toy in her mouth. Jess scooped her up in a hug and then ruffled the fur on her head. Bubbles dropped her toy, gave an excited bark and attempted to jump onto Jess's lap.

'The start-up costs shouldn't be much,' said Erica, watching Jess trying to calm the puppy. 'Maybe a thousand. Five hundred each.'

'We can do that,' Jess agreed. 'I can build a website. You can sort out the advertising.'

'Yeah, the marketing's the easy bit. I'll talk to Gran, see what equipment we might need. That'll be more than the initial thousand.'

Jess waved Erica's concerns away.

'We can afford it. It'll be fine. And I can quit my job.' She grinned, giving Bubbles a rough cuddle.

'How was Steve otherwise?'

Jess's smile faded.

'Oh, he seemed distracted. He said things were okay, but I don't think they are. But, how can they be? He's been grieving his wife for months and suddenly she's back. After he's been so shaken up. Maybe she's still acting weird. He wouldn't talk about it much, just something about a strange man.'

'What? She was having an affair?'

'Who knows. That could explain why she faked her own death.'

'There's no evidence to say she faked her own death. Anyway, for an affair, much easier to just break Steve's heart, take the baby and go start a new life.'

'True.' Jess glanced down at the phone in Erica's hand. 'Are you going to call the hospital or registrar or whatever?'

'Yeah. Should I do that now?' Maybe best to get it over with, thought Erica. Even though she couldn't say she was calling from an official company yet.

'Might as well. Just to see if there is a death certificate. If it's all official.'

Erica nodded, her mouth suddenly dry. She made herself another cup of tea and took her phone into the living room to make the call in private. The room was filled with bits of skirting board and part of the wall was bare where Marshall had taken away the old boards but not yet replaced them. Erica wondered briefly how long this job had been going on for. It seemed obvious from stepping foot in there that the work had been interrupted.

Taking a sip of tea and a deep breath, rehearsed words repeating around her head, Erica dialled the number she'd found online.

16

'I don't know how she did it,' said Erica, walking back into the kitchen. 'But apparently her death certificate is real.'

'You remember Romeo and Juliet?' Jess asked. Erica stopped, glancing down at the puppy, now collapsed on Jess's feet. She was keeping her warm, at least, although Jess would have preferred it if Bubbles wasn't quite so heavy.

'Yeah? This isn't about you and Marshall, is it?'

Jess rolled her eyes.

'Don't be silly. You remember Juliet takes a drug to make her look dead? She fakes her own death but Romeo didn't get the memo?'

Erica smiled.

'Ah yes. I remember the memo scene well.'

'Well, who's to say Steve's missus didn't do that? Taken this drug, appeared dead, got the death certificate, woken up—'

'Is that before or after her autopsy and funeral?'

Jess stopped.

'There was an autopsy?'

'No.' Erica grinned. 'Just wanted to see your reaction.' She sat back down at the table and Bubbles lifted her head to greet her.

As Erica went to speak, the puppy jumped up and gave one loud, high-pitched bark. There was a knock at the front door.

Jess went to answer it. Her mind whirring with the possibilities of fake deaths and drugs that she just assumed the person at the door would be selling something. She peaked through the peep hole and her chest gave a flutter. There was a distorted Marshall, running a hand over his stubble, glancing back at his van parked on her driveway. With a smile, she opened the door.

'Hello, stranger.'

Marshall's lopsided smile turned into a grin.

'Hey there, beautiful.' He stepped inside and she closed the door behind him. His hands were on her before the door was shut. They kissed, gripping each other tight.

'Ric's here,' Jess said as they broke apart. 'Come meet her.' Unable to help herself, Jess ran her fingers down Marshall's chest. It was becoming a habit. He wore only a t-shirt and she could feel the warmth of his skin through it.

'Okay.' Marshall let Jess lead him into the kitchen. Erica looked up as they entered, her gaze landing on Marshall and for a moment Jess fretted over what she would think.

'You must be Erica,' Marshall said.

'And you must be Marshall?' Erica glanced at Jess for help. Jess nodded at her.

'Yup.' Marshall gazed affectionately down at Jess. 'How's it going?'

'We're opening a paranormal investigation agency.' Jess grinned, moving in and wrapping her arms around Marshall's waist.

'You are? That's great!' Marshall looked to Erica. 'Is there money in that?'

'Apparently. Maybe,' said Erica.

'And it looks like Steve's wife faked her own death.'

'We don't know that,' added Erica.

'I don't know what else it could be,' said Jess. 'Ric called up the authorities. There's a death certificate and everything. She was officially dead and now she's alive. How else do you explain that?'

'Twins?' Marshall offered.

Twins! Jess cursed herself. She'd forgotten that explanation. Erica nodded in agreement.

'We should probably find out if she's a twin before we go in suggesting she's a time traveller who can somehow bring herself back from the dead,' said Erica.

'Maybe in the future they do have something, a machine or drugs, that can bring you back from the dead,' Jess suggested. Marshall squeezed her gently, which was probably supposed to be encouraging but in that moment felt a little patronising.

'A cure for death? Why not.'

Jess glanced up at the man towering over her. He accepted things so easily that she wondered again if he was mocking them. There was no malice in his soft expression, just an easy-going nature. Would that get annoying at some point? Could she live with it being annoying? Gazing over his thick arms and big hands, his soft eyes and lips, remembering his gentle and rough touches, Jess figured she could live with it. For now.

Marshall let go of Jess to crouch low and ruffle Bubbles' ears as the puppy bounced around him. 'I'll let you get on with it then. I've got skirting boards to fix.' He straightened and Jess stopped him leaving, pulling on his shirt and kissing him.

They watched as he left the room.

'Well, he seems nice.'

'He's gorgeous,' Jess told Erica, sitting back down at the table. 'And we're going on our first date in a few hours, so let's wrap this thing up. What's our next move?'

୧୦୯

Showered, wearing her new blue dress, her hair styled and make-up on, Jess checked herself over in the mirror. Nerves fluttered in her stomach and bowels. This was silly. They'd seen each other naked. They'd spent the last day and night talking, only stopping to make love. This date was nothing other than a formality. A chance to go out together, be around people, eat nice food and not have to clean up. It was a chance to dress up and impress each other. That was what was making Jess nervous.

What if Marshall realised she had nothing else to give? What if tonight was the night he became bored with her? Ordinarily she wouldn't mind too much, but she wasn't ready for it to be over. Not only did she feel this was only the start, but something deep inside her clawed and yearned for him. It had been a long time since she'd been in a relationship, but she could have sworn she hadn't felt like this with Paul. Or the boyfriend before him.

Jess sat down on her bed and stared into her own reflected eyes.

She didn't want to think too hard about the implications of those feelings. That way led to heartbreak.

There was a knock at the front door. Jess spent

an extra moment sitting still, before she took a deep breath, exhaling slowly through her mouth. Brushing down her dress, she picked up her new heeled shoes and made her way down the stairs.

Jess froze as she opened the door. Marshall's eyes widened as he looked her up and down, but she hardly noticed because she was doing the same to him. He was wearing jeans still, but they were clean of the dust, dirt and paint splotches she'd become used to. His shirt was a button up, soft blue and fitted. He'd shaved, leaving his face smooth and making him ever so slightly unrecognisable.

Jess smiled.

'Well. Hello.'

Marshall gave her his now familiar lopsided smile.

'You look incredible.' His gaze travelled up and down her again.

'Do we have to do this?' Jess asked, picking up her bag but hanging onto the door.

'You don't want to go out?'

'It's just that…we could stay in.'

Marshall shook his head.

'No. I want to go out into the world with you. Come on.' He offered her his hand. She took it, his grip gentle but firm around her fingers as he pulled her out of the house, stopping only to allow her to lock the front door. 'Where's the pup?'

'Ric took her home, to give us some space. So we don't have to rush back.'

'That was good of her.'

Jess shrugged.

'Her parents are in love with Bubbles. There's a high risk I won't get her back.' She looked up into Marshall's eyes. 'It's a risk I'm willing to take though.'

Marshall laughed and led her down the driveway to his van.

'Where are we going?' Jess asked as she settled into the passenger seat.

'There's this new steakhouse I want to try. What do you think?'

'Thank God. I thought you were going to suggest an Italian.'

Marshall raised an eyebrow as he pulled out into the road.

'Not in a pizza mood?'

'I think all my first dates have been in Italian restaurants. I now take it as a sign of impending doom.'

It seemed to Jess that the city was busier in the evening than during the day. She blamed the student population. Damn young people, she thought. Coming out at night, having fun. She swerved to miss a group of young women, flashing more skin than cloth, giggling amongst themselves. They were oblivious to Jess but she noticed a couple of them checking out Marshall. Jess put her arm through his, drawing him close. He looked down at her quizzically before pulling away. Before Jess could react, he draped his arm comfortably around her shoulders, stroking at her bare skin with his thumb. Smiling to herself, she leaned into him as they walked to the steakhouse.

The new restaurant had a red neon sign above the large doors. Jess spared it a fleeting look and then stopped. Marshall's arm slipped off her as he continued forward.

'What's up?' he asked, turning to go back to her.

She stared up at the sign.

'Nothing,' she murmured. She was going to look away. She was going to take Marshall's hand and go through the doors with him, when the neon sign flickered again. 'Did you see that?'

'What?'

'The sign flickered. It's probably meant to though, right?' Jess didn't look at Marshall. She was fixated on the restaurant sign.

'I don't know. It's probably just a power surge.' Marshall gave a gentle tug on her hand.

Yes, a power surge, Jess told herself. The bowel loosening fear the sight brought over her was probably just a silly memory from the flickering lights in Steve's house. Jess wanted to shake it off but her breath caught in her throat.

'Jess?' Marshall's voice was full of concern and managed to wretch Jess's attention away from the sign. She looked down and movement behind Marshall caught her eye.

There were people going in and out of the restaurant. It was a busy evening. But for some reason, she looked behind Marshall and immediately focussed on two familiar figures.

Jess straightened and moved to hide behind Marshall's bulk. Peering round, she watched the figures as they paused, talking, holding hands.

'What the hell, Jess?'

Jess looked up into Marshall's eyes, now hardened, the concern gone. She stepped back.

'I'm sorry. It's just—'

'What?'

'That's Steve and his wife.' Jess wasn't sure what to do. Marshall turned to look at the couple as they began to walk away in the opposite direction.

'You want to say hi?'

'No. No, I don't think so.' Jess shook her head, calling herself all the swear words she knew. What was she doing? Tonight was about Marshall. So what if Steve and his was-dead-just-a-few-days-ago wife were also having a date night? She couldn't scare Marshall off. Without thinking, she gripped his hand. He squeezed back.

'Let's go eat,' she told him. He didn't need much prodding. Silently, he led her towards the restaurant door. Jess allowed herself one last glance back up at the neon sign and watched it flicker again. A power surge, or a design feature. It had to be.

Someone walked straight into her, their body rebounding from her, pushing her back a few steps and causing her to lose contact with Marshall.

'I'm so sorry,' came a male voice. Jess looked up at the man who had walked into her. Or had she walked into him? She hadn't been looking where she was going, relying on Marshall to guide her.

'Sorry. My fault,' she said. The man seemed small but that was probably because he was standing next to Marshall. He was taller than Jess, he must have been at least six foot, with dark hair. He wore a long coat that mostly covered his clothes but his bright blue eyes were the thing that kept Jess's attention.

He gave her a small smile and moved around her at speed, pausing outside the door to the restaurant and then rushing away. Marshall and Jess watched him go.

'Wonder why he was in such a hurry,' Marshall mused. 'Hope it wasn't the food.' He carried on to be seated, but Jess remained staring out of the door. As the man had left, the red light reflected into the street from the neon sign above had flickered. He'd gone in the same direction as Steve and Rachel.

Jess stared a few moments more, but the light didn't flicker again.

Steve

Steve should have felt guilty eavesdropping on his wife, but he couldn't help himself. Rachel had shut herself in the nursery and every instinct in Steve forced him to stand on the other side of the closed door and listen intently. Visions of his wife climbing out of the window cradling Joe almost made him push through the door, but he held back.

Downstairs, in the kitchen, the phone rang. Steve let it ring. Rachel didn't shout out, she didn't even complain. He could hear her murmuring to their baby, although he couldn't make out the words.

The ringing stopped.

A second later, his pocket began to vibrate and his ringtone sang out. Steve jumped away from the door, yanking his phone from his pocket. It was an unknown number.

The nursery door opened and Rachel stood in the doorway, hands on her hips.

'It's him, isn't it,' she said.

He looked up, meeting her eyes.

'No. He rang on the landline before. He doesn't have my number.'

Steve shrunk back under Rachel's glare.

'Where do you think he got the landline number?' she hissed. Behind her, Steve could just make out the sleeping bundle that was Joe in his cot. Rachel positioned herself protectively between them. The sight made Steve's chest hurt.

'Aren't you going to answer it?' Rachel asked.

'Should I?'

The phone was still ringing, but it would go to voicemail soon.

'Yes.' Rachel folded her arms. Steve turned away to answer the phone. 'Stay here,' Rachel ordered.

Steve glanced at her as he moved the phone to his ear.

'Hello?'

'Hello, Mr Green. Is your wife there?'

Steve blinked.

'Yes.' Should he say more? Should he be keeping things from this man or from his wife? It concerned him that he had to ask that question.

'Is she listening?'

'Yes.'

'May I call you Steve?'

'Erm, yes.'

'Good. Steve, can you move away from her?'

'No.'

Rachel narrowed her eyes.

'Who is it? Is it him?' she asked loudly.

Steve froze, as if she were on the other end of the phone and couldn't see him.

'She knows I called?' came the man's accusing voice.

Steve swore silently. He'd had enough. He wanted to get out of here. To take Joe and just leave. They'd go to his mother's near Manchester. He could start again. Give Joe a good childhood instead of whatever this might lead to. Would he need a divorce? Would a divorce be possible if everyone thought his wife was dead?

'I wish you hadn't told her, Steve. But I suppose you had to. I can understand that. I can't keep anything from my wife.' The man sighed.

Rachel held out her hand, asking for the phone. Lost in thoughts of death certificates and divorce solicitors, Steve handed it over. As he let go, he realised what he'd done and made a small noise.

Rachel shot him a look of disgust that would have broken his heart only a couple of a weeks ago. Now, all it did was make him angry.

'Detective Cavanagh?' Rachel said into the phone. 'I do wish you'd stop calling my husband.'

She paused as the detective spoke, her eyes glistening. 'Look. I don't care what you have to say,' she continued. 'You know why I came back. Surely you understand the love of a parent for their baby. Ask your wife.' Rachel gave a small smile. 'I would appreciate it if you'd leave me be. I'm not hurting anyone here. You can leave me. I won't create a fuss, there'll be no problems. And if you take me back, I'll find your wife and we can have a nice discussion about the love between a mother and her baby.'

Rachel didn't wait for a response. She hung up the phone and threw it back to Steve.

'I'd love a cup of tea,' she told him, before turning back into the nursery and closing the door.

17

There was a man standing outside Steve's front door when Erica pulled the car up. Jess didn't seem to notice at first.

'Got the details?' she asked, rummaging through her bag.

'Hmm? Yup.'

'Good.' Jess sat back, lifting her head and closing her eyes. 'I'm very interested to see what Rachel has to say about this death certificate thing. I bet she won't explain it though.'

Erica felt Jess looking at her, but she kept her eyes on the strange man standing by Steve's front door. 'It's wrong that I'm so excited about this, isn't it? But just think, even if there's no ghost, we can still make a job out of this. Jess Tidswell and Erica Murray, Private Investigators. I wonder if you need qualifications for that. Maybe we should just stick to the ghosts. Hey, maybe there's a P.I. we could develop a connection with. To hand over when a ghost case turns into something like this. Hey.' Jess nudged Erica. 'Are you with me?' Finally, Jess followed Erica's gaze to the front door. 'Who's that?'

'No idea.'

Erica got out of the car, watching the man. He was in a long brown coat, but underneath he appeared to be wearing casual jeans and a shirt. It seemed strange attire, so strange that Erica hardly noticed his short dark hair or the concern on his face as he gave them a cursory glance. Erica studied the long coat, wondering why it felt like she'd seen it before recently.

'Excuse me. Can I help you?' Jess called out.

Brave, thought Erica. She didn't think she could stand on someone else's doorstep and act as if she owned it.

The man held up a finger to silence Jess. Erica sighed. Well, that was that. Half-heartedly, she reached out to stop Jess but her friend was already jogging over to give the man a piece of her mind.

'Don't you put your finger up to silence me. How dare you! Who are you?'

The man didn't move. He was bent over, listening against the front door. Erica frowned.

'What's going on?' Jess continued. 'Excuse me.' She leaned across the man and knocked on the door.

Finally, he straightened, mouth open to argue, but he froze as he looked at her. Slowly, as if he didn't want to, he turned and looked straight at Erica. Her stomach turned as their eyes met.

'Shit,' the man said.

A loud bang made them all stop and look around.

'What was that?' Jess cried. She rapped on the door again, harder this time. 'Steve? Are you there?'

The door flung open and Steve appeared, breathing hard, tears in his eyes.

'She's gone. She took him.' Steve looked at the strange man, his expression changing. 'Who—are you him?'

'What?' Jess pushed Steve back into the house.

232

Erica went to follow but the strange man leapt past her. She couldn't be certain, but she was sure he was purposefully not looking at her as he rushed past. He disappeared around the corner. Erica watched the space he'd occupied for a moment, before following Jess into the house.

Jess was rushing around just as much as the strange man. She ran from window to window while Steve stayed in the middle of the hallway.

'What's going on?' Erica asked.

'Rachel ran away with the baby,' Jess told her, running out of the back door.

'She just ran past me with him. Ran past me, out the back door and she's gone. She said...she said... This is my fault.' Steve's body shuddered. 'Is it my fault? Why did this have to happen?' He gave another shudder, as if his knees were about to give way.

Erica spared Steve a glance before following Jess. Out into the garden, through the open back gate, where someone ran into her. Stepping back and waiting for her vision to focus, Erica looked up into the ice blue of the strange man's eyes. She blinked.

He stared at her for a moment.

'Shit,' he muttered, looking her up and down with a pained expression. Erica could almost feel offended. He gave her one last look and then turned and ran.

Erica shook her head and looked around.

'Jess?' she called.

Raised voices came from down the road, in the direction that the man had gone. Swearing under her breath and pretty sure this was a bad idea, Erica jogged to find them.

Around the corner were more townhouses, circling a small green park with a climbing frame, swings and a roundabout. By the gate was Rachel, holding her baby close to her chest. The man and Jess approached her.

Rachel was glaring at the man, allowing Jess to circle round and attempt to get behind her, despite the playground fence.

'You don't want to do this,' the man told Rachel. 'If you do this, you'll be worse off.'

Rachel barked a laugh.

'How can I be worse off? You don't know, you have no idea. But you're brave, I'll give you that. I didn't think you'd follow me here.'

'If I hadn't, someone else would have done.'

Rachel shrugged.

'You're a father. You have a child. You must understand this.'

'Don't give me that,' the man almost laughed. 'That baby is part of your new life. A new life you were never supposed to have.'

Erica looked at the man in shock, when she turned back to Rachel she expected the woman to have tears in her eyes. Instead, Rachel looked at the man with scorn and pure hatred.

'I'm not a threat anymore,' she growled.

'Yes. Yes, you are.' The man seemed to sag. 'I can tell you're going to make this difficult. More difficult than you already have. But wherever you go, whenever you go, I will find you and I will take you home.'

'This is my home now.'

'Then why fake your own death?'

Aha! Erica and Jess looked at each other triumphantly, although they both managed to stay quiet.

Rachel noticed them for the first time.

'And what about them?' she asked quietly, her voice hard as she gestured to Erica and Jess. 'They know. What will you do with them?'

Erica glanced at the man and was taken aback to find him smiling. Not a cocky, self-assured smile she might have expected, but a small, secret smile. His eyes searched for her and then he snapped back to Rachel, turning his back on Erica.

'That's not your concern,' he told her.

Rachel had used his momentary lapse of concentration though, and held something in her hand. The man's eyes widened.

'No! Don't!'

The world went white.

Erica opened her eyes and closed them again. The world was too bright, colours dancing under her eyelids.

'Jess?' she called out. She tried opening her eyes again, slowly this time, crunching up her face in preparation for the bright pain. She winced as the outside world hit her again. Slowly, her vision returned. She blinked, trying to dislodge the floating colours. As she began to see clearly, Erica found she was still near the playground. Off to her right, Jess was hunched over, her hands on her knees, opening her eyes and then scrunching them closed again. Between them, closer to the playground gate, was the man. He wasn't blinking, he didn't seem disorientated. Had he not seen that light? His head hung low, as if in sorrow, and his hands were dug deep into the pockets of his long brown coat. His shoulders heaved in a sigh, and then he turned to look right at her. She blinked at him. The man turned to Jess.

'Are you all right?' he asked. Although he glanced at Erica again, he seemed reluctant to speak to her.

'No, no,' muttered Erica to herself. 'I'm fine. Don't you worry about me.' She rubbed at her eyes.

Jess joined her.

'Are you okay?'

Erica nodded.

'You?'

Jess gave a nod and turned back to the man.

'What, the fuck, was that about?' she asked, keeping her voice low as if in respect of being so close to a playground, despite there being no one around.

The man studied her.

'Jess, right? Boy, you haven't changed much.'

The two women gawped at him.

'What do you mean, I haven't changed much? How do you know my name? Who the hell are you?'

The man gave a weak smile and his gaze landed on Erica. She expected it to flitter away, as it had been doing all this time, but it lingered. She found herself unable to look away from those light blue eyes, so tired and worn, and gentle and kind.

'Err, what year is this? Right.' The man scrunched up his eyes. 'Have you met him yet? No, wait, of course you have.'

Jess stiffened beside Erica.

'Who?'

'Marshall.'

Finally, Jess was lost for words. She opened and closed her mouth, before snapping it shut. She took

236

a step back, gripping onto Erica's sleeve as the man approached them.

'I'm sorry. This must seem so strange.' He looked at Erica with such sadness in his eyes that Erica's breath caught in her throat. 'It wasn't meant to be like this,' he murmured to her and only her. 'But I suppose, it will now always have been like this. I do hope I haven't changed too much. She's right, I shouldn't have come.' He paused, gazing at Erica. 'What if this is our only chance, now? What if this is it? And I've changed our future. Then I guess I need to say it now, and I want to say it now, because I didn't know you now. I only know you as you are now from photos and what you've told me. You're beautiful, Ric. You always were, of course. You always will be. But as we haven't met yet, you are beautiful. I always wished we'd met sooner.' He gave a little laugh.

A small voice in Erica's mind told her to step away, to join Jess and leave this man who was obviously mad, but something in his voice and eyes had frozen her to the spot. She couldn't move, she could barely breathe.

'Should I introduce myself?' he murmured.

Was he talking to himself? Should she answer? He smiled at her and her stomach twisted.

'It was a funny story, how we originally met. I don't think we'll have that anymore. I wonder what else will have changed. Not much, I hope. I can bear losing our first joke, but not you, or… I can't lose us.' He swallowed hard. 'Detective Sergeant Rick Cavanagh.' He held out his hand. 'Hello, Miss Erica Murray.'

Erica looked down at Rick's hand. He withdrew it before she could consider shaking it.

'No. No, no. You're right. I shouldn't do this. We shouldn't do this.'

There was a silence as they stared into each other's eyes.

'Erm, excuse me?' Jess's voice broke through. Neither moved. 'Hello? Erica? Detective man? What the hell is going on? Where did Rachel go with the baby? Hello?'

ഇരു

They made their way back to Steve's house, Rick marching along in front, leading the way. Erica followed, watching his back.

'What the hell was that about? Do you know him?' Jess hissed beside her.

Erica shook her head.

'Never seen him before in my life.' Yet, as she said the words they sounded wrong. Had she seen him before?

'Oh. Wait.' Jess stopped walking, forcing Erica to stop and turn back.

'What?'

'I saw him. Last night. I went out with Marshall and I saw Rachel and Steve coming out of the restaurant we were going into. This bloke followed them out. I bumped into him.'

'So that's how he knew who Marshall was,' Erica offered with a shrug of her shoulders. She frowned, looking down at the ground. 'Maybe he's an old friend of Steve's.'

Jess shook her head.

'Didn't you hear what he was saying? He sounds insane.'

'Maybe he is.'

'Then we need to call the police. This man is going around saying he's a detective, what if Steve believes him?'

There was a moment of silence as they began walking quickly back towards the house. Rick the detective was at the front door step.

'Remember when we were just hunting ghosts?' Erica murmured.

ഔ

Steve sat on his sofa, nursing a hot tea. Jess had put a slug of whisky into it, not that Steve seemed to notice. 'So,' Jess began, standing in the middle of the room, her arms crossed. 'What the hell is going on? Shouldn't we be calling the police?'

'I am the police,' said Rick, seating himself at the opposite end of the sofa to Steve and giving the man a sad glance.

Jess gave Erica a look that plainly asked if she could believe this. Erica wasn't sure what to believe.

'Do you have ID on you?' Jess questioned him.

Seemingly oblivious to her stern voice, Rick reached into a hidden pocket in the inside of his trench coat and pulled out what looked like a wallet. He flipped it open to show an ID badge and then flipped it shut.

'Err, I didn't see that. For all I know, that was a library card.' Jess took a step towards Rick but he held up his hand to stop her.

'I can't show you the details.' He struggled with some inner voice. 'Although you've already seen so much, so why not.' He handed the card holder to Jess who flipped it open. 'I'm truly sorry, Mr

Green,' Rick told Steve. 'I will find her, I will bring your baby home. I swear.'

Steve didn't respond. He sipped at his tea, staring blankly at nothing. Rick wrung his hands between his knees. Slowly, he looked up at Erica and seemed a little startled that she was watching him.

'Ric. Erm, Erica.' Jess sidled over to Erica and showed her Rick's ID. Erica tore her gaze from the man to look down at the photo of him. There were his kind blue eyes and his soft dark hair. Erica sighed, fighting back the urge to smile.

Jess nudged her and pointed to a date on the card. It was eleven years in the future. Erica frowned, her stomach dipping. She slowly caught Jess's eye.

He's from the future. The words crept into her mind and stayed there as the logical part considered them before brushing them aside.

No, there had to be an explanation for this.

'The date on this is wrong. It says it was issued eleven years from now,' Erica told the room. Jess glared at Rick.

'Yes. It was reissued after I…well, I lost my old one. That's a good story. You enjoyed that one.' He smiled at Erica and then remembered himself, losing the smile and looking down at the carpet. 'I really shouldn't be here. This is all wrong.' He went to take back his ID. Jess snatched it away.

'You're telling us you're from eleven years in the future?' Jess asked, holding the ID high and away, as if the detective were Ruby. Rick could easily reach up and take the ID, which he did. Despite that, Jess continued to glare defiantly.

'Thirteen, actually. I guess that does no harm.'

Rick rubbed his hand down his face. 'This is ridiculous. We get training for this.' He glanced at Erica. 'And I need to stick to it. I have to go. I'll call you later, Mr Green. If I'm going to get your baby back, I need to talk to you, but not while the girls are here.'

Steve gave the smallest of nods, not looking up.

'Girls?' Jess almost growled.

Rick flashed a smile at Erica and something in her chest hurt.

'We weren't meant to meet this way,' he told her again in a soft voice. 'We were supposed to meet in a few more years. I should have known this would happen. I knew the name Steve Green rang a bell, but I didn't think. I should have asked you. I wonder if we'll still meet.' His eyes grew distant. Then, with one last affectionate look at Erica, the detective turned and left the house. They heard the door close behind him.

'Shouldn't we have stopped him?' Jess's voice was getting close to a shriek as she looked between Steve and Erica.

'You saw his ID number,' Erica told her. 'Call the police. Check it out.' She looked at Steve, her mind whirring. They needed to get this sorted out as soon as possible, if only so she could get away and have a good think about what had just happened. 'And report the missing baby.'

18

Jess drove Erica home, the silence heavy in the car as both women sat deep in thought. Jess glanced at Erica a couple of times when the traffic allowed. Her friend was staring out of the window, her brow creased.

'What do you think?' Jess murmured, her voice sounding loud in the vacuum.

'I think this is beyond us now,' said Erica without looking round. 'This isn't about ghosts, and that's why we got involved. There's nothing paranormal about this. We should step back.' She finally turned her head to look at Jess, but Jess kept her eyes on the road. 'You've called the police. I don't see what else we can do.'

'I can be there for Steve,' said Jess, although her mind was thinking of much more.

'Well, yeah. But other than that...' Erica drifted off and looked back out of the window, at the houses and trees and shops trundling by.

Jess sighed, hard enough to nearly scream.

'But it just doesn't add up.' Her fingers tightened around the steering wheel, and she was forced to take control and slow down as the lights ahead turned red. 'His ID had a date eleven years in the future and yet the police knew about him. They confirmed he was a detective. Not with them, but still. How does that work?' Stopped at the lights, she bodily turned and stared at Erica until her friend was forced to meet her eye. 'I think we need to talk to your grandmother's elf friends.'

'Fae,' said Erica. 'They're not elfs, they're fae.'

'Same thing, isn't it?'

Erica shook her head.

'Definitely not. Never call them elfs. You'll die a horrible and painful death.'

Jess smiled, waiting to see the humour in Erica's eyes, but there was none. Her smile faded and she turned back to the road, pulling away as the lights turned green.

'All right. Fae. We should ask them.'

'Ask them what exactly?'

'About this detective man. Ask if it's possible. They said Rachel was out of our time. Maybe this man really is from the future.'

'It would make more sense to ask them if they could tell where Rachel had taken the baby,' murmured Erica.

'Yes!' Jess thumped the steering wheel. Next to her, Erica jumped and looked at her. 'We should do that. The cemetery, right?'

Without warning, Jess hit the indicator and immediately turned down a side road. Erica gripped her door handle.

'What the hell are you doing?'

'Turning around. We're going to the cemetery to talk to the fae.'

'And what about the police? If we stay involved in this, the police might suspect us. I really think we need to back off, Jess.'

She was right, Jess knew she was, but she didn't slow down.

'Jess. It's a missing baby. The police take this stuff really seriously. They'll find him,' Erica told her gently.

Jess shook her head and was surprised when tears stung her eyes. She sniffed hard.

'Don't you want to know?' She wanted to sound excited but there was a tremble in her voice. 'What if Rachel is from the future? Maybe she's taken the baby there.'

'Then there's no way we can follow her and no way we can bring her back.'

Jess slowed the car.

'I wonder how she and the detective got here. Maybe—'

'No!' Erica bellowed. 'Nope. No. Whatever you're thinking, no. Now, please, take me home. You need to get Ruby from school. And aren't you seeing Marshall tonight? You have a life to get back to. We'll sleep on it. Rachel's not going to harm her baby. Wherever they are, they'll still be there tomorrow. We'll talk about it in the morning. We'll figure it out then. Okay?'

Jess struggled. She did have to pick up Ruby, and she was already running late. She sniffed again, blinking back the hot tears.

Erica's hand squeezed her arm.

'It'll be okay,' she murmured.

Jess gave a nod.

'I know,' she said in a small voice. 'I know.' Although she didn't quite believe herself.

There was another silence.

'What was going on between you and that man? Detective Rick,' Jess asked.

When Erica didn't reply, Jess glanced over at her. Was it her imagination or was there colour in

Erica's cheeks? She certainly had a faint smile on her lips. 'Ric? Don't tell me it was love at first sight.' Jess grinned, forgetting herself.

'Of course not,' Erica told her. She turned to look at Jess. 'Has that ever happened to you?'

'Marshall.' Jess nodded. 'You've never fallen in love at first sight?'

'No,' murmured Erica. 'Never. I don't think you can. You think you loved Marshall as soon as you saw him, or did you just want to get him in your bed?'

'Well...' Jess shifted in her seat. 'Okay, good point.' There was another pause. 'So.' Jess glanced back at Erica. 'Do you want to get Detective Rick in your bed?'

Erica smiled and turned away, looking out of the window where Jess couldn't see her face.

'It'd be awkward, you know,' Jess told her. 'Rick and Ric. You'd be forever known as Erica just so you'd know who people were talking to. It'd be awful.'

Erica didn't respond. She kept her face to the window.

'His name is unfortunate,' she said eventually.

'Do you Rick take Ric,' Jess imitated.

Erica raised an eyebrow at her.

'Oh, come on. I only smiled at the man, and you're already marrying us off.'

'You heard what he was going on about. Sounds like something happens between you in the future. All that "this isn't how we meet" rubbish.'

Erica's face fell.

'You think it was rubbish?'

'Oh. I didn't mean... Sorry. What did you make of it?' Jess exhaled slowly. She needed to think before she spoke. Erica seemed genuinely put out by the idea that this man might not be what he said he was. She would have to watch that. Erica wasn't one for getting heartbroken, she was too practical about it. She often broke up with her boyfriends before they had the chance to break her heart. While Jess knew she'd been hurt, she'd seen the tears, Erica was good at protecting herself. So it seemed strange that she should be so taken with this man who was unknown to them, who acted so strangely.

Maybe she was just flattered by his words, the way he had looked at her and known her. Jess couldn't begrudge her that, she'd feel the same. But there was something about the whole situation that set Jess's teeth on edge. This man could hurt Erica as much as Rachel was hurting Steve, Jess realised. That was it. Jess wouldn't let that happen. She'd need to keep an eye on her friend.

Or maybe Erica was right. Maybe they should stay out of this from now on. That would keep Erica out of harm's way of this man. Jess could continue looking into it. She'd need to stay close to Steve throughout this, after all. The man needed a friend right now.

At the next opportunity, Jess turned the car around.

Erica looked at her with surprise.

'Now what are we doing?'

'I'm taking you home. Like you said, I need to pick Ruby up. In fact, we might need to pick Ruby up on the way. If that's okay?' Jess glanced at the clock, her stomach knotting when she saw the time.

'Of course.'

Another silence fell between them, this time comfortable and less thoughtful.

'The police are checking in on Steve now?' Erica asked.

'They should be. They didn't seem fussed about the strange detective man. Just confirmed that he did work for them.' Jess shrugged. 'But yeah, they should be at Steve's by now. I'll call him later and check he's okay.'

'There you go. That man's nothing to worry about. They know what they're doing.'

Jess rolled her eyes to herself.

'If you say so,' she murmured.

'It's a missing baby, Jess. They'll do whatever they can.'

'Yeah.' Jess's stomach had dropped at Erica's reminder of little Joe. She wondered where he was right now. Where was Rachel? For a moment, she allowed herself to consider what time they were in. Were they thirteen years in the future? I bet it looks no different to now, she thought. Maybe the cars would have a different style, but the houses and shops would be the same. Maybe there would be less green. That was usually the main change. In thirteen years' time, Jess had no doubt that she'd be the one telling young people that all this used to be fields.

Steve would need more than a phone call later. But she couldn't leave Ruby. Marshall would look after her, she knew, but she didn't want to be so reliant on him so soon. She worried about trapping him, pushing him away, scaring him off. She swallowed. No, she couldn't ask him to babysit again. Steve had to have family somewhere. Someone who could come and look after him during this awful time. She would ask. She would offer to call them. But that was all she could offer.

She repeated that to herself a few times to make sure it went in.

She glanced at the time again as she turned down the road to Ruby's school. The police would probably still be there. She'd wait until Ruby was settled at home, then she'd call Steve.

There was nowhere to park outside the school. They were too late to grab a space, so Erica jumped out and went to wait for Ruby while Jess circled the car around. This wasn't her favourite part of being a parent.

∞⌒

'How are you?' Jess asked. Steve had answered the phone with hope, as if she might be Rachel. Disappointment might as well have dripped through the receiver.

'Okay. I guess.'

'Well, no, I know. Of course you're not okay.' Jess sighed and rubbed the hem of her top between her fingers. 'How did it go with the police? What did they say?'

'I told them everything that happened. They said they can't do anything. It's Detective Cavanagh's case.'

'What? That's ridiculous. He's not even...' Jess stopped herself and took a deep breath.

'It's his case so there's not a lot they can do,' Steve said.

'Not a lot they can do? What does that mean? They can search for Rachel, can't they? Isn't that what they do when someone goes missing?'

'It's his case,' Steve repeated. Jess bit her lip. She was saying too much, overwhelming him. She took a deep breath.

'Okay. What do you know about him? Do you trust him?'

'I...I don't know. I have to though, don't I? What else can I do?' Steve sounded close to tears. 'He called me before, told me not to trust her. I should have listened to him. But I thought I could trust my wife. I should have been able to trust my wife.'

'Of course you should have,' Jess told him gently.

'Even though she wouldn't talk to me. It felt like she didn't want to be anywhere near me. She became so protective of Joe.' Steve's voice cracked as he said his son's name. 'I should have known something like this would happen. I should have seen it coming.'

'You couldn't have seen this coming,' Jess said. 'No one could have. You had your family back.'

'But—'

'Hindsight is a wonderful thing. But you need to stop beating yourself up. There's no way you could have known.'

'Detective Cavanagh told me he's after her to arrest her, for murder.'

Jess opened her mouth to speak but no words came out. Her heart pounded. She pushed the phone into her ear.

'What do you mean?' she asked feebly.

'I don't know.' Steve's voice quivered. 'That's all he told me. That's all he said.' There was a pause. 'I didn't want to know. I couldn't bear it. I don't think he would have told me anyway.'

'No. No, probably not,' Jess murmured. Against the white noise that was blaring in her head she could hear Marshall and Ruby laughing about something in the living room. Jess clenched her eyes shut. 'What do you need me to do, Steve? What can I do?'

The silence stretched out long enough for Jess to wonder if Steve was still there, or whether he'd curled up in a ball on his kitchen floor. When he spoke, the sound came so suddenly that she jumped.

'Nothing. You've done enough. You don't need to be involved anymore. At least it wasn't a ghost.' Steve choked on a forced laugh and Jess's heart broke.

'I'm so sorry, Steve,' she murmured. 'I want to help. Do you have family nearby? Anyone visiting?'

'I'm fine.'

Jess took that as a no.

'What are you doing tonight?'

'I'm fine, Jess. I'll be fine.' Jess could hear the effort it took for Steve to keep his voice steady.

'I'll come round tomorrow, as soon as I can. Maybe you could get a hotel tonight?' She couldn't bear the idea of him alone in that townhouse, the nursery dark and empty.

'I can't. What if she comes back?'

Damn, he was right.

'Okay. I can't come over tonight, but first thing tomorrow. As soon as I've dropped Ruby off at school. Okay?'

'You have work.'

'Screw that. I'm quitting anyway.'

'I don't want to cause a bother.'

Jess actually laughed at that.

'Steve! No arguing. This might be entirely selfish of me, but I need to know you're okay. So

I'll be there tomorrow. Don't worry about smartening up or anything stupid like that. I'll come round, make you a cup of tea and I'll be there to talk if you want. Or I can clean up. Or something. I'll bring you food. Okay?'

'Thank you.'

'Okay. Oh, hey, did you get a phone number for that detective?'

'No. He said he'd be round tomorrow. He's coming tomorrow.'

'Good. Okay. Right, well, don't do anything silly. Try and get some sleep. Put the TV on or something. And if you really need to get out, you can... You can come here.' Jess pulled a face at herself. She really didn't want Steve in the house, there was no room, but what else could she do?

'Thank you, Jess. I don't know... Thank you.'

They said goodbye and hung up. Jess stared at the phone for a moment before blindly turning and leaving the kitchen. She walked into the living room to the sight of Marshall sitting in the middle of the sofa. On one side, Bubbles took up half the sofa, her head resting on Marshall's knee, his fingers deep in her fur. On the other side, Ruby was curled up against him, his arm wrapped around her shoulders. He looked up and smiled at Jess, but the smile quickly faded.

'Anything I can do?' he murmured.

Jess took in the scene and smiled weakly, a warmth growing in her chest and spreading through her chilled body.

'You're doing it,' she told him.

Steve

Steve spent two hours sitting at his kitchen table, looking at his phone after hanging up on Jess. It was dark by the time he stirred. His back ached and his legs were numb. He came to gently, looking around the kitchen. Moving slowly, stretching out his limbs and cracking his neck, he put the light on and stopped and stared once more.

The house was silent. In the middle of the kitchen table, the new baby monitor sat lifeless. He couldn't take it. The darkness, the silence, the knowledge that the cot upstairs in the nursery was empty. But he couldn't leave. What if she came back? Crying, gripping their child, asking for forgiveness.

Steve frowned.

He wouldn't give it to her. The pain in his chest flared with rage. There would be no forgiveness for this. There would be no more chances.

The silence was bearing down on him, his head aching from its weight. He couldn't stay here.

She wasn't coming back. The thought made his chest hurt more, but he had to admit it. He knew, deep down, that it was the truth. She was never coming back.

Steve turned and walked out of the house, having enough wits about him to grab his coat and keys, and to lock the door behind him.

He wasn't sure where he was going. The world had always looked different at night, and now the low light of the street lamps gave everything an other-worldly glow. He knew this world. He had walked in it before, but those had been happy times. Now the shadows mocked him, the breeze in the branches of new trees planted by the developers rattled and swayed as he walked past. He walked between the townhouses and reached the main road. Head down, he walked along the pavement as traffic roared past him. The constant loud noise was a comfort. He could barely hear his own thoughts over them, but still the thoughts were there.

What would he do now? Where would he go? He'd have to sell the house. Maybe he'd change his job. Maybe change city. He could go north and start again, somewhere busy with cafés and people and commuters, where he wouldn't have to think about everything he'd lost. A new life. Maybe he'd meet someone new. Maybe they'd have a child. A fresh start. A new chance.

He couldn't bear to even consider the possibility that he'd never see Joe again, so he simply pushed that from his mind, his future plans already taking it as fact.

But as his future plans ran away from him and his new family formed in his mind, the pain became overwhelming. He stopped and looked up at the now black sky. The lights around him made it impossible to see the stars.

'You all right there?'

Steve wheeled round, knocking himself off balance. He put out his arms and teetered to the side. The man leaning out of the window of the police car narrowed his eyes.

'You okay, mate?'

Steve didn't know how to answer. He knew he should say he was fine, but the words wouldn't come. His hands and lips trembled, his eyes filling as he attempted a nod.

The policeman frowned.

'Have you been drinking?'

Steve wanted to laugh. No. But he should have had a drink. He shook his head.

'Where are you off to?'

Steve shrugged.

'Come and take a seat in the back of the car.'

Part of Steve's mind rebelled against this. He didn't want the trouble this could bring. He wasn't drunk. He was fine. Despite that, he obediently got into the back of the police car, sat back and closed his eyes. The tears came freely, the sobs wrenching through his aching chest. The policeman sat for a moment and allowed it to happen. Then he pulled back onto the road. Steve didn't ask where they were going. He didn't care.

19

Erica sat down on the sofa, next to the armchair which currently held her grandmother who was looking down at a magazine on her lap.

'You don't have your reading glasses on,' Erica pointed out.

'That's because I'm not reading.'

'You're just looking at the pictures?'

Minerva looked up at her granddaughter.

'Shouldn't you be in work?'

'Shouldn't you be at home?'

'I'm waiting for your dad to take me.'

'I called in sick.'

Minerva gave a sly smile.

'I didn't know you were ill, poor love.'

'I'm not.'

'So, you lied?'

'Yup.'

Minerva grinned.

'I'm so proud of you.'

Erica laughed.

'I'm proud of me too.' Her grin faded and she looked down into her mug of tea. 'Jess wants to start a paranormal investigation agency.'

'I know. Eolande told me. You should do it.'

Erica snapped her head up to look at her grandmother.

'That's it? No "but how will you make money?" or "you can't be serious?". Just, yeah do it?'

Minerva shrugged.

'You're two savvy young women. You'll make it work.'

'That's not how business works, Gran.' Erica sipped her tea.

'And you know that.' Minerva pointed her magazine at Erica. 'See, you're off to a flying start.'

Erica paused.

'Do you think there's money in it?'

'People buy strange things, why not finding out if their house is haunted. That's what you'll be doing, right?'

'Right.'

'And you're the best person for that job.' Minerva's expression fell. 'Any news on that poor boy and his baby?'

Erica shook her head and checked her phone just in case. There were no messages from Jess.

'Nope. I haven't heard anything. I told Jess we should leave it alone, but...'

'But?'

Erica hadn't meant to say "but". She'd meant to stop and never mention Detective Cavanagh to her grandmother, but the word had just slipped out as her thoughts had meandered back to him.

'But...I don't know, the poor man has lost his baby. And from what Eolande and Alfie say, Rachel is a time traveller.'

Erica squirmed a little as Minerva narrowed her eyes, studying her granddaughter.

'Yes,' she said slowly. 'Yes, he might need help that the police cannot give him.'

Erica met her eyes. What did she know?

258

'Do you think we should help?'

Minerva shrugged.

'If you can. Time travel isn't something we've ever come across, though. What do you think you could do?'

Erica sighed.

'Eolande could help?' She gave her grandmother a sly look. Minerva raised an eyebrow at her.

'Quite possibly she could, but I doubt she would.'

'Why not?'

'She has her reasons. Why don't you ask Alfie? He'd be very willing help you. With whatever you want.'

Erica stared at her grandmother as Minerva broke into a grin. 'He's a handsome man.'

'All fae are attractive. You told me that.'

'Attractive and lustful,' Minerva agreed.

'Exactly.'

'And for good reason. They're good at what they do, you know. And if what they say is true, and you're going to give your heart to someone one day, don't you want to have some fun first?'

Erica's mind immediately flashed back to Rick.

'When they say that, about my heart belonging to another, I mean, they can't possibly know that. Can they?'

Minerva sighed and lowered her voice.

'You're not to tell your mother this. Or anyone, for that matter.'

Erica leaned closer.

'Okay. I won't.'

'Eolande told me when your grandfather was about to…leave us.'

'But it was a sudden heart attack. No one knew.'

'I think your grandfather knew. I think we all know, when our time is coming to an end, on some level. But Eolande knew too. Did your mother ever tell you that he organised and paid for his funeral the week before he died?'

'No.'

'I didn't understand why he was doing it at first. I would ask him and he would just tell me that he needed to make sure I never had to go through organising such a horrible thing. The day he went to sort it out, a week before he… Well, I went for a walk in the cemetery. I don't know why. It was so peaceful, walking among the trees. That was when I met Eolande, and when she told me what was about to happen. She was a rock, there for me throughout the whole thing. She kept away when I needed space and to be alone, and she was there when I needed holding.' Minerva smiled to herself. 'It's not our place to ask how they know these things, it's enough to just accept it.' She looked up at Erica. 'Accept it. You're going to fall in love one day. Falling in love is an incredible thing. It makes your heart feel so full it'll burst, and then it'll drag you so low you'll cry. And at some point, you'll regret not saying yes more often. Trust me, it's a terrible thing to have to wait for the death of the man you love before you can start having that sort of fun. You need to have it now. As well as then.'

Erica nodded.

'I'm sorry that you went through that. With Granddad. That we couldn't be there for you.'

'It wasn't your or your mother's place to be there for me the way Eolande was. You're my girls, my blood. Eolande is something else.'

Erica looked up at her grandmother and

hesitated, wondering how much to say.

'There's a detective looking for Rachel,' she started.

'Well, good.'

'I think he's a time traveller too. Maybe from Rachel's time.'

Minerva placed her magazine down on the small table beside her chair and gave Erica her full attention.

'Well, why you didn't mention that before?'

'Well...'

'Well?'

'There's something about him, Gran,' said Erica with a sigh. 'The way he looks at me. The things he says. He doesn't make a whole lot of sense but he seems to say that we're together in the future.'

Minerva's eyes widened.

'What's he like?'

Erica smirked.

'Tall, dark and handsome.'

'A bit cliché.' Minerva sat back, a sparkle in her eyes. 'But he's from the future and maybe not even our timeline. I wonder when you're supposed to meet him.'

'He told me we didn't meet like this. He seemed quite upset that we might not meet how he remembered it.'

'Yes.' Minerva's smile faded. 'Of course, there's a chance now that he's changed the timeline so much that you don't even end up together.'

Something twisted in Erica's gut.

'You think so?'

Minerva studied her granddaughter.

'Maybe. Maybe you should stay involved in this case if this detective is involved and you want to get to know him. And if that's the case, you don't want Alfie there. I'm not sure how you can help. Why don't you ask this detective what you can do?'

'Yes, the authorities love it when they're on a really important case like child abduction and two civilians ask how they can help.' Erica frowned. 'Actually, they do ask for help don't they? Maybe we could.'

'You could,' said Minerva, pointedly. 'What's Jess up to? You've already told her you don't want to be involved, haven't you?'

Erica opened her mouth to protest. 'I know you, Ric,' Minerva interrupted. 'You make a decision, the decision that you think is right and you announce it. But right by whose standards? Society's? Who gives a crap what society thinks you should do. Go to school, get a job, stay in that job until you retire and die. Pah!' Minerva leaned forward eagerly. 'You have a chance to break that, Ric. I tried to but society was less forgiving back then. Your mother's trying and she got further than me. But you, Ric. You did well in school and we're so proud, but we don't want you stuck in that job until you retire. And you know damn well that if you change job, go somewhere else, you'll still be stuck doing the same thing. This business stuff, that's the future. Life is short, so why don't you get on with it?'

Erica had sat back during her grandmother's tirade. Minerva left enough of a pause to let Erica think she could respond. Just as Erica opened her mouth, Minerva continued.

'You need to stop and think before you make decisions, but not the way you usually think. Instead of thinking what's right, think about what you want.

Do you want to stay in this crap job of yours?'

'Well...no.'

'Do you want to go do the same job somewhere else?'

'No.'

'Do you want to be your own boss?'

'Yes.' Erica smiled, the idea filling her with a buzz.

'Do you want to work with Jess?'

'Yes. She's my best friend.'

'Do you want to keep doing this marketing stuff?'

'No.' Erica snapped back, surprised. 'I don't.' She looked at her grandmother.

'Do you want to start a paranormal investigation agency? Ah! Don't think. What's your gut and your heart telling you?'

'Yes. Yes, I do. I want to see if we can do it.'

Minerva clapped her hands and laughed.

'Do you want to help Steve get his baby back?'

'Yes.'

'Do you want to see this detective again?'

'Yes.' That was the easiest one, Erica thought. The word slipped out before Minerva had finished with no hint of question in Erica's mind. 'Yes.'

'And you told Jess you didn't want to.' Erica blinked at her grandmother, trying to take everything in. 'Ric, you know Jess. What do you think she's doing right now?'

'Shit.' Erica jumped up and grabbed her phone, unlocking it and bringing up Jess's number. She stopped and turned back. 'Thanks, Gran.'

Minerva waved her away, picking up her magazine.

Erica ran into her bedroom and closed the door behind her as she held her phone to her ear. The ringing continued long enough for Erica to know Jess wasn't going to pick up.

'Hi.'

Erica jumped.

'Jess! Where are you?'

'Why? What's wrong.'

Erica could hear the roar of traffic in the background. Wherever Jess was, she wasn't home.

'Where are you?' she repeated.

'Out. Why?'

'You're at Steve's, aren't you?' That roar of traffic was the dual carriageway that skirted the new development. Erica could almost see where Jess was standing, by Steve's front door. Or maybe by her car.

'Maybe. You know. Just to check he's okay.'

'Okay. Well, I've changed my mind.'

'About what?'

'What you said. I think we should be involved. I think we should help Steve more than just you being a friend for him to lean on.'

'Really?' Erica could hear Jess grinning. 'Are you sure?'

'Yup.'

'What made you change your mind?'

Erica stopped herself mentioning Rick.

'Gran did. She pointed out some things to me. Also, I think we need to sit down and properly talk about this investigation agency idea of yours. If we're going to do it, we need to get started.'

There was a silent pause and Erica wondered what Jess was doing.

'Okay. Great. Are you at work today?'

'No. Are you going in?'

'No.'

Another pause as Erica contemplated what that meant.

'We really should be going into work. Just because we want to leave doesn't mean we stop going in. There are clients depending on us.' She cringed, hearing herself and glanced over her shoulder, half expecting Minerva to be standing there ready to smack her around the head with her magazine.

There was no one there. Erica took a deep breath and closed her eyes. What was her heart telling her?

'I guess you're right,' said Jess. 'I'll go in today. I'll just tell them there was a hiccup at Ruby's school, that's why I'm late. Have you already called in sick?'

Erica opened her eyes.

'Don't go in,' she said. 'Your friend has just had his baby abducted. You can't possibly go into work. Get a sick note from the doctor if you must.'

'Really? What about you?'

'I already called in sick but I'll go in. Show face. Then tonight, we're talking about this. We need a business plan. We need to look at the finances.'

'We're both quitting,' Jess squealed down the phone. Erica pulled the receiver from her ear, grinning.

'Let me know how things go with Steve. I'll go into work.'

'Good luck.'

'You too.'

Erica hung up and her shoulders sagged. How had she managed to do that? She'd started the morning with a day alone with her thoughts and now she was headed back to the office. But not for long, she thought with a smile.

'Everything okay?' Minerva asked from behind. Erica spun round and gathered the small woman up in her arms, giving her a squeeze.

'Very. I'm leaving my horrible job.'

'What?'

Erica placed her gran back on the ground as they both turned to look at Erica's mother. 'You're doing what?'

'Err…'

'You're quitting your well paid, steady job when you have nothing to go onto? Why?'

'To, erm, start a paranormal investigation agency with Jess.'

Esther stared between Jess and Minerva before flinging up her arms.

'What? Mum! What have you been saying to her?'

'Nothing, love, honest,' said Minerva, holding her hands up in defeat. 'Well, nothing much.'

'Nothing much? She's quitting a good job for what?' Esther was shouting now. The dogs appeared behind her. One sat down with a small cry.

'A job that I hate, Mum,' Erica told her, trying to not feel judged by the dog. 'A job where I'm not appreciated. Where the boss's mate gets the job I earned. In a workplace full of men. Men who, it seems, don't think a woman can do their job.'

'I thought you were going to start your own marketing agency,' her mother said sadly. Erica relented with a sigh.

'I was.'

'Do both.' Minerva looked between her daughter

266

and granddaughter with a grin and a shrug. 'Why not? You should diversify your income.'

Erica blinked at her.

'I should what?'

'Diversi—'

'I heard what you said. How do you know about that sort of stuff?'

Minerva's grin dropped, giving way to a dark look.

'You think I'm old and past it, but people ran businesses back when I was your age.' She lifted her magazine as if to hit Erica. Erica flinched away with a smile.

'Okay. Sorry.'

'Could you do that?' Esther asked.

'Yeah. I could.' Erica stared at the carpet, trying to imagine it. Marketer by day, ghost hunter by night. A thrill ran through her. 'I should. I will.' She looked up at her mother and grandmother with a smile.

'What's going on?' Her father walked into the hallway, nearly tripping over the dogs. 'You realise we have rooms in this house, don't you? Big rooms with comfy seats where you can have conversations and everything without tripping people up and getting in the way.'

'Sorry.' Esther gave her husband's cheek a kiss.

'Sorry!' Minerva said.

'Come on, I'll get you home,' he told Minerva, opening his arms to gesture for her to lead the way. Minerva handed Esther her magazine, the dogs following her towards the front door.

'Sorry, Dad. Right, I have to go to work.'

'The good work or the bad work?' Erica's mother asked.

'Bad work. I guess I'll have to work out my notice now.'

'But it's extra money and for a good cause,' her mother reminded her.

'Ha!' came Minerva's voice, causing Erica to hesitate.

'Yeah. We'll see.' She gave her mother a kiss and rushed past to get changed into more suitable clothes.

20

Jess stared down at the phone in her hand and grinned, her mind filled instantly with worries and plans and excitement. But those were for tonight. Right now, she had a friend to see. She checked the time. It wouldn't be long before she'd have to go home. Marshall was there finishing off the skirting, but he had another job to get to and she didn't want to leave Bubbles alone for too long.

She knocked on the door and waited, placing her phone back in her pocket and watching the cars on the nearby main road. She looked up at the door. There were no shadows moving behind the glass. She knocked again, and again looked up the road, waiting.

When the door didn't open, she looked up at the house. The windows were all shut, the curtains open and still. Jess frowned and knocked again, louder.

Without pausing, she opened the letterbox with some difficulty and shouted Steve's name into the house. Hugging herself, she watched the door.

There was still no movement. No one answered.

Jess pulled her phone back out and called Steve's number. It rang. She held her ear to the door, wondering if she'd hear the ringtone from inside, but there was only silence and the ringing in her ear. After it went to voicemail, she hung up and tried his landline. From inside the house, the phone rang. She listened to it, straining to hear footsteps on the stairs or the click followed by Steve's voice.

It just rang and rang.

Flutterings of panic descended on Jess. She hung up. Not knowing what else to do, she banged on the door.

Should she knock on the neighbour's door? She stared at the neighbouring townhouse. What if Steve was inside? What if he'd done something stupid?

Should she call the police?

Tripping over her own feet, she rushed to the neighbour's door and banged on it. It opened slowly and a face peered out.

'I'm sorry,' Jess breathed, unable to catch her breath. 'I'm sorry, but Steve. The man who lives here.' She gestured to Steve's house. 'Have you seen him? Do you know where he is? Only, he isn't answering the door.'

'Probably in trouble with the police,' said Steve's neighbour, an older woman who eyed Jess suspiciously. 'The police are always round. He's trouble that one. You should stay away from him.'

Jess glared at her.

'His wife was killed a few months ago. He was left alone with their newborn baby. And now he's not answering the door. Did you see him last night? Were the police here?'

'No.' The woman closed the door and Jess listened as she locked it. With a sigh, Jess pressed some buttons on her phone and held it to her ear.

'Hey.'

'Hi.' Jess bit her tongue. Why did the tears have to come now? Why couldn't they have come before she made the call?

'What's going on? Are you okay?'

'No. Steve isn't answering the door and his neighbour's a horrible old woman.' She shouted the last part, hoping the neighbour would hear. She walked back to Steve's front door, feeling guilty about calling his neighbour horrible. 'I don't know what to do.'

Marshall sighed thoughtfully down the phone.

'And he has no friends or family you could call?'

'No.'

'And there's no sign that he's home?'

'No.'

'Does he have a car?'

Jess wheeled round but spotted the old navy Vauxhall in Steve's parking spot.

'It's still here.'

'You're worried he's inside and something's happened?'

'If someone had taken Ruby... ' Jess couldn't finish the sentence without sobbing. She stopped as her voice broke.

'Call the police,' said Marshall.

'Really?'

'You're worried and you have reason to be. Call the police.'

Jess looked out towards the main road.

'There's a police station here. Should I go there?'

'Might be quicker,' Marshall agreed. 'Do you want me to come with you?'

'No. No, I'm okay.'

'Do you want Erica to go with you?'

'No. No, she had to go into work. No. Thank you. I'll be okay.'

'Okay. Let me know how it goes, all right?'

Jess smiled, wondering fleetingly if it was too soon to talk commitment with Marshall.

'Thank you,' she murmured. They said goodbyes, Marshall putting on a strong tone although he was obviously worried, and they hung up.

Jess took a deep breath, gave the townhouse one last glance, and began to walk over to the police station, calling Steve's mobile over and over.

It was a new building, made of shiny colours and glass, or so it seemed to Jess. The large glass doors slid open automatically as she approached. A long desk greeted her and a woman in uniform sat behind it. She looked up and smiled as Jess crept in.

'Can I help you?'

'It's my friend,' said Jess. She cleared her throat. 'He lives over there.' She pointed back to the new development of townhouses. 'His wife died a few months ago. He's alone with the baby, except the baby was abducted, and now he's not answering the door. His car is there. He's not picking up his phone and his neighbour's a bitch and won't talk to me, and I don't know what to do.' It all came out in a rush but the policewoman took it in her stride, nodding along.

'What's his name, love?'

'Steve Green.'

The policewoman made a note.

'And when did you last see him?'

'Yesterday. You're not going to wait twenty-four hours, are you? He lost his wife, his baby's been taken. What if he's...' Jess trailed off. She wouldn't mention that it was Steve's wife who took the baby.

'Of course. We'll look into it straight away. He

only lives over the road, you say? Hang on a sec.' The woman vanished into the building beyond the desk and Jess fidgeted.

'Thought I recognised the name,' said the policewoman, returning, staring down at a file in her hand. 'He was brought in last night. He's safe and sound, don't you worry. He's in the cells.'

Jess stared at the woman, unsure of which reaction to give first. She exhaled in a rush.

'He's safe?'

'Yup.'

'Thank God. But he's here? In the cells? Why?'

'Sorry, I can't give out that information. You'll have to talk to the detective involved. Detective Sergeant Cavanagh.'

Jess's stomach plummeted.

'Can I see him?' she asked, her mouth dry.

'Take a seat, I'll give him a call.'

Blindly, Jess moved to where the policewoman gestured, taking a seat on one of the new, plush chairs that was fastened to the floor over to one side of reception. She stared at the two doors that led into the station.

After a short wait, the door opposite her opened and Detective Cavanagh wandered through, his eyes scanning the room until they met hers.

'Ah, Miss Tidswell.' He held out a hand to her. She took it weakly. He gave it a gentle squeeze and turned to the officer on reception. 'Can you give us a minute?'

The policewoman nodded.

'Would you like a drink, love?' she asked Jess. Jess shook her head, giving the woman a smile.

Rick moved over to Jess and sat beside her. They waited for the policewoman to leave.

'Are you okay?' he asked.

Jess looked up at him and realised she was trembling.

'No. No, I'm not okay. Where's Steve? What's going on?'

'Steve's fine. He's down in the cells.'

'But why? What's he done?'

'He was found last night wandering the streets and seemingly drunk. It turns out he hasn't been drinking. I reckon it was a form of shock. We kept him in anyway. I wanted to keep an eye on him. For the same reasons I assume you're here?'

Jess looked down at the floor and nodded.

'I can take him home. Look after him. You can't keep him in cells after everything that's going on.'

Rick studied her.

'Maybe. But I need to talk to him first. I need to go over some things with him. I was just about to do it. Then I'll take him home, make sure he's okay. Then you can visit him.'

Jess's eyes widened.

'I can't see him now?'

'No.'

'Why not?'

'Miss Tidswell, Jess, this is a police investigation and—'

'And Steve's done nothing wrong! He's the victim! This is how you treat victims?'

'Jess, please. I understand that you're concerned —'

'Concerned? I'm bloody livid!' Jess stood up and glared down at Rick. 'You won't tell us what's going on, you won't let Steve go home and I'm guessing you won't find Rachel and Joe. What's the point of you?'

Rick ran a hand down his face, rubbing at the dark stubble on his chin.

'There are protocols I have to follow.'

'According to your protocols, you shouldn't have met us. You shouldn't have met Erica. To hell with your protocols. You won't even tell us what's going on.' Jess growled, thinking about what Steve had told her last night. Could Rick legally tell her about Rachel being a murderer?

'I'm sorry, Jess, I really am. Go home. I'll get Steve to give you a call when I drop him off.'

Rick stood and herded her to the door.

'No! Either let me see him or tell me what's really going on.' Jess tried to stop herself from being walked out of the station but Rick seemed to suddenly be everywhere and there was no avoiding him.

'I'm sorry, Jess. Go home.'

'Would you tell Erica?' Jess spun round and faced Rick defiantly. He hesitated and looked down at her.

'I couldn't. Please don't bring her into this. It would get too messy.'

'Too late, she's involved. She wants to be involved. We're going to find out what's going on.' Jess pointed a finger at Rick. 'And you're going to get Joe back.'

Rick leaned away.

'And what if you two weren't involved but I still get Joe back? How's that?'

Jess opened and closed her mouth.

'Well, that would…be…okay, I guess.' She dropped her pointed finger. 'Fine. Yes. Find Joe.'

'That's what I'm doing, Miss Tidswell. That's what I'm doing.' Rick gestured out of the door again. Jess went to argue further but there wasn't anything else to be said.

'Fine,' she mumbled, turning and leaving. She strode out to the road and stopped, staring at nothing, wondering what just happened.

ഩരു

Marshall jumped as the front door opened and Bubbles leapt up from the sofa, barking. He followed the dog out into the hallway, where Jess absent-mindedly stroked Bubbles as the puppy bounced around her.

'What happened? Did you find Steve?'

Jess's eyes focussed and she gave Marshall a weak smile.

'He's at the police station,' she murmured.

'Are you all right?' Marshall held out his arms to her. She sank into him, holding him tight. He breathed in her hair, kissing the top of her head.

'No,' she murmured into his t-shirt. 'I'm not.'

They embraced a moment longer.

'Come on, I'll make you a cup of tea.'

Jess pulled away and took a deep breath.

'I might need something stronger.'

'We can do that. I can pick Ruby up from school, if you like.'

'No,' Jess said, a little too fast. Marshall couldn't help taking that a little personally, but she was so shaken that he realised it probably had little to do with him. Her friend's baby had just been taken by a woman who was supposed to be dead. Of course Jess was acting a little strangely.

'Fine. But I'll drive you to and from the school.'

Jess nodded, wandering into the kitchen, Bubbles

at her heels.

'Okay. Ruby'll like that. She likes your van.'

So do you, thought Marshall fondly. But that Jess wasn't in the house right now. He couldn't think that way. He filled the kettle and clicked it on as Jess took a seat at the table.

'Do you want to cancel our date tonight?' he asked.

'Do you mind?'

'Of course not. I can leave you and Ruby be, if you prefer?' He didn't want to offer it, but it was the right thing to do. Sometimes the right thing was an arse.

'No! No, please, stay with us.'

Marshall glanced at Jess's big eyes and his chest swelled, stomach twisting.

'Sure,' he told her, keeping the grin off his face.

Steve

'Hi, Steve.' Rick walked into the small room, nudging the door closed behind him with his hip. He set the two coffees on the table and sat opposite Steve.

Steve blinked at the drink in the disposable cup in front of him.

'Why am I here?' he croaked.

'You're not under arrest. I know this is an interview room. Sorry, it was all that was available right now. You're not being interviewed. I'm worried about you, Steve. You're going through something traumatic, that I don't think you fully understand, and I just don't want you left at home right now. Last night is testament to that. We can't have you wandering the streets. The officer on duty genuinely thought you were drunk and lost. Now, I know you weren't. I know you're in shock and I don't blame you. But I have a responsibility to protect you and not enough resources to do it properly. So, here we are. Drink the coffee. It'll help.'

Steve picked up the drink with a trembling hand and sipped. The heat was almost unbearable, burning at his throat and stomach. It took some of the pain away from his chest.

'When can I go home?' he asked, his voice

clearing.

'When I think you'll be safe,' Rick told him, cringing as he watched Steve sip again at the coffee. 'This isn't a run of the mill abduction as far as the police in this station are concerned. I can't just put out a request for all forces to keep an eye out for your wife.'

'Because you're a time traveller,' murmured Steve.

'Because she's from the future.' Rick nodded. 'She won't be coming back here, once I find her. You understand that, don't you? I think it would be best for you if you accept that your wife is dead. She died in that car accident. Although that was no accident.'

'Because she faked her death.' Steve stared down at the table. The words were in his voice, but he still couldn't believe them.

'Exactly,' Rick agreed. 'The man who hit her and thinks he killed her? That's real.'

Steve frowned. No. Rachel wouldn't have done that. Not his Rachel.

'How did she do it?'

'She's clever. As I'm sure you know. There's something quite intoxicating about an intelligent woman, don't you think?'

Steve's eyes flickered up to meet Rick's.

'The driver claimed there was a flash of light and so he stopped. He has no memory of hitting anything. I believe she did it in a panic, and didn't stop to think about the repercussions. Like, how much she'd miss her baby. So, here we are.' Rick sat back and sighed. 'Like I said, I think it better that you just believe your wife is dead. I'm going to get your baby back, arrest Rachel and that'll be the end of it. Okay?'

'Who did she kill?' Steve's voice broke again, but he had to know.

'I don't think it's important,' Rick said gently. Steve looked up at him, balling his hands into tight fists.

'It is to me.'

Rick sighed again, harder this time.

'A friend of hers. An old school friend.'

Steve frowned.

'Why?'

'I can't tell you, Steve.'

Steve shook his head.

'I don't believe you.'

Rick shrugged.

'You don't have to. It is what it is. All you need to concern yourself with is your son. I'm going to get him back. And I have a plan for that, but I need to know you're not going to do anything stupid. Drink up, I'll take you home.'

21

Erica shifted in the driver's seat, her work shirt stifling her. With an exasperated sigh, she turned down the radio—the voices were beginning to grate on her—and she stared at Steve's front door. Why wasn't anyone home yet? Jess had told her he'd been arrested, but how long could they possibly keep him when they had nothing to charge him with and no staff to look after him? She was close to getting angry when a car pulled up behind her.

Erica ducked down a little in her seat, watching everything from the rear view mirror. The car was a Ford with a shiny look about it that suggested the police. Erica's stomach jolted as Rick got out of the driver's side. He looked up at the townhouses and stretched his back. At first, she had put her strange feelings towards him down to his attractiveness but as she watched him now, this time travelling detective, she wondered if it had more to do with whatever it was that allowed her to sense spirits. She thought that was a skill honed during her childhood, spending time in her grandmother's house which had been home to a number of ghosts. Her grandmother had always scoffed at that. It wasn't a talent to learn, she'd told Erica on a number of occasions. It was something you were born with. Something in your blood.

Erica studied Rick in the rear view mirror. Was that all this was? Erica picking up the same energy around Rick as Eolande and Alfie had picked up around Rachel? Erica glanced at herself in the wing mirror. If that were the case, why hadn't she felt this way around Rachel?

Steve got out of the passenger side and Erica ducked down further. The two men wandered over to Steve's front door, Rick letting Steve go first, speaking to him. Steve didn't look like he was listening. His eyes were down and distant, the very vision of a broken man.

As they opened the front door, Erica took a deep breath, held it and opened the car door. Steve walked into the house, oblivious, but Rick heard her. There was a pause as they stared at one another. Rick was the one to break the silence.

'What are you doing here?' he asked gently, giving Steve a cursory glance before moving towards Erica. She closed the car door behind her and swallowed.

'We're involved in this too. Jess and me,' she told him, her voice smaller than she'd have liked. 'I want to help.'

'You want to help? The best thing you can do is to stay away.' Rick stopped a few steps away from her.

'Why? Steve's all on his own. He needs people here with him.'

That made Rick hesitate and Erica knew she was right. Still, he shook his head.

'No. Go home, stay away. That's the best thing.'

'For who?' Erica narrowed her eyes and took a step forward. 'Who is that best for? Steve? Me? You?'

Rick sighed and glanced back to the open front door. Erica couldn't see Steve, but that didn't mean that Rick couldn't.

'Ricci, please.' Rick took a step closer and stopped himself. 'We can't be around each other. Not now. Not like this. It's going to screw everything up, if it hasn't already.'

'Screw what up?' Erica threw up her arms. She was so tired of him talking in riddles.

'Us. Our future,' said Rick. Erica's heart pounded, silently urging him on while scared of what he might say. 'We don't meet this way, Ricci. Not that I remember. I've already changed so much by coming here. Who knows what. And if we aren't together anymore… I can't risk this more than I already have. Please. Stay away.' Rick turned and walked up to the front door.

Erica's eyes stung with tears.

'Then you shouldn't have come here,' she called after him.

Rick stopped and turned back to her.

'I know.'

'I don't know you. I didn't ask this to happen.' Erica strode towards him. 'But Steve asked us to help him and that's what we're going to do.'

Rick looked her up and down and gave her an easy smile. Erica didn't know whether to kiss or punch him.

'You don't have to help, Ricci. I've got this.' Rick's eyes had softened and Erica could truly believe that one day she would fall in love with this man, if she hadn't already.

'You know where Rachel is?' she asked, crossing her arms over her chest. Rick glanced down at her arms and then back to her eyes.

'I have some ideas.'

'And what happens to Steve when you go after her?'

Rick rubbed the stubble on his chin and sighed. All of her anger fled and Erica tightened her grip on herself.

'Fine. You'll stay here and look after Steve. But that's it. And we're not talking anymore.'

'Fine. Great. Thank you.'

She thought he might say something more, but instead he continued into the house. She followed a few steps behind.

'Where do you think Rachel is?' she asked.

Rick held up a finger and she stopped walking.

'We're not talking anymore, remember?'

'Right. Because you're from the future, where we're a couple.'

'You're my wife.'

Erica opened and closed her mouth.

'We get married?' she asked after a moment's thought.

'We're not talking anymore.' Rick walked into the kitchen where Steve sat at the table. Erica followed.

'You think Rachel went back to your time?'

Rick gave Erica a warning look. She shut her mouth and sat at the table, turning her attention to Steve.

'What can I do to help?' she asked.

Steve didn't respond. Erica sat back in her chair. She was no good at this. This was more Jess's area of expertise. 'Shall I call Jess?' she offered. Steve blinked but said nothing. 'Once for yes,' Erica muttered to herself, pulling out her phone and bringing up Jess's number.

The phone rang and rang. After a while, Erica admitted defeat and hung up.

'She's probably picking Ruby up,' she said. 'I'll try again later. Tea? How about a cup of tea?'

Steve gave a single nod.

Thank God, thought Erica, standing up a little too fast. Something to do that would keep her hands busy. She began pottering around the kitchen, working out where the cups were. She brushed up against Rick, leaning back against the counter. He moved and she found the cups in the cupboard behind him.

'Do you want one?' she asked.

'Please.' Rick was staring down at something on his right wrist, next to a gold watch. He fiddled with it.

'What's that?'

'No talking,' said Rick.

'But—'

'Nope.'

'Is that what helps you travel through time?'

Rick looked up straight into Erica's eyes. The cool blue sunk into her and for a moment she forgot what she was doing.

'Milk, one sugar, please,' said Rick pointedly, jolting her back.

'Right. Right.' She went back to the kettle.

'Steve?' Rick sat opposite Steve at the table, where Erica had been sitting. 'Steve?'

Steve glanced up at Rick.

'Have you noticed anything changing around here? Any shadows moving, any pictures that have changed, anything in a different place to where you left it?'

Steve blinked and shook his head.

'I don't think so.' He scrunched his face up. 'No.'

'Good,' said Rick.

Erica pressed her mouth shut, desperate to ask why.

'Why?' asked Steve. Erica exhaled in a rush.

'If your wife has gone into the past, she'll likely have changed things in the timeline. Something will be off. It could be as little as a different kettle being purchased.' Rick gestured to the kettle as Erica poured water into the cups. 'Or as significant as you living in a different house.'

'Would he know that? If we were in a different house to the one we started off in? We wouldn't remember the old house, surely,' said Erica, placing their tea on the table.

'There's always an adjustment period. It often feels like déjà vu.'

'Oh. That's…not comforting at all.' Erica leaned back against the worktop and sipped her tea. Rick smiled at her, lingering a moment.

'I haven't noticed anything,' said Steve. 'But I've been in a police cell since last night.'

'All right.' Rick took a gulp of tea. 'Point made.'

'I don't mean to be rude,' said Erica. 'But if you do find her, what are you going to do? You came here to find her and look how that turned out.'

Rick raised an eyebrow at her.

'Well, it's nice to have you on my side.'

Erica felt her cheeks begin to burn. She shouldn't have said that, but no, it was a good point. She stood by the question, so she said nothing, working hard to maintain eye contact with the detective. Rick took another gulp, screwing his eyes shut against the heat as he swallowed.

'I maybe wasn't as quick as I should have been. But that stops now. I'm going to grab Rachel, get Steve his son back and you're going to stay here and look out for Steve while I'm gone. I'll come back, give you the baby and then I'm gone. Out of here. And you won't see me until we meet properly. Hopefully,' Rick added quietly. Erica took a deep breath, wondering which bit troubled her the most, the not seeing him again or the way he'd said "hopefully" under his breath. 'Right.' Rick slammed his hands down on the table, making both Erica and Steve jump. 'I'm going to have a quick look around, check nothing is out of place, then I'll be going. Stay here,' he told Steve. 'Stay with Ricci, whatever happens. And I'll bring your son back to you. Okay? But, remember what we talked about. Forget about your wife. Maybe talk to Ricci about the new life you could start.' Rick gave Erica a slight nod but she just pulled a face at him. What a thing to tell the poor man.

'Okay.' Erica sat in the seat Rick had vacated, placing her cup of tea gently on the table next to Rick's empty cup. Her fingers lingered.

She listened to Rick leaving the kitchen behind her, his footsteps on the stairs and allowed herself a moment to imagine never seeing him again. 'I might just give Jess another call,' she said.

'She'll be home with her family. With her girl,' said Steve, head hanging low. 'She's busy.'

'Yeah, but she'll want to know about this.' Erica studied Steve. 'She's found someone, you know. I remember when she first became a single mum, she didn't think she'd ever find someone who would have her, her daughter and all her baggage. But she's found someone. You should have seen her.

The grin on her face. She's happy and excited, and he's lovely. You'll get that. When you're ready. You'll find someone else who will love you and Joe, who will make you feel excited again.'

Steve's eyes were watery, tears brimming but not falling, as he looked up to meet Erica's gaze. She swallowed at the sight of them, at the red puffiness around his eyes in such contrast against his pale skin. The man looked exhausted.

'If I get Joe back,' he murmured.

'You will. Don't you worry about that.' Erica hoped she was right, sending a silent prayer out into the universe.

22

Jess pulled out her phone just as it stopped ringing. It was Erica. On autopilot, Jess went to call her back and then stopped herself. No. She didn't want Erica's opinion right now. She wouldn't approve of where she was, but this was something Jess had to do. Bubbles followed her closely, pausing far too often to sniff a patch of grass.

Jess paused at Erica's grandfather's grave in the cemetery, giving the gravestone a small, respectful smile. The man had never had a bad word for her, even when she'd discovered she was pregnant, even when she'd broken up with Paul. He'd given only encouragement and even a secret offer of money to help her put a roof over her head, food in her daughter's belly and find a future for her and Ruby. Jess had loved him like he was her own, but now wasn't the time to reminisce.

'I'll come back,' she whispered to him. Sat beside her, watching the flies zoom past intently, Bubbles gave an excited bark. Jess ruffled her ears.

Moving on, towards the secret garden, Jess pushed open the gate and stepped inside, pulling it closed behind them.

The silence was immediate. The roar of traffic disappeared, leaving only bird song and the rustle of leaves as the light breeze moved through them. It was peaceful and serene, except for the eyes Jess could have sworn were watching her through the trees.

Bubbles lifted her head and growled. Then there were only shadows, the sinister feeling of being watched somehow lifted. Jess glanced down at Bubbles who was hesitant. The dog looked up at Jess and gave an uncertain wag of her tail.

'Come on,' Jess told her in a hushed voice. She led Bubbles over the clearing full of long meadow grass, to the bench, where she sat. Bubbles, seemingly now comfortable, went to the end of her lead and began investigating, snorting loudly when a piece of grass went up her nose. Jess watched her half-heartedly, her main focus was on the tree line.

After ten minutes of nothing happening other than Jess having to prise open Bubbles' mouth a number of times to pull out sticks and leaves, Jess wandered over to the trees. Bubbles followed.

'Eolande?' Jess called softly. 'Are you there? I don't know the protocol for this.' She looked down at Bubbles, as if she would know. 'I'm sorry,' Jess continued to the trees. 'But I need to speak to you. Please?' There was a long pause. 'Eolande? It's about that woman, who you said was not from our time. Well, she's taken the baby. Okay, so it's her baby, but she's run off with him. We don't know where they are. Steve is devastated. That's the baby's dad. Please, Eolande. I just want a little help to find her. That's all.'

Jess waited in the silence.

Bubbles gave a growl, moving back against Jess's leg. Jess looked from her to where the puppy was looking. Alfie leaned against a tree off to their left, examining his fingernails.

'Does it have to be Eolande or will anyone do?'

Jess stiffened and Bubbles began barking at the man. Alfie laughed at the dog. As he lazily approached them, Jess's fingers gripped the lead. She shouldn't have come. Why did she come here? She took a step backwards, pulling Bubbles with her.

'Would you like me to silence her?' Alfie asked, staring straight into Bubbles' eyes as the dog barked frantically.

'No!' Jess dipped down, wrapping her arms around Bubbles and hushing her. The puppy buried her head into Jess with a whimper. 'Is Eolande not here?'

'She's here.'

'Can I talk to her?'

Alfie gave her a slow smile.

'Why not talk to me?'

Jess looked back to the trees behind Alfie.

'Can you help?'

'Maybe. What do you want?'

Jess considered her options. She could just walk away now. Take Bubbles and go home and forget all about this. But she'd come this far, and Alfie or Eolande were bound to tell Minerva about her visit. She was already in trouble, she might as well see what she could get out of it.

'Do you know where Rachel Green is?'

That slow smile stayed on Alfie's face.

'The time traveller?'

'Yes.'

'No.'

Jess sighed.

'Okay, well, great. Is there any way you can find out? She's taken Steve's baby.'

'Who is also her baby.'

'Yes, but without talking to Steve about it. She just swooped in and took him.'

'Her own baby.'

Jess huffed.

'It's abduction, whether the mother or father took the baby,' she snapped. 'Things like that need discussing. You don't just grab your baby and zip into a different time without talking about it first. I should know.'

Alfie raised an eyebrow. Jess wasn't going to give him the satisfaction of explaining herself on that one. She knew what she meant. 'Plus, she's wanted by the police. We don't know if the baby's safe,' she added.

Alfie nodded.

'You know, the fae are well known for taking children. We take your babes to bring up as our own. Or perhaps we seduce your kind, lure them into our world to create our own babes.'

Jess gritted her teeth.

'What are you getting at?'

Alfie shrugged.

'You're asking abductors where the abductor has gone. There is irony there.'

'You knew she was a time traveller when Minerva and Erica didn't. Is there no way you can tell where she's gone?' Jess wanted to get back on track but immediately regretted bringing up Erica's name. Alfie's eyes brightened at the mention, the smile that seemed to be permanently plastered to his face broadening.

'Maybe if Erica came here and asked me.'

There was something iridescently charming about Alfie in that moment that made Jess both shiver with revulsion and feel drawn to him at the same time.

'No. She's not here. She won't be here. Can you help me or not?'

Bubbles was losing patience. She squirmed away from Jess and Alfie, crying. Jess positioned herself between her puppy and Alfie, and gave Alfie a defiant look.

'I can't. That's not quite in my skillset. But Eolande might be able to.'

'Then can I see her?' Jess shouted. She hadn't meant to shout, but it was either that or scream.

Alfie held up his hands in submission. He blew Bubbles a kiss, making the dog bark and whimper, and then disappeared back into the trees.

When he was gone, Jess backed up and lowered herself to put an arm around the dog.

'I'm sorry, Bubs. We shouldn't have come here. I'm sorry. We'll go. In a second. We'll go home, okay?' she whispered, rubbing the puppy's ears as Bubbles cried.

'No, you shouldn't have come. But humans are so prone to mistakes, this one can be forgiven.'

Jess moved between the fae and her dog. Eolande watched without expression. She stood tall and beautiful, watching Jess. Bubbles gave a small whimper but didn't bark, instead cowering behind Jess's legs. Jess had to get her out of there.

'I'll make it quick, and I'll be gone.' And you'll never catch me doing this ever again, Jess thought. 'Rachel Green, the time traveller. Do you know where she is?'

'I can find her.'

Jess's heart lightened.

'You can? Well, can you then? Please?' she

asked, the words coming out in a rush.

'No.'

'What?'

'It is not my place to do such a thing. The abduction of this child does not concern us.'

'What?' Jess squealed. 'But…I…Okay.' She looked down at Bubbles, trying to regain her composure. 'Why did you come to the house in the first place? Surely that didn't concern you either?'

'That was a favour for Minerva. Nothing else.'

'Well, this is a favour for Minerva too.'

Eolande crossed her arms.

'Do not put words in my lover's mouth.'

Jess hesitated, trying not to think about Minerva and Eolande being lovers.

'Please,' she said. 'Please. I don't know what else to do.'

'That is also not my concern. Is there anything else?' Eolande glanced behind Jess to Bubbles.

'But—'

'If there is nothing else, then please leave here.' Eolande turned and wandered back into the trees.

Jess opened her mouth to call after her but no words came. The anger was a tight ball in her gut, making her trip over what word to use. "Oi" and "hey" came to mind, but she knew nothing good would come of them. She gripped Bubbles' lead and went to leave the garden.

'Goodbye, Erica Murray's friend.' Alfie's voice floated to them but Jess didn't turn around. She rushed from the garden, through the gate, Bubbles running on ahead and pulling her, eager to be away from the fae.

They stopped at Erica's grandfather's grave so Jess could catch her breath.

'Worthless, damn fae,' she muttered before snapping her mouth shut. What if they'd heard? She freely admitted that she was clueless about the fae, she had no idea what they were capable of. Before coming, she'd promised herself that she wouldn't tell Minerva or Erica about this visit, but now she felt compelled to tell Erica. If only to warn her away from Alfie. Surely Erica wouldn't do something so reckless and stupid as to give in to his advances, no matter how strong the pull of his charm. Jess groaned.

Then she yelped and jumped away, wheeling round to face whatever attacker had just placed a hand on her shoulder.

There was no one there.

Breathing hard, searching around, Jess could see no one. Then, Bubbles began to bark. Not the frantic fearful barking she'd given to the fae, but an unsure, protective bark. Jess watched her as Bubbles barked and barked at the empty space next to the gravestone. A chill washed over her.

'Okay, Bubs. Time to go home, I think. Ruby and Marshall are waiting for us.' Jess welcomed the warmth that those two names gave her, thawing the chill of the cemetery. A family was waiting for her at home. Right now, she needed them. She needed to hold Ruby and to be held by Marshall. Jess pulled Bubbles away, back towards the car, trying to keep calm.

'Come on, Bubs. Back home for something to eat and a nap for you.'

Bubbles came easily, trotting and pulling Jess towards the car, just as eager to get home and away from this place. Jess got her safely in the car before slumping in the driver's seat and turning on the ignition.

She jumped as her phone rang, and Bubbles gave out a solitary bark. With trembling fingers, Jess answered the phone.

'Hey, Ric.' There was a shake in her voice that she just didn't have the energy to hide.

'Hey. Are you okay?'

'Not really. Are you?'

'Sort of. Where are you?'

'Erm…'

'Can you come to Steve's?'

Jess sat upright.

'Steve's? Why? Are you there?'

'The detective is going to get Rachel back. I have to stay here with Steve and I'm out of my depth,' Erica whispered those last words. 'Can you get here?'

'Sure. I need to pop home first.'

'Where are you?'

'Erm… When do you need me?'

'About half an hour ago.'

'Okay. I'm on my way. I just need to check if Marshall can look after Ruby.'

'If not, I'll call my mum. I'm sure she'll understand and won't mind. Let me know.'

'Okay. Speak in a bit.' Jess hung up before Erica could ask any more questions. She took a deep breath, staring straight ahead at nothing. Bubbles barked again, snapping her out of it.

'Right. Right. Here we go.'

Slowly, Jess pulled out of the cemetery, back onto the road and back, it seemed, into the real world.

Steve

Steve stared at nothing. The table stared back at him but he didn't see it. His whole body was numb, his mind quiet and still. Above his head, he could hear Rick opening and closing drawers and cupboard doors. He was in Steve and Rachel's bedroom. Steve listened to the footsteps as Rick moved into the nursery. He blinked, his eyelids were itching, his eyes so dry. He wished he could cry, just to give them some relief, but the tears wouldn't come anymore.

Silently, his mind was putting the pieces together. Rachel wasn't coming back, he knew that as a fact, deep in his gut. Teetering on the edge of that thought was the idea that he might not see Joe again.

All of the passionate and hurried conversations during their first flurry of love played out before him. How reserved she'd been when he'd asked her questions. Where did her parents live? When could he meet them? He never did meet them. That made sense now. He had questioned over and over why she didn't want anyone from her family at their wedding. Why hadn't it bothered him more? He'd been a fool.

Steve put his head in his hands, elbows on the table. Still, fresh tears wouldn't come.

Rick came down the stairs and into the kitchen. He didn't speak but his movements filled the silence in the room. Steve was aware that the detective and Erica were exchanging looks. It didn't help that there seemed to be a connection between them. Something invisible but strong. Strong enough for Steve to feel it despite not being able to feel hunger or pain or even the grief that he knew should be wracking his body.

'She's in the future,' said Rick, fiddling with that thing on his wrist again. 'Nothing seems out of place or much changed so I don't think she's in the past. She wouldn't want to risk any big changes, she wouldn't risk not having Joe, right?' Rick looked at Erica for confirmation but she just shrugged.

'Right,' murmured Steve, not looking up but watching them from the corner of his eye.

'Right. So, I'll pop back to my timeline and check with my colleagues. See what they have. I'll check at her parents and all her usual hangouts, see what I can find. I won't be long.'

Erica nodded and looked at Steve.

'Jess will be here soon,' she told him.

Good, thought Steve. That would make things less awkward, even if just a little. Jess would know what to say. She'd know what to do.

'Good. Stay right here. I'll be back.'

Erica snapped her head round to Rick and smirked. He gave her a warning look.

'Who did she kill?' asked Steve, unable to contain the question as his mind fiddled with that piece of the puzzle. Both Rick and Erica turned to him.

'What?' asked Rick, avoiding the question.

'The friend she killed. What was their name?'

Steve looked up and directly into Detective Cavanagh's eyes.

'You really don't need to know that. And it's an open case, I can't tell you,' said Rick, turning his attention back to the device on his wrist. 'I'm sorry, but you can't know that. I'll be back as soon as I can.'

'Well, you're a time traveller. Surely you'll be back in a second?' Erica asked, watching him. Rick gave her a small smile that made Steve look away and back to the table.

'It doesn't quite work that way. It isn't quite that neat.' Rick looked at Steve. 'Take care of one another.'

The light above their heads flickered on for a moment. Then there was a flash of light. Erica looked away but Steve didn't feel the need. He blinked a few times to rid himself of the coloured dots dancing in his vision and then he sank back into himself as Erica made yet another round of tea.

23

Erica sat at Steve's kitchen table, consumed by the silence. The more she tried to think of something to say, a conversation starter, anything to bring sound back into the world, the more her mind went blank. She'd made them both fresh cups of tea. Steve hadn't touched his while she had already finished hers.

'Who did she kill?' she asked eventually, her voice small but sounding loud in the vacuum of the kitchen.

Steve stirred and glanced up at her.

'Her friend. An old school friend.'

Erica raised her eyebrows.

'Why do you want to know who they are?' She rubbed a spot on the table top. An indentation, likely from where something had been dropped.

Steve looked back to the table.

'I don't know.'

'Rick, erm, Detective Cavanagh seemed to suggest he was only from, what? Ten, thirteen years in the future. That means that there's a Rachel here in our time.'

Steve frowned.

'Is that why you wanted to know?' Erica asked. 'You want to find her friend and warn them? I can see why Detective Cavanagh wouldn't tell you. It'd be heroic but who knows what it would change.'

Steve met her gaze.

A knock at the door made them both jump.

'That's probably Jess.' Erica stood up slowly. She hoped it was Jess.

Jess gave her a sad smile as she opened the door. The relief on Erica's face must have been obvious.

'I'm here,' said Jess with some forced enthusiasm.

'Everything okay?' Erica asked, stepping back to allow her in.

'Sort of.' Jess seemed about to say something but she stopped.

'Is Marshall looking after Ruby and the puppy?'

'Hmm.' Jess avoided looking at her. Erica watched her friend go into the kitchen and greet Steve. There was something Jess wasn't telling her. She never had been good at keeping secrets, especially from Erica. She followed Jess into the kitchen and found her friend sat in her seat. She watched Jess pull her laptop from her bag.

'Cuppa?' she asked.

'Please.'

Erica turned her back on the table, once again going to the kettle. She was beginning to feel she was developing a relationship with the device. The worn silence settled back on the room. Erica sighed.

'What are you doing?' she asked as Jess booted up the laptop.

'I thought I'd get started on our new business. While we wait. I hope that's okay?' Jess asked Steve who gave the faintest of nods.

'Okay' Erica frowned. 'I was just telling Steve...' Erica stared at the cups. What had she been telling Steve? 'Oh, that there must be a Rachel already in this present. If a Rachel came back to here, and Rick, erm, Detective Cavanagh, is only from ten years or so in the future.'

'Right.' Jess was preoccupied with her laptop.

'So,' Erica continued, looking at Steve. 'Why don't you find Rachel. The now Rachel. Start again. Fall in love. I mean, she'll be something like ten years younger, but still. Maybe then she won't...' Erica drifted off, hoping she didn't have to finish that sentence.

Jess looked up, glancing between Steve and Erica.

'Won't what?' she asked.

Erica twisted her lips.

'Kill her friend,' murmured Steve. He sat back. He was still staring into space but at least he was upright now.

Jess's eyes widened and she slowly turned back to Erica. Erica gave her a small shrug. What else could she do?

'It's an option,' she told Steve. 'You couldn't tell her Joe was hers, but you'd know. Maybe on some level, she'd know. Of course, you couldn't really tell her anything about Joe's mum. And in hindsight, it would be incredibly messy. How old was she? She might be too young in this timeline. Probably just best to put it all in the past.' Erica quickly made the tea and handed out the cups, plonking herself in a chair and looking to Jess for help.

'I think you probably do need a plan,' said Jess slowly, turning from Erica to Steve. 'What will you do when Joe's back? Where will you go?'

Steve didn't reply.

'You own this house, don't you?' Jess continued.

'You could sell. Prices are good at the moment. Sell and use the money to start a new life. You could go anywhere. Where would you like to go?'

Steve didn't respond but he appeared to be thinking.

'I could save her,' he murmured eventually.

Erica groaned inwardly. Where was her time machine, she wondered. So she could go back and stop herself saying all that rubbish.

'No, Steve. Remember? We decided that would be a bad idea. Plus, I don't think Detective Cavanagh would approve. You'd be changing everything,' she told him.

'For the better.' Steve turned to her and his eyes focussed. It was eerie enough to render Erica momentarily speechless.

'But what if her friend's death means something wonderful happens later on down the line?' Erica thought furiously.

'They could be an organ donor,' Jess offered.

'Jess is right.' Erica could almost see Rick's disappointment in her, and the thought made her sick. 'Rick is right. You need to start a new life. Forget about Rachel.'

Steve gave a small shrug and went back to staring at the table. Erica turned to Jess.

'Can I help with anything?' she asked, her voice a little too high-pitched.

'You mean, with the business?'

Erica nodded.

'There's loads you could do.' Jess glanced at Steve. 'But maybe now isn't the right time. I'm just researching time travel. Feel a bit useless being left behind.'

'Yeah.' Erica joined Steve in staring down at the

table. There had to be something they could be doing. When she looked up, Steve was staring at Jess's laptop.

'Can you look her up? Rachel?'

Jess caught Erica's eye over the top of the computer.

'I don't know.'

'She probably gave you a fake name,' Erica told him.

'What if she didn't?'

'Got any biscuits in this house?' Erica scraped her chair back and went hunting through the cupboards. Where was Rick? Why wasn't he back yet?

'I could just do a quick search,' said Steve.

'Nope.' Jess moved her laptop away from him. 'Steve, that way lies madness. I'm telling you.' She wrapped her arms around the computer as Steve tried to pull it towards him. 'Get back and take a deep breath. Think about what you're doing. This isn't just about finding your wife. You're talking about finding the woman who killed someone, a friend. A woman who lied to you. A woman who ran away rather than face up to what she did. A woman who stole your baby boy from you.'

'He's her baby boy too,' said Steve, but he sounded unsure. He sat back, looking lost.

'I think you need to stop thinking so much about Rachel being a woman you love and I think you need to focus on being angry with her. Where's the anger, Steve? She faked her own death. She haunted you, for crying out loud! She gave no thought to how you were feeling or how her actions would affect you. Why aren't you angry about that?'

Steve's jaw firmed but then he relaxed, his eyes

filling with tears as his chin twitched.

'Why did this have to happen?' he managed to say before the first tears fell.

'Oh, Steve.' Jess moved over to put an arm around him. 'I'm so sorry.' She held him for a moment as he cried.

Erica found a roll of tissue and pulled off some sheets, handing them to Steve. He blew his nose, wiping roughly at his eyes.

'How did you meet her?' Erica asked, placing a plate of biscuits in the middle of the table. If they were going to have to wait for Rick, they'd do it with some relative comfort. Steve gave a small smile. Jess and Erica helped themselves to the biscuits.

'During a storm. I was walking through town, down by the water. It was so dark, even though it was only about two in the afternoon. It wasn't quite raining yet but there was thunder. And then there was a flash of lightning. I stopped because it made me jump and then there she was, walking around the corner, looking cold and lost.'

Erica and Jess both paused in their eating, Erica with the biscuit near her mouth, ready to bite. Jess swallowed her mouthful.

'So, there was a flash of light and then she appeared?' she said gently.

Steve heaved a sob.

'That's what happens, isn't it? Did she disappear in a flash of light with Joe?'

Erica nodded.

'She'd only just arrived and there you were,' breathed Jess. 'It's actually quite romantic.'

'I bought her a coffee. The rain came while we were talking. Except...' Steve took a deep breath.

'She wasn't talking much. I would ask her questions and she would turn the question back on me.'

'You couldn't have known,' Erica told him. 'How could you? No one could have ever guessed.'

Steve nodded once.

'The signs were there though,' he murmured.

'Oh, they always are.' Jess brushed away his words with a gesture of her hand. 'When me and Paul were together, all the signs were there. I just didn't see them until we broke up. Sometimes, you ignore the signs because actually, you just want to be happy and in love. Or, in my case, not a single mum. Then, when reality hits, you feel like an idiot for ignoring them. Except, you're not an idiot. You're human. That's all. And for those years, you were happy. That's what you need to remember.'

'She must have loved you,' agreed Erica. 'She stuck around. She stayed with you when the world and time was her oyster. She stayed with you. She married you.' Erica stopped. She was in danger of feeling sorry for Rachel. The woman had found her new life and a new happiness, until something had made her throw it all away.

'When did things start to change?' she asked Steve. 'How soon before she faked her death?'

Steve shrugged and finally took a sip of what must have been lukewarm tea.

'I don't know. Nothing changed. Except… Oh, except that she started refusing to leave the house. She became paranoid. I thought she had post-natal depression. I mentioned it to the midwife. It started in the hospital. The day after Joe was born.'

Erica wondered when Rick had shown up. Had she seen him around the time she gave birth? Or had her maternal instincts been enough to make her act so differently? Erica couldn't believe Rachel had faked her death without good reason.

'She could have had post-natal depression,' said Jess. 'I did. It's common. Babies turn your life upside down. And that's when it's a normal life. Who knows what Rachel went through.'

'I know I should be angry, but I still love her,' murmured Steve, as if to himself.

'Of course you do,' said Jess gently, placing a hand on his.

Erica checked the time on her phone. Where the hell was Rick?

24

It was coming up to two hours since Detective Cavanagh had left for the future. The silence had returned to the kitchen but it was easier now. Erica was on her phone, although Jess couldn't see what she was doing. Steve was on his second cup of tea and reached for a biscuit. Jess stared at her laptop screen and the articles about time travel she'd pulled up. None of them were helpful.

'Oh.'

Jess looked up at Erica. She'd put her phone down. 'When you arrived, you looked like you needed to say something. Is everything okay at home? With Ruby and Marshall?'

'Hmm? Oh, yeah. They're fine.' Jess kept her head down. Was she going to tell Erica? She wasn't sure yet. She needed more time to think.

'What was it then?'

Jess paused, allowing the silence to fill the gaps and hoping that Erica might forget what she'd been asking. 'Jess?'

No such luck. Jess sat up and fidgeted. The memory of Alfie's smile and haunting eyes returned to her. She had to tell Erica. She had to warn her away.

'Well, and I know you're not going to like this and I know I'll be in trouble, but, well, I went to the cemetery today.'

Steve looked between the women, chewing on his biscuit.

'My cemetery? Gran's cemetery?' Erica asked, her voice flat, her eyes dark. Jess nodded. 'Why?'

'Because Detective Cavanagh wouldn't let me help and I needed to help, and Eolande was the one who told us Rachel wasn't from our time, so...' Jess drifted off.

'You went looking for Eolande?' Erica pushed her empty cup away.

'Maybe.' Jess felt herself tense, as if Erica would jump across the table to her and she needed to spring away.

'Did you find her?'

Jess nodded and Erica closed her eyes.

'Gran's going to kill you.'

'I know.'

'And then she's going to kill me.'

'I'm sorry. I wasn't going to tell you but—'

'Eolande will have told her, I bet.'

'But—'

'She didn't hurt you, did she? They're dangerous, Jess. You can't just go wandering in there alone.'

'Actually, I had Bubbles with me. But—'

'Was Bubbles any use?'

'She protected me. She was actually terrified of them. Oh, and she—'

'Them?'

Jess stopped and sighed.

'Alfie turned up.'

The colour went from Erica's cheeks.

'What happened?'

'Okay, but you have to let me talk. No interruptions.'

'Go on.'

Jess took a deep breath.

'Eolande wouldn't see me but Alfie came and talked to me. Then Eolande showed up. Turns out they're both useless and neither would help. But! I need to tell you a couple of things.'

'Okay.'

'First of all, that Alfie is scary. He said he'd only help me if you were there. He's creepy as all hell, Ric, but he's charming as all hell too. My grandmother would say he's the devil. Please, please don't have anything to do with him.'

Erica nodded.

'What's the other thing?'

She's not listening to me, thought Jess. Not really. Had she already made her mind up about Alfie? If she had, Jess hoped she'd made the right decision.

'Bubbles. She was barking at all sorts in that cemetery. Not always her scared bark. Sometimes just her protective bark. It made me wonder.'

'What?'

'Maybe she can see dead people.'

Erica smiled.

'Dogs are supposed to be sensitive to these things. Our dogs don't bark like that, but maybe that's because they're used to it.'

'Right. Exactly. But Bubbles isn't. Maybe we could take her with us on jobs. She can be a team member.'

Erica grinned.

'Brilliant! We'll need a job first though.'

'What's this?' asked Steve.

'We're setting up that paranormal investigation

agency I told you about,' Jess said. 'So we can help people the way we're helping you. Well, no, the way we would have helped you, had there actually been a ghost.'

Steve gave a weak smile.

'I can't believe I thought the house was haunted.' He gave a small laugh.

That was something, thought Jess. He's laughing. It's not much, but it's a start.

'It would have been so much easier if it had just been a ghost,' Erica pointed out.

'What would we have done?' Jess asked. She couldn't believe they'd gotten this far without her asking what they'd do when they encountered an actual ghost.

'Find us a job and I'll tell you,' said Erica.

'You're on.' Jess opened up a new tab on her laptop and tapped away at the keyboard.

'How on earth do you search for paranormal investigation clients? Are there job boards?' Erica asked. Steve gave a chuckle. It sounded sad, but it was another laugh. The atmosphere in the kitchen was lightening. All they needed now was Rick to show up.

Jess paused to give the detective a chance, but nothing happened.

'I'm searching recent news stories and forums. I found a few sources the other night. There's bound to be someone local who's having trouble.'

'Is there?' Steve asked. 'I don't think I would have told anyone if I hadn't been worried about the state of my mind. If I hadn't had Joe to consider, I wouldn't have asked.'

At the mention of Joe's name, the oppressive atmosphere returned and Steve looked back down to the table. Jess kept searching, desperately trying to find a piece of information to bring the conversation back round.

'Oh, here we go. Someone posting in a forum about hearing strange noises. Not just in the night but during the day too. They can't figure it out. They're sure there's a logical explanation but their partner says it's the spirit of her dead uncle who used to live in the house. Turns out they moved into the house after his death.' Jess looked up at Erica. 'Sounds promising.'

'One's a sceptic. Means they might not be up for paying.'

'I suppose it depends on how much they don't want Uncle living with them,' said Jess.

'If there is a ghost and if it is the uncle.'

The light above their heads flickered on and made all three look up. The light went out.

'What was that?' Jess asked, the hair on her arms standing on end.

'A power surge?' Erica peered out of the window, but it was hard to tell if anyone else was having trouble.

The hallway lit up and then fell back into shadows.

Together, Jess and Erica left the kitchen and waited in the hallway.

Another crackle and a flash of light flickered through the living room doorway. Steve appeared beside them.

'It's the detective,' he said, wringing his hands. He pushed past them into the living room, standing by the doorway. Erica and Jess forced him inside a step so they could stand beside him. They left the centre of the room clear as that's where the ball of light was floating.

Jess glanced sideways at Erica, wondering if she could feel anything otherworldly from the ball. Jess couldn't, but it's unnatural state was leaving a trail of goosebumps down her arms. Sweat crept down her back and she had to unplaster her tongue from the roof of her mouth. She flexed her fingers, unable to keep her hands still.

The ball of light spread and there was a flash. Jess raised her hands to protect her eyes. When she lowered them, a blunt sound rushed from her mouth.

In the centre of the room was Rachel, bent over, breathing hard and playing with a device around her wrist.

'Rachel?'

Steve's voice broke through Jess's shock. Rachel looked up at Steve and gave out a whimper.

'Where's Joe?' he asked. Rachel shook her head. Jess went to move forward but Rachel held out a hand.

'Don't come closer. Don't. Stay there. I can't…' Rachel looked at Steve. 'He's safe. He'll always be safe,' she told him. 'I'll never let anything happen to him. I promise. I'll always keep him safe and loved. I have to go. He's coming.'

'You can't have him,' said Steve, his voice surprisingly steady. He took a step forward so he was level with Jess. 'Bring him back. Right now.'

'Don't come closer!' Rachel screeched. She gave the device on her wrist a smack. 'Don't come closer. I love you,' she shouted. Jess assumed that was meant for Steve.

The light was building from her wrist and Rachel straightened.

'No. No, no, no,' said Jess, stepping forward again.

'Don't come closer, I said,' Rachel warned her. Then she closed her mouth and studied Jess. 'You're her, aren't you?'

'What?' Jess screamed. 'Where's Joe? Where did you leave him?'

Rachel grinned.

'Bye.'

The light grew, encompassing everything around Rachel.

'No!'

Jess didn't think. If she'd stopped to think, she definitely wouldn't have done what she did next. Which was to jump forward, throwing herself at Rachel, as if somehow she could keep her there, in that room, in that time. Rachel's laughter filled her ears and then there was a rushing noise. The white light blinded her until it was all she could see.

'I'm glad you're coming with me,' said a voice. Rachel's. It was Rachel's voice. Thinking was becoming hard. Jess screwed her eyes shut against the bright light. It all hurt so much. Her stomach twisted, the biscuits and tea rising up in her throat. Her limbs felt long and heavy but she couldn't move them. There was pain at her shoulders, as if claws were digging in deep. Her mind screamed at her. She had to get out of this. She had to be free of whatever this was.

'I'm glad you're coming with me,' came Rachel's voice. 'He won't do anything with you there.'

Steve

Erica screamed as the white flash of light vanished and with it, Rachel and Jess. She ran forward into the room, dropping to her knees as if Jess was just on the other side of the carpet.

Steve stood motionless. The detective had failed. There was no Joe, there was no Rachel. There was just him and his grief, the pain that hung heavy over his body, and this house. This damned house. He turned away from Erica, leaving her kneeling on the carpet, breathing too hard and too fast. He returned to the kitchen, sat at the table and pulled Jess's laptop over. He would put the house on the market. He couldn't stay here. He would travel light. He wouldn't need much. Everything else he would leave. Rachel's clothes. Her meagre belongings that made so much sense now. The nursery. Joe's abandoned toys that he never got a chance to play with. He'd leave it all the way she had. He would start a new life. He'd move north. Maybe as far as Scotland.

He stared at the laptop, unsure of where to start. No, he shouldn't be starting with the computer. If he was going to start a new life, he needed to pack.

Steve made his way up the stairs. Erica had stopped screaming now. That was a mercy. She was mumbling and crying. She'd come to accept it soon, he thought. Jess was gone. Just like Rachel. Just like Joe.

He stopped in the bedroom. It was getting dark. He flicked on the light and found his old duffel bag. The one that predated his relationship with Rachel. Opening the drawers, he began to throw underwear and t-shirts inside. He found his jeans in the wardrobe and threw them in too. What else did he need?

Something made him look up. A flicker of movement. Had Erica followed him?

He stopped and listened. No. Her voice was coming from downstairs still. She was talking frantically on the phone. He wondered for a moment who she had called. The grandmother they'd brought that one time, Jess's new man, the police maybe? Steve smiled. The police couldn't do anything. Detective Cavanagh had proved that.

Another flash of movement. It was in the hallway. Steve wandered blindly through, memories of the baby monitor crackling returning to haunt him. Not a ghost, he thought. Surely not.

There, in the hallway, was a figure. A translucent woman. She didn't notice him, but why would she? She was holding a baby boy. She was holding Joe. Steve peered closely at the woman. It was Rachel, gurgling back at their son as she lifted him up. She spun round slowly, making baby Joe laugh. She looked away, smiling, although Steve couldn't see what she was smiling at. Then she looked directly at him. He stumbled backwards, but their eyes didn't connect. She wasn't looking at him, she was looking at someone else. She was smiling at someone who standing close to Steve. He moved quickly out of the way, but there was no one there.

'Rachel?' he murmured, approaching the figure. 'Rach?'

She couldn't hear him. She didn't react. Her mouth moved, forming words, but he couldn't hear her either.

This is it, he thought. I'm going mad. It's finally happened. Steve leaned against the wall, watching his happy wife and the shining eyes of their baby, as he slid down to sit on the floor.

The image flickered and then it was gone.

On the other side of the hallway, Erica watched from the stairs.

'It was Rachel,' said Steve, his tongue feeling too big for his mouth.

'I know. I saw her.'

'You did?' Steve flinched. He couldn't be going mad if Erica saw her too. 'Was she a ghost?'

'No. No, it seemed more like a hologram or something. Or…'

'What?'

Erica looked at him.

'A memory. Maybe this is what Rick meant about seeing something different in the house.'

'What do you mean?'

'She was looking at someone. I'm guessing you. Do you remember that happening? What you just saw?'

'No.'

'Then maybe that's what Rachel would have been doing right now if all of this hadn't happened. If you were still a happy, safe family.' Erica rubbed at her forehead and wiped the wetness from her cheeks. 'That's what she's doing. She's going back to change something. She's altering our present. That must be it. Why else would we see flashes of a time that hasn't happened. That can't happen.'

'She's putting it right,' said Steve, settling back down. He would let her. He would sit here and wait for her to put things right. He'd wait for her to come home.

He was aware of Erica watching him, but he didn't care. He wasn't moving.

'The only way to do that is to get rid of Rick,' murmured Erica. 'She can't.'

'She has to,' whispered Steve, closing his eyes.

25

Erica wondered if she would burst. She needed to do something but couldn't think what. She'd called home but no one had picked up. She'd called her mother's mobile, but it had gone to voicemail. They were busy. What if Rachel had already done the deed? Would she kill Rick? What about Jess? Erica couldn't stand still. She left Steve on the stairs and returned to the kitchen. There was Jess's laptop on the table. Was that any use? She didn't know. She walked back into the living room.

'Please come back, Rick,' she murmured. 'Please be okay.'

The living room light flickered. Erica wheeled round. 'Rick?'

The light went out with a clink and then back on before flickering again. Maybe it was Rachel coming back. Is that how it worked? Once Rachel had got rid of Rick, would everything just change or would she return, triumphant? Would she bring Jess back with her?

A beam of light appeared in the hallway. It was coming from the kitchen.

Erica made her way into the hall. There was the same ball of light, just beside the kitchen table. This time, Erica didn't approach. Above her, Steve shifted. She glanced up to find him watching, on his hands and knees, crouching low.

Please be Rick, she thought. If this was Rachel returning for some reason, Erica was outnumbered.

Light from the ball spread and there was the bright flash. Erica shielded her eyes and hesitated before lowering her arm. She wasn't sure she wanted to see who was there.

She gave a yelp when she peered at the figure, blinking back the splotches obscuring her vision. Rick looked around the kitchen, his gaze landing on Erica.

'Is she here?' he asked. Erica, tears filling her eyes, threw herself at him, wrapping her arms around his neck. He caught her, holding her tight.

'Rachel took Jess,' she managed to say into his shoulder. Rick's hold on her tightened.

'Are you okay?' he asked, his lips brushing her hair. She nodded. He was so warm and solid, she didn't want to let go. There was a smell of sweat and cigarette smoke about him that made her want to bury her nose into his neck to breath him in. Rick let her go and she forced herself to stand back.

'There was something strange, on the landing. We saw Rachel, but she wasn't really there. She was happy, holding the baby. It was like a ghost but it wasn't.'

Rick gave a singular nod.

'A memory. The timeline is starting to right itself. She's gone into the past.' He began fiddling with the thing on his wrist.

'Do you know where?'

Rick sighed. He didn't.

'I think she's gone back to get rid of you,' said Erica.

Rick looked up at her.

'So she can go back to how it was,' he said. 'Before she faked her own death.'

'Exactly. When did she see you? Steve says she changed after giving birth but that could have just been, you know, giving birth.'

Rick sat down at the kitchen table and took the last biscuit from the plate in the middle.

'I was at the hospital. I didn't think she'd seen me, but maybe she did.' Rick rubbed his face.

'She has Jess. We need to find her. Where do you think she went?'

'There are a number of places she could have gone. We'll check the hospital first though, yeah?'

'We?' Erica's stomach dropped.

'Oh, I think we're past all that saving the timeline crap, don't you? She's taken Jess and we've not only talked but we've touched. You might as well come with me. You can grab Jess while I deal with Rachel.'

'Travel into the past?'

Rick gave her a sweet smile.

'I won't let anything happen to you. Trust me.'

And she did trust him. She trusted him with her life. This strange man who she'd only met days ago, professing to being her future husband, who she knew nothing about. Erica grinned.

'What are we waiting for?'

'You can't.'

They both turned to Steve. 'She has to put this right,' he told them. 'We have to give her a chance to put this right. That's what will happen, isn't it?' He pointed up the stairs. 'If she does it, I'll get her back. Her and Joe. Happy again. Won't I?'

'She'll kill me,' Rick told Steve. 'I'm the price of that happiness.'

'It's worth it,' said Steve.

Erica couldn't breathe. What was he planning? There were no weapons in the house, but that didn't mean he wouldn't try and do them damage.

'You don't mean that,' she told him, her voice strained. 'You wouldn't want someone to die just so you could have Rachel back.'

Steve pulled a face.

'Rachel and Joe. My wife and child.'

That was harder for Erica to argue. She moved to stand between Steve and Rick.

'Well, this is my happiness, I think. And I'm not going to let you or Rachel take him.' Erica wasn't sure what Rick was doing behind her back, but she hoped he appreciated that.

Steve looked appalled.

'You came here to help me,' he told her.

'To help get rid of a ghost. I'm not going to let you kill someone.' Erica nearly laughed.

Steve shook his head.

The light above their heads flickered. Steve's eyes widened.

'No! Don't.'

'Every second we stay here is a second wasted,' came Rick's voice in Erica's ear. His arms slid around her waist and everything went white.

As the light faded back to colour and normality, the world span and Erica could no longer keep the insides of her stomach inside. She scrambled away from Rick and threw up, on all fours, her stomach cramping and heaving until she was spitting up bile.

Rick's fingers slid across her neck and he pulled the hair from her face, his other hand on her back. Erica was at once horrified and comforted. Her throat burning, her nose filled with vomit, Erica sat back and tried to hide her face from Rick. He only smiled at her and handed her a tissue.

'Sorry. It's always bumpy the first few times. You get used to it.'

Erica couldn't talk. She took the tissue and began to wipe at her face, blowing the bile from her nose. She looked around.

This world didn't look much different to the one they'd just left. They were in the city centre, at the hospital. She could see the familiar cityscape out of a nearby window, and the sterile but old corridors were a big giveaway. A nurse walked past and then jogged over when she spotted them.

'Are you okay? What happened? Did you leave your room?' She looked down at Erica's stomach and then at Rick. Erica frowned, putting a hand on her sore gut.

'Early days,' said Rick. 'Sorry about the mess.'

'Oh, that's no problem. Are you on a tour?'

'Yes, we didn't quite make it to the toilets. We got a bit lost.'

'I'll say. They're over there.' The nurse pointed in the opposite direction. 'Don't worry, it happens. We'll get this taken care of. Have a sit down,' she told Erica. 'I'll get you a cup of water.'

Erica, still reeling, could only nod and allowed Rick and the nurse to guide her to a small room with a couple of chairs and a desk. She sat on a chair and the nurse disappeared and reappeared in moments with a paper cup of water. 'Take it steady. Let me know if you need anything. How are you feeling?'

'I'm fine. Thank you. I'm sorry,' said Erica. The nurse smiled.

'How far along are you?'

Erica opened and closed her mouth.

'Eleven weeks,' said Rick.

'I had an awful first trimester too. Don't worry, it should pass. And it's all worth it in the end.' The nurse smiled and then went to clear up the mess Erica had left in the corridor.

Erica looked at Rick.

'What?' It was all she could think of to say. Rick smiled.

'We're in the maternity ward. This is where Rachel gives birth. They're used to women being sick here.'

'Eleven weeks?'

'You actually didn't have too much morning sickness,' said Rick. 'But there were a couple of times when you did what you just did. It was when you were tired of being pregnant and decided to just eat what you damn well wanted.' He grinned at the memory. 'And she's right, it does pass and it is worth it. Feeling better?'

'Not really.'

'Well, I need to find me. Come on.'

Erica followed shakily, taking her cup of water with her.

They found Rachel's room. Erica didn't dare glance in, she just took Rick's word for it. They hid around the corner as Rick peered out every now and then. He checked his watch.

'Any minute now I should come and find her,' he said. He checked around the corner again. 'There.'

Erica peered around and saw Rick, another Rick, looking exactly the same as the Rick she was with, hanging around the corridor. He peered through the slightly open door of Rachel's room and then walked away.

'That was it?'

'Yup. I didn't want to arrest a woman who had just given birth. I'm full of mistakes on this job, huh? I promise I'm actually a really good detective. Come on.' He led Erica down the corridor, following his past self.

'But Rachel's that way.'

'Yes, but our Rachel is going to try and kill this Rick, so it's him we need to follow.'

They followed him, right out of the hospital and down the street.

'Huh.' Rick stopped and scratched the back of his neck. 'No Rachel. This isn't where she came.'

'Then where is she?' Erica turned, looking around at her city from just months ago. She wondered where her past self was right now. Rick sighed.

'Maybe she saw me another time. Out of her window, perhaps, when I followed them home.'

Rick stopped to think. Erica waited next to him, shifting her weight from one foot to the other.

'I guess we sort of have all the time in world to figure this out, right? Given that we can time travel. Except that before you said you'd only be gone a moment and you were gone hours.'

'Yeah, I'm sorry about that. That's not really how it works.'

'So, we don't have all the time in the world, do we?' Erica sighed, looking up the road. 'We need to figure this out now, don't we?'

'Yup.' Rick pulled out a small tablet from his pocket and slid his finger around on the screen. He lowered it and put it away as Erica leaned in to look at it.

'Seriously? I can't look?'

He looked at her with soft eyes.

'Don't you want any surprises?'

Erica couldn't help but smile as Rick put his arm around her waist again. She could get used to this.

'Where are we going?'

'There's one big momentous occasion that Rachel can definitely change. And if she doesn't know where I was when she felt like she was being watched, then this is where she'll go.'

'Okay.'

Erica was overcome by the bright light again. She tried to relax into it this time but somehow that made it worse.

As the light faded and colours returned, Erica doubled over and dry heaved. There was nothing left in her stomach to come out. Rick stood over her, hand protectively on her back, but when she glanced up, gripping her abdomen, she saw his attention was elsewhere. She slowly straightened, her stomach rolling.

They were on a street at the edge of the city and the traffic was moving steadily through. Erica looked at Rick.

'This is where Rachel died. Or, no, where she pretended to die,' she said.

Rick didn't answer. He took her hand and led her down the road.

'There. There she is.' He broke into a run, dropping her hand. Erica tried to keep up but her stomach cramped with each step.

The distance between them grew and Erica only caught up because Rick had stopped. He looked to the other side of the road from the edge of the pavement. In-between the cars driving past, Erica saw Rachel but Jess wasn't with her.

'Where's Jess?' she hissed.

'That's not our Rachel,' Rick said. 'That's this time's future Rachel, and she's about to fake her own death.'

26

'I'm not coming with you.' Jess crossed her arms, defiantly lifting her chin.

'Fine by me,' said Rachel with a shrug, turning and walking away. 'But without me, you've got no way of getting back home. Not that that'll matter soon.'

Jess gave a small, contained scream of frustration as she watched Rachel leave. She jogged to catch up.

'What if I stole that thing on your wrist, huh?' Jess tried. 'Then I could go home and leave you stranded here.'

'If you like.' Rachel held out her wrist to Jess. 'It won't make any difference even if you did know how to use it.'

Jess deflated.

'Fine. Well, what are we doing here?'

Rachel didn't respond, she carried on walking. Jess followed her as they turned into a street she recognised. A main road, lined with parked cars, leading into the city where the traffic was heavy but steadily moving. Rachel walked down the street, casually looking in shop windows.

'Just up here,' she said. 'Now. I need you to do me a favour.'

'Why on earth would I do that?' Jess asked.

'Because if you don't, the timelines will be messed up. Anything happens to me here, without my plan taking effect and Joe will never see me or Steve again.'

A chill ran over Jess.

'Okay, fine. What do you want me to do?'

'Your detective is here somewhere. If you see him, I want you to grab his attention, anyway you like. Scream, shout, beg him to save you for all I care. Just get his attention.'

'Distract him, you mean.'

'Exactly.'

That didn't sit well with Jess, but the idea that baby Joe was somewhere lost in time without either of his parents was too much to bear. Rachel had already reassured her he was somewhere safe, but without Rachel returning to wherever she'd left him, he would be truly lost.

'Fine.'

'Good. Here we go. You go on ahead, find your detective.' Rachel stayed near a shop entrance but urged Jess on. 'See that coffee shop, there?'

'Yeah.'

'Somewhere outside there. Hang around there and see if you can spot him. Go on.'

Jess walked on, trying to look normal. The more she thought about it, the more awkward she felt, the more her walk seemed silly. Were people watching her? Could they sense something was wrong. Maybe they'd report her for suspicious behaviour. Then what? She could hardly explain that she was from a few months in the future, and if they'd be so kind, she'd quite like a Detective Cavanagh to come and take her home. She'd be arrested and given some sort of medical. Maybe she'd be put in a hospital, did they still do that kind of thing? Thrown into an asylum. No, that didn't happen anymore. Jess stopped. She'd overshot the coffee shop. Making her way back, she peered at the faces around her, searching for Rick. If nothing else, he'd protect her. She'd have some explaining to do, but he'd look after her. It was his job, after all. Something niggled at Jess. That was what Rachel wanted. Why? What did she need to distract Rick from doing?

There he was. Eyes lingering on her for slightly too long, a hint of recognition and then a turned back. This wasn't the Rick she knew. This was the Rick of a few months ago. At this stage, she'd take any Rick. He was avoiding her, trying to protect his own timeline. She opened her mouth to speak to him when she glanced across the road and saw Rick and Erica. With a loud hoot, Jess rushed forward, stopping only to wait for a break in the traffic.

She'd be waiting a long time. After a moment, she called to Erica.

'Ric! Erica!' She waved her arms. Erica didn't hear her. She looked pale and sickly. Had they just arrived? It seemed to Jess as if she and Rachel had been here for hours. A car honked as it drove past. 'Fuck off!' Jess shouted after it before turning back and shouting to Erica. Rick had gone from Erica's side. Jess paused, lowering her arms. The Rick she'd been told to distract had turned to look at her, and now Jess could see the other Rick crossing the road further up. 'What the hell is going on?' she muttered. She stepped out into the traffic and a car screeched to a stop before her.

Someone grabbed her arm and yanked her backwards. She pulled it back and spun to give that person a piece of her mind. Rick grabbed onto her wrist and held her tightly. Jess closed her mouth. Rick wasn't looking at her, he was looking beyond, into the crowds of people down the street.

'Where is she?' he asked.

'Who? Erica's over there.'

'No, Rachel.'

'There,' Jess pointed. 'She told me to come up here and find you. To—'

'Distract me.'

'Yeah.'

'You're doing a great job. I'm about to completely miss Rachel running into the road and being hit by a car. Probably a car swerving to miss you.' Rick let go of her wrist and moved away, jogging down the street.

Jess looked at the cars rushing by.

'Shit.' She ran after Rick. 'There's two of you here.'

'Yeah, I was following her when she got hit by the car.'

'You could have stopped her.'

'Then all of this would be over.'

'But I'm here, ruining it.' Jess slowed down.

'You have to be here. I mean, I didn't know you were a future Jess doing this. But I remembered you being on this street at this time. I thought that strange.'

Rick stopped and pulled a gun from inside his trench coat.

'What in the holy fuck are you doing?' Jess screamed. 'What is this?'

'Get down,' Rick told her. 'Get back and get down.'

'Do all police have guns in the future? Time

travel and guns? This isn't real. None of this is real. I'm going to wake up soon, back in my old flat with Ruby and this will all have been a dream. I'll be back in my crappy life soon, going to a job I hate and there'll be no lost babies, no faking anyone's death, no damn fae, no time travel and no fucking guns.' And no new house, she thought. And no Marshall. Her stomach turned. No Bubbles. No new business.

Someone screamed. Tyres screeched. Horns honked and then there was a loud bang.

It seemed as if time had stopped and for a moment, Jess wondered if that was possible. Had Rachel or Rick done this? But no, people were still moving, albeit slowly. Everyone had simply paused at the same time. When the gun had fired. Now the world came back to life. The cars on the road were still stopped but people on the street were moving, two crowds forming. One near a shop window, the other in the road.

Jess rushed towards them and then stopped, wondering which to go to. Where had Rick gone?

There, at the crowd closest to the shops. Rachel was on the ground and Rick was at her head telling the people to back away.

'Someone call an ambulance!' someone shouted.

Jess caught glimpses of red as the crowd jostled. A couple of men pushed the people back.

'Give us some space. And get an ambulance! And the police. Someone call the police. She's been shot!'

Jess glanced at Rick but there was no one accusing him.

'I am the police,' he announced, fishing around in his pocket and bringing out his ID which he whipped around quick enough for no one to read properly.

Seriously, Jess thought. You'd have thought they've have given him appropriate IDs for the times he was going to. Except, he was chasing a time travelling fugitive. Jess looked down at Rachel as she breathed hard, stunned, gripping her leg. Rick hadn't known where in time he'd be chasing her to.

He'd shot her in the leg. Blood was rushing from the wound, no matter how much Rachel gripped at it. Someone wrapped their coat about it but the blood soon soaked through.

'Everyone step back. Is there an ambulance on the way?'

Someone told him there was. There were two ambulances.

Jess turned and looked at the other crowd in the road. There was no blood. Rachel lay on the tarmac, not moving. A few people were crying loudly, trembling violently and moving away. Erica leaned over Rachel and then stepped back, away from the body, turning to meet Jess's eye.

'Didn't she see the car?' someone asked.

'She just ran out.'

Erica ran and lifted Jess up in a tight hug. Jess wrapped her arms around her friend.

'You're my Jess, aren't you?'

'Only if you're a future Erica.'

They both laughed and hugged again.

'Don't you ever do that to me again,' Erica warned, letting Jess go. 'I mean it.'

'Oh, don't you worry. I'm not doing this ever again. I'll leave the time travelling detective to you.'

The ambulances and police turned up within minutes. Jess and Erica tried to ignore the limp body of Rachel in the road, although the cries and tears would haunt both of their dreams for months to come. Paramedics saw to the man driving the car that had hit her.

Rick let the paramedics do what they had to for the other Rachel's leg. Someone seemed to mention the fact that the two women were identical, although Jess thought she heard a paramedic mention something about twins.

The police talked to Rick about the gunshot wound, but moved away quick enough. Jess watched curiously. How much did the present police force know about their future time travelling colleagues?

Erica and Jess huddled close, keeping Rick nearby at all times. When told that Jess and Erica couldn't join Rick and Rachel in the ambulance, he again flashed his ID. Jess was pretty certain that he implied that Jess and Erica were going to be taken into custody with Rachel, but it got them in the ambulance together so she didn't argue. The idea of taking a separate police car was, at that moment, terrifying.

It was cramped in the back of the ambulance and the paramedics were reasonably sharp with them. They didn't complain though, bandaging up Rachel as best they could with so little space. Rachel kept quiet for the entire journey. By the time they reached the hospital, the anger had faded from her expression, her eyes were dull as if the fight had gone.

They were left alone in a hospital corridor while they waited for a doctor. It was likely that Rachel needed surgery to remove the bullet that was lodged in her leg.

'I understand you're desperate,' Rick said to her. Erica and Jess sat a little further down the corridor, giving them some space, but they could still hear every word. Rick wasn't being exceptionally quiet about it. 'I'd be desperate too. But you knew this would happen before you met your husband. You knew this would happen before you got pregnant. But you went ahead and forged a new life anyway. You have no one to blame but yourself.'

Jess glanced at Erica. She was watching Rick with soft eyes. Jess smiled. Maybe she didn't have to worry about her getting involved with Alfie after all.

'You've been so reckless. Going into the past and starting a new life. There are laws about this. They'll be added to the charges against you. Who knows what damage you've done. What you've changed.'

Rachel gave a wry smile.

'And what about you, Detective? What about what you've changed by coming after me?'

'You didn't really give me much of a choice, now, did you?'

'You could have sent someone else. I'm sure any of the other little detectives would have been happy to do this for you. But no, you had to come. Why's that, Detective? Hmm? Haven't told your fancy girl that, have you?'

Jess did a sideways glance at Erica.

'That's none of your business. You're under arrest and you're not escaping this time. This time, you're going to trial and you'll be going to prison for a long time. These charges just keep adding up.'

'You don't have to do this,' Rachel said.

'Well, that's just not true. Now, you tell me where your son is.'

'No. He's safe. Why should I tell you?'

'Really? You want him growing up without you or his father?'

Rachel gritted her teeth. 'You're going to prison, Rachel,' Rick continued. 'Give your boy a chance. Give your boy his father.'

Rachel turned her face away, and Jess imagined she was holding back the tears. Her chest ached in sympathy. Right then, in that moment, she wanted nothing more than to go home and hold Ruby.

'I want a deal. I'll tell you where he is, but I want a deal,' said Rachel. Jess reeled. She was using her baby as leverage. Jess shook her head and turned away. She didn't want to hear anymore. She just wanted to go home.

Steve

The house was too quiet but it was different this time. This time it was unreal. Had the last few months been a dream? Maybe Steve had never met Rachel, he'd never had a son. For a brief moment, he wondered whose house he was sitting in. Whose living room was this? He sat forward on the sofa, unable to relax in this strange house. He shook his head, trying to dislodge the thoughts. This was real. This was his life.

He sat back. Maybe it would be better to believe this wasn't his house. He wished he could go home.

The house crackled with static electricity. Steve stood up and waited. The landing light flickered on and off.

He ran, taking the stairs two at a time.

'Rachel?' He fell into the nursery and stopped.

Jess smiled and offered him a baby wrapped in a soft green blanket. Beside her, Erica and Detective Cavanagh watched him. Steve blinked, his heart pounding against his ribcage. Tears pricked painfully at his eyes as he approached the baby and looked at the child's face.

A sob wrenched through him and his shaking arms lifted to take his son.

'Hi, Joey,' he murmured, looking down into his baby boy's eyes. The tears fell freely, one dropping onto his son's cheek as the baby opened his eyes and looked up at his father. Steve wiped the tear away.

No more tears, he decided. No more bad tears. He'd cried enough. This was where it ended.

'Where's Rachel?' he asked, not taking his eyes from his boy.

'Back in my time,' said Rick. 'In custody. It's all over.'

Steve nodded, still not looking up. It was all over. He expected more tears to come then, grief for his lost wife and the happy family he'd yearned for. No tears came. He was done crying for her. He held his son close and looked up, meeting Rick's eyes.

'Thank you,' he murmured, glancing at Erica and Jess. Jess smiled, her eyes watery and chin tight from holding back tears. She gave him a nod and Steve grinned back at her.

The bad times were behind them, he thought. It was time for something happy, and something new. A new beginning.

27

'Mummy's being weird,' said Ruby as Marshall walked through the front door. He ruffled her hair.

'What's she doing?' he asked, dropping his tool bag by the door.

'Singing and dancing.'

Marshall laughed.

'Sounds like your mum to me.'

Ruby shrugged.

'She's doing it differently.'

'Show me.'

Ruby led Marshall into the kitchen. His bulk and shadow over her was familiar now, and a comfort. Ruby wasn't sure which she liked best, the way Marshall talked to her or how happy her mother was when he was around. Bubbles gave a bark and rushed over to say hello to Marshall, her tail wagging so hard her body wiggled.

'Are you staying tonight, Marshall?' Ruby asked.

Jess, who had been dancing from the fridge to the hob, stopped in her tracks and stared at Marshall wide-eyed.

'You'll have to ask your mum about that,' said Marshall with a smile as he roughly rubbed Bubbles' head. Ruby liked that about him too. He was always smiling.

'Mummy?'

'Hmm?' Jess took a swig of beer from an open bottle on the counter.

'Can Marshall read me a story tonight?'

'Oh. Yeah. If he wants to, I don't see why not.'

Ruby looked up at Marshall and beamed.

'See. You can stay tonight.'

She skipped over to the dining table, plonked herself on a chair, picked up a crayon and returned to her drawing.

Jess gave Marshall a subtle shrug.

'I guess you have to stay the night,' she murmured as Marshall moved past her.

'Well, if I have to.' He leaned over and kissed her.

'Yuck!' Ruby laughed and stuck her tongue out. Jess stuck her tongue out back at her.

'What are you yucking at? Go wash your hands.'

Ruby jumped up and ran out of the kitchen, thundering up the stairs.

Jess immediately turned to Marshall, wrapped her arms around his neck and pulled him down for a kiss.

'I quit my job today.'

Marshall, hands on her hips, leaned back.

'Ah, that explains the dancing. Ruby said you were acting weird. I don't see much of a difference to be honest.' Marshall pressed his lips against hers. 'Although I love seeing you this happy.'

Jess grinned up at him.

'I love being this happy. I hope it lasts.' She stroked the back of his neck with her finger. 'I registered our new business today too and made a start on a new website. Erica sent me over a full marketing plan. We're in business.'

'That's fantastic.' said Marshall, kissing her again. 'What time is Paul picking up Ruby tomorrow?' He pulled Jess close and kissed her neck. 'I think we should celebrate.'

Jess stopped and pulled away.

'I think we should too, but I was also thinking that Ruby could stay here this weekend.'

'Isn't it Paul's weekend to have her?' Marshall asked, following her as she moved back to the hob to stir the chilli in the pan.

'It is. But…'

'But you need to have her close right now. Of course. Right, in that case we could have a day out to celebrate.'

Jess looked up into Marshall's eyes. Smiling, she wrapped her arms around him again.

'What did I do to deserve you?'

Marshall laughed.

'I can think of some shit you've been through.'

'Oh, yeah, that.'

They kissed again, Marshall's hands moving down her back.

'Oh, yuck. You're kissing again.'

They broke apart with a jump.

'Don't be rude,' Jess told her daughter, returning to the hob. 'Hey, sweetie. Are you looking forward to going to your dad's for the weekend?'

'Yes.'

Jess looked at Ruby over her shoulder.

'Because if you like, I can ask your dad if he'd mind you staying here. With us. We can have a fun weekend together.' Jess had to stop herself from adding "as a family". She glanced up at Marshall and caught him secretly smiling to himself.

'Yes, please! Could we go to the zoo?'

Jess turned to Marshall.

'Marshall? Would you like to come to the zoo with us?'

'I'd love to,' he said.

Ruby cheered, bouncing in her chair at the table.

'I'll give Paul a ring,' said Jess. As she reached for her phone, it lit up and buzzed. She turned her back on Ruby and Marshall and opened the message.

The house is on the market. Me and Joe are leaving now to stay with my mum in Manchester. Thank you for everything. Send me an invoice for the investigation. I've emailed you a testimonial. Take care. Steve x

Jess smiled, gripping her phone and holding it to her chest.

'Back in a moment,' she murmured. Marshall and Ruby didn't hear her. They were too busy sitting at the table, Ruby showing Marshall a game on Jess's tablet. Jess watched them secretly for a moment, smiling, before walking out of the room.

28

Erica sat on the park bench and looked up at the evening sky.

'Everything okay?' Rick sat beside her.

'Not really,' Erica admitted, watching two dogs playing together.

'We did it. I got my perp, we got Steve's son back. I'd call that a success.'

'Tomorrow I have to go back to my horrible job,' said Erica. And you're leaving, she added silently.

'Which job is this?'

'Goldbrick Communications. Another marketing agency.' Erica sighed. 'They've passed me up for promotion twice now. I've handed my notice in, but I still have to go back in tomorrow.'

'Oh, those bastards.' Rick smiled. 'Would it help to know that in my timeline, you quit that job to start a paranormal investigation agency?'

'What do you mean, in your timeline? You're in this future, aren't you? I thought you were my future.'

They locked eyes. The ice blue of Rick's softened and became sad.

'I really hope that's still the case,' he murmured.

'If you still remember me, right now, then surely we still end up together. Nothing's changed. Or, let me guess, is that not how it works?'

Rick reached up and stroked her cheek.

'No, that's pretty much how it works. And I hope you're right. I was such an idiot for coming here, for jeopardising us. If we're still together when I get home, you're going to kill me.'

Erica laughed.

A comfortable silence settled on them.

'Back in the past,' said Erica, carefully, 'Rachel said something about why you came back. Why you did this. Is something going on? Are you in trouble?'

Rick's smile faded and he looked away, up at the sky.

'I can't say,' he said.

'Why not? Because I'll kill you?' Erica nudged him playfully.

'Something like that.' He looked back to her. 'I do love you, Ricci. More than I think you know. I need you to promise me something.'

'What?'

'Find me.'

Erica raised an eyebrow.

'How did we meet, in your time? Before this?'

Rick grinned and looked down at the ground. Erica studied him, wondering what memories were playing in his mind.

'I don't know if I should tell you. If it happens, it happens.' He looked back at her. 'But I want you to find me. It won't be me as I am now. You changed me, for the better.' He gestured to himself. 'And I won't know who you are, of course, because present day Rick hasn't met you yet. But you'll know me. If I don't ask you out, because I'm an idiot, then you ask me out. I promise I'll say yes.'

'Ha!' Erica looked at him sideways. 'What if

you don't? Like you said, it's not you you. When I find you, you won't look at me the way you look at me now.'

'Maybe. But I will. It won't take long.' Rick winked at her. 'So, you promise?'

Erica nodded. It was the easiest promise she'd ever made. What did he think she'd been planning since they'd returned to the present?

'I promise.'

Rick hesitated.

'It's so hard not to kiss you right now, but I think that might ruin everything.'

Without thinking, Erica leaned forward and kissed Rick. Her hand moved to the back of his neck and he quickly relaxed into it, his hands finding her waist. They bumped noses as the kiss broke.

Rick gave her a questioning look.

'You know, just in case I don't find you,' said Erica with a smile. She leaned forward and kissed him again quick.

'See you soon,' he murmured.

Erica's smile fell.

'Yeah. I hope so.' She looked up into those blue eyes. 'When? When do we meet?'

'You know I can't tell you,' he whispered, kissing her again. 'But I can't wait to meet you.'

Rick stood and began to walk away. Erica watched him go, her whole body aching, screaming at her to follow him. He turned back to her, fiddled with the device on his wrist and was soon swallowed by a bright light.

₭ℛ

Erica walked through the cemetery to her grandfather's grave. Her grandmother hunched over the gravestone, her lips moving as she talked quietly. She smiled as she caught sight of Erica.

'Hi, Gran. Escaped from the home again? Does mum know you're here?'

'No. But you can tell her. Stop her from worrying.'

'You need to start using that phone we gave you.'

'I can't get the buttons to work.' Minerva sniffed. 'What are you doing here?'

'Just wanted to come say hi to Granddad,' said Erica, looking around. 'You're busy, though. You're talking to him?'

Minerva almost pouted.

'Oh, sweetheart, you still can't see him?'

Erica shrugged, holding back the tears that had been threatening to come since she'd left the park bench. 'Never mind. You will,' Minerva continued. 'I'll leave you two together.' She smiled at the air beside her and left in the direction of the secret garden.

Erica studied the space Minerva had been looking at.

'Hi, Granddad. I'm sorry I can't see you yet. Or hear you. I quit my job. That's what you said I should do, isn't it? I wish we could talk properly.' Erica sighed. 'He left, Granddad. I know he had to. Of course he did, but I miss him. I can't stop thinking about him. I know it'll go with time, but it won't will it? I need to find him.'

'You'll find him.'

Erica spun round and stopped as Alfie approached.

'What do you want?' she asked.

'It sounds to me like you might need some help.'

'What? You can help me find him? I'm assuming you know who I mean. You seem to know everything about me, so why not?' Erica crossed her arms. Alfie stopped in front of her.

'I could help you find him, but that's not what I meant. You're hurting, and I can help with that.'

'I don't want your help with that,' said Erica quickly. Alfie flashed her a charming smile.

'You'll change your mind.'

Erica growled.

'I'm sick of this. I'm sick of men telling me what I'm going to do. I will find Rick, but only because I want to. This.' Erica gestured between herself and Alfie, 'is not going to happen. I don't want your help. I don't need your help. That's that.'

Alfie mimicked her posture, crossing his arms.

'And everything I've told you so far hasn't been true?'

'That's not the point,' said Erica, although she could feel her argument falling flat.

'I won't hurt you,' said Alfie. 'And there's no force here. That's not how this works. When you're ready, when you want to, here I'll be. But I'm not going to stop being a part of your life now. We can be friends, can't we?'

'Friends is a strong word,' said Erica. 'Acquaintances. Maybe.'

Alfie grinned.

'See you later, Erica Murray.' Alfie walked past her, in the direction of the secret garden. Erica watched him go.

'I wish I could see you. I'd love to know what you think of them,' she muttered to the empty air.

She glanced down at the gravestone. 'See you later, Granddad.' She turned back to her car, walking slowly, looking up at the bright sky and listening to the birds singing.

Their song was joined by her ringtone. She smiled, answering her phone.

'Hey, Jess.'

'Hey. Guess what. How would you like to go to a house on the other side of the city and check out if there's a poltergeist making a family's life miserable? You can sense poltergeists, right?'

'One way to find out, I guess.'

'Is that a yes?'

'We'd be a shit paranormal investigation agency if we didn't,' said Erica. 'Are these paying clients?'

'Yup. Accepted my initial rate and everything.'

Erica smiled, her shoulders dropping as she relaxed.

'Are you at home? I'll be right there. We can discuss our game plan.'

Erica hung up and stopped walking. Closing her eyes against the warmth of the morning sunshine, she turned. As she opened her eyes, she saw a figure standing by her grandfather's gravestone. His hair shining in the sun, his shirt sleeves rolled up in a way that tugged at Erica's memories. He lifted an arm and waved to her.

ഇൻ

Author's Note

I desperately wanted to set this story in Bristol. That's where Erica and Jess live. But I needed to bend reality to fit the story, so some parts aren't quite true to how you'll find them if you go searching.

But, please do go searching because Bristol is a magical and beautiful city.

If you do fancy a tour:

- ◆ The cemetery is based on beautiful Arnos Vale Cemetery (although as far as I'm aware, there is no secret garden where the fae live).
- ◆ Steve Green lives in the one of the colourful townhouses in Charlton Hayes, near Patchway, which were being built when I started writing this.
- ◆ The police station is based on Patchway Police Centre, on the A38
- ◆ Rachel faked her death on Gloucester Road.
- ◆ And Erica and Alfie have a coffee sat outside on Brunel Quay, which is definitely worth a visit and a drink.

Book Two in the Erica Murray Mystery series is coming in 2019

Get regular updates and access to exclusive and early goodies by signing up at:
www.jenice.co.uk/updates

If you enjoyed this book...

Authors love getting reviews.
It's one of the best ways to support authors you enjoy.
I would really appreciate it if you could leave a review of this book on Amazon or your favourite distributor.

Acknowledgements

This book wouldn't be possible without the three most important people in my life; mum, dad and my Chris (I love you).

Special thanks to my mum who helped to inspire so much of this story, first by uttering the words,
    'Erica Murray would make a great penname,'
and then by researching our family history.

Massive thank you also to the friends and family who are always there when I need them, supporting me and my writing, most notably, Joanne, Elliot, Carly, Abi and Ryan.

Other Books By
J E Nice

The Last War Trilogy
It starts with a scream...

It starts with a scream.
People are going missing in Drummbek castle. It's
something castle maid Tabitha can't ignore, and
she's determined to find out what's really going on.

Meanwhile, in the Wastelands, exiled veteran
dragonslayer, Del Thorburn, knows exactly what's
going on and she's on her way home to finish what
she started.

What happens will change their lives, and the lives
of those they hold close and love, but if they think
that'll be the end of it, they're sorely mistaken.
Some dragons just won't die.

Get the first book in the trilogy,
Matter of Time,
for free at
www.jenice.co.uk/updates

Printed in Great Britain
by Amazon